Moscow, Midnight

Also by John Simpson

Fiction
Moscow Requiem
A Fine and Private Place

Non-Fiction
The Disappeared: Voices from a Secret War
Behind Iranian Lines
Despatches from the Barricades
Strange Places, Questionable People
A Mad World, My Masters
News from No Man's Land
The Wars Against Saddam: Taking the Hard Road to Baghdad
Days from a Different World: A Memoir of Childhood
Not Quite World's End: A Traveller's Tales
Twenty Tales from the War Zone
Unreliable Sources
We Chose to Speak of War and Strife

Moscow, Midnight

John Simpson

JOHN MURRAY

First published in Great Britain in 2018 by John Murray (Publishers)
An Hachette UK Company

1

© John Simpson 2018

A CIP catalogue record for this title is available from the British Library

ISBN 978-1-47367-449-3
Trade Paperback ISBN 978-1-47367-452-3
Ebook ISBN 978-1-47367-450-9

Typeset in Adobe Garamond by Hewer Text UK Ltd, Edinburgh
Printed and bound in Great Britain by Clays Ltd, Elcograf S.p.A.

John Murray policy is to use papers that are natural, renewable and
recyclable products and made from wood grown in sustainable forests.
The logging and manufacturing processes are expected to conform
to the environmental regulations of the country of origin.

John Murray (Publishers)
Carmelite House
50 Victoria Embankment
London EC4Y 0DZ

www.johnmurray.co.uk

To: julian@litagency.co.uk
Subject: Help!

Hello Julian,
The last time we met, I opened up to you about the trouble I was in, and you said it could be written up into a half-decent novel which you, as my agent, could flog to a publisher.

Well, I've written it, and here it is. It just needs a final couple of chapters. You'll see I've done it like a thriller, complete with short sentences and hard-boiled gags. That way, if there's a fuss I can say 'Why is everyone taking it so seriously, for God's sake? It's just a bit of entertainment.'

I'm hoping it'll provide me with some measure of protection. After all, if I'm sent to join the choir invisible now, this book will make it pretty clear who's responsible.

Best regards,
Jon.
PS: You could always start it with this email . . .

One

Everything that follows really happened. It feels good to get it off my chest.

We'll start in Paris.

Imagine a café in the Thirteenth, cavernous and decorated with badly painted pictures of forests and mountains. Sitting in the gloom at a back table is a biggish, ramshackle bloke with an empty coffee cup and half a glass of Ricard in front of him, scribbling away at a rate of knots.

That's me.

Dismiss any thoughts of the Champs-Élysées or the Louvre from your mind: the Thirteenth is neither grand nor glamorous, and it's not the kind of area tourists bother to search out. This part of it is mostly inhabited by Vietnamese and Cambodians, refugees from way back.

It's twelve thirty-five now, and I've been sitting here since ten, writing and ordering a carefully spaced out succession of *noisettes* (which doesn't mean nuts, as you might reasonably expect, but little cups of fierce black coffee).

I'm waiting for someone to come in on their own, sit down near me, and order something moderately expensive: *steak frites*, perhaps, with a half-bottle of red, and a coffee and a glass of something throat-rasping to end with. It's a familiar enough sight in Paris at lunchtime. When the customer has finished, he or she will call for *l'addition* and the waiter will bring it on a little round gun-metal dish, then wander off to do something completely different in another part of the café. The customer will peer at the bill to make sure it's correct, put the necessary cash into the dish, add a bit more for service, and head off.

That's the chance I've been waiting for all morning. In the brief space of time between the moment when he goes and the waiter makes one of his passes down this end of the café, I'll get up, walk a bit too close to the now abandoned table, scoop the contents of the metal dish into my pocket, and head out through the main door.

It's paralysingly scary the first time you do it, but after the ninth or tenth go it becomes natural – automatic, even. The key thing is to pick the right place to sit. After that, everything's dead simple. And if you can abandon all sense of right and wrong and concentrate purely on your own survival, you can even enjoy yourself. For me, this is entirely a matter of life or death.

I'm not, you see, the person I once was. I used to live a civilised and fairly honourable existence in London. I might not have been well off (too many ex-wives for that), but I'd never have dreamed of stealing anything. Even forgetting to return my books to the London Library would bring me out in a sweat. And yet now I live solely by chiselling and theft.

Oh well: 'He must needs go that the devil drives.' There's a vast range of half-remembered quotations which hang in my brain like suits in a wardrobe, waiting to be picked out at the relevant moment. Not, of course, that suits are exactly my thing nowadays.

After I leave here in the early afternoon, the devil will drive me to some entirely different part of Paris: possibly the Third.

4

I'll wander round a bit, doing some legitimate shopping, and by then it'll be time for pre-dinner drinks. Maybe I'll go somewhere around the Rue du Parc-Royal, where I've spent some happy times in the past. I won't do any lifting (that's the expression I find myself using), just in case someone I know spots me. But after an honestly acquired drink or three I'll head off somewhere else where people have money, like the Sixteenth, and do it there.

I still look reasonable enough, though I could do with a haircut and a beard trim. My increasingly stained and ragged clothes will be all right as long as the lights are low. With luck, everyone will think I'm an author down on his luck. God knows, they'll be right: I'm the author of my own misfortunes. Afterwards, with hopefully a couple of hundred euros in my pocket, I'll head back to my apartment block for the night. I don't actually have an apartment, but I live there all the same. I'll explain later.

Anyway, while I've been writing these words, a heavily built character in a dark blue suit, which would have fitted him better around the chest and stomach five years ago, is sitting a few tables away from me, getting down to business with a *confit de canard* and a half-bottle of Beaujolais. He looks gloomy, he's balding, and a faint line of sweat has gathered along the twin furrows of his forehead. A southerner, I should judge: he'll have shaved this morning, yet on his cheeks and chin there's already a definite dark fuzz which matches his suit.

Personally, I would have thought it was too hot for duck at this time of year, but he's giving his a proper mauling. Maybe it helps me in my criminal project to feel superior to this completely unexceptional middle-class chap. But it's unfair: after all, I'm more than a bit inclined to sweat myself nowadays, especially when I'm worried. I'm worried now.

5

He pushes the empty plate aside and orders a *noisette* and a glass of Poire Williams – something I'm rather partial to myself, as it happens. Looking at the cheap Casio watch on his hairy wrist, he downs both quickly and calls for the bill. As soon as it arrives he pays, makes a lot of noise getting up, and shoulders his way out of the restaurant.

My moment has arrived. I've been careful to pay my own bill beforehand, so I'm all ready. I pack my notebook and biro away and lurch across to the table he has left, as though I'm finding walking a bit difficult. I don't bother with the coins – I just palm the twenty-euro note and the ten-euro one, and scrunch them up in my hand. It's another perfectly executed operation.

Except that it isn't. The pair of illicit, early middle-aged lovers sitting at a table in the darkest of the café's corners should have been gazing into each other's wrinkle-surrounded eyes, but instead one of them – the bloke – catches sight of my operation.

'*Attention! Qu'est-ce que tu fais? Arrête ça!*'

Bugger. I lurch off at a rate of knots and make it to the entrance, but the waiter – Vietnamese, I imagine – is quick off the mark and blocks me. I try to push him away, but he clings on. In the end sheer weight tells, and once I get through the door I'm off. I don't run much nowadays, but it's amazing what you can do when you're scared. And I'm really, really scared.

At the next corner I look round, chest heaving, and spot him in his white apron heading my way. He's short and bow-legged but seems pretty fast on those curved pins of his, and I get the impression he's a determined kind of character. The Vietnamese tend to be, as President Johnson discovered. I run on, finding unexpected reserves of strength in my own legs, but each time I look round he's still behind, and seems to be getting closer.

Then he makes his big mistake. He stops and shouts something: 'Stop thief,' possibly. Once upon a time that would have been enough for the entire street to gather, looking for a lamp post to hang me from. In today's Paris, though, everyone is so scared of getting involved that they just ignore him. An elderly lady stops to look at me as I run past, but I glare back threateningly and she turns towards a shop window instead.

That's the waiter's last throw. He stands looking in my direction for a while, then drifts away. Fortunately for me, there are no cops around for him to appeal to; there never seem to be nowadays. Presumably they're all looking for suicide bombers. I feel able to drop into a fast walk, chest heaving and legs trembling, and at the end of the street I come to the Boulevard de l'Hôpital. Only twenty yards or so away there's the familiar sign of the chain store Monoprix. Whipping in through the main doors, I head for the men's department, select a pair of cheap black trousers from the rail and go into a booth to try them on.

No one actually helps me, of course. It's the same in every store throughout the advanced world: you can't find an assistant if you happen to want one, any more than you can find a cop. Don't think I'm complaining, though – all these things make my life as a thief and a renegade a lot easier.

Now I can sit in my booth with the curtains shut, waiting for my breathing and my pulse rate to reach the low hundreds, and for anyone who might just possibly have followed me in the shop to lose the scent. I've resigned myself to using thirty of my hard-won euros to buy the trousers. As it turns out, though, there's still no assistant around and I don't have to after all.

So, like the good citizen I no longer am, I put the trousers back on the rack and head out into the boulevard. The street seems remarkably clear of anyone waiting with handcuffs and a warrant. I head for the nearest Métro station, trundle down the steps on my wobbly legs, and hop on the next train without even noticing where I'm going.

I've got away with it again. But only just, this time. I'll need to be a hell of a lot more careful in the Sixteenth this evening. Running through my mind, keeping time to the movement of the train like a metronome, is a song. I suppose it's because the blood is still pounding through my head.

> *The pulse of an Irishman ever beats quicker,*
> *When war is the story or love is the theme;*
> *And place him where bullets fly thicker and thicker,*
> *You'll find him all cowardice scorning.*

It's an Irish folksong, probably written by some patronising Protestant bastard like the ones in my own family, and for some reason (money, I assume) Beethoven did an arrangement of the rather charming tune. It's become an earworm for me: I can't put it out of my head. But please don't think I find it relevant to myself: my career has often placed me where bullets have flown thicker and thicker, and I haven't scorned cowardice in the slightest.

And by the way, if you decide to stick with me in the book that follows, you'll find me quoting all sorts of irritating little tags and catches, left over from a grand but wasted education. If you can't put up with it, and there's no reason why you should, I suggest you step off the Métro now and leave me to it.

Two

So what turned me into an outlaw, stealing cash, barrelling into perfectly harmless waiters, and generally behaving like a Millwall fan on his first away fixture? Well, it's a long story, but I hope that by the end of this screed you'll be able to understand the whole difficult business. What I really want is your sympathy, of course, but I accept that you might want to hold back on that.

The best place to start is my old flat in Chelsea, early one morning last April, when I still had a job and somewhere to live, and all the food and drink I needed, and friends who didn't shun me; well, one or two of them. It's a surprisingly roomy first-floor place in a red-brick block which was built in the year Conan Doyle came up with his ludicrous explanation for how Sherlock Holmes had survived the Reichenbach Falls. Nowadays, of course, I'd never be able to afford anything remotely like this place on a journalist's salary, but in the early 1990s property prices in Chelsea crashed, and foreign buyers were still just an estate agent's orgasmic dream. At that precise moment a dear old auntie of mine in County Wicklow chose to die and leave me some cash, and I managed to chisel a mortgage out of my reluctant bank and snapped it up.

This flat, which is in the Royal Hospital Road, is the only thing I possess that's of any serious value. (I don't count the four eighteenth-century oil portraits of my Irish ancestors, which I had to pack away because one of my three wives complained that they put her off making love to me. Well, something clearly did, so maybe she was right.)

The place is nice enough, but since I'm a bit of a slob it's desperately untidy. My auntie from Wicklow would have said it lacked a woman's loving touch. So do I, but we needn't go into that just now.

There are more unwashed plates and glasses than one solitary inhabitant should probably generate, and various bits of abandoned clothing are lying around. I blame television: if it didn't put out all those watchable if trashy series, I wouldn't have to do so much eating and drinking lying on the couch.

Maria, my cleaning lady, possibly Albanian, is perpetually horrified at the way I live, but since she can't actually speak English she is only able to register alarm and reproach by her facial expression and hand movements, like an actress in a silent movie. I pay her extra, to assuage my guilt, and can't be arsed to check whether she is here illegally. I'm not a police tout, after all.

This was last spring. At that immeasurably distant time I had a proper bed to sleep in, and although my life wasn't fantastic I at least didn't have to steal from other people to keep going. And no one wanted to kill me. Apart from my most recent ex-wife, that is.

It was nine twenty-six, and the morning light was seeping in around the edges of the curtain. I lay sprawled in that last and most pleasurable stage of sleep, when you're sufficiently awake to know that you can stay in bed for a good half an hour longer, and can kid yourself that you've earned it.

So of course my mobile rang. Blindly, I patted the bedside table – keys, reading glasses, some coins, a paper cup which still held some whiskey and water, a ludicrously long biography of Napoleon which had sent me to sleep the previous night – before I reached the epicentre of the noise. The coins rattled on the floor and the whiskey and water began to seep around.

'Who the fuck is that?'

There was a deep guffaw at the other end. I recognised it at once.

'What sort of time do you think this is, you evil South African bastard?'

Barend Malan was a large, bearded cameraman, constructed rather along the lines of Henry VIII. I had shared iron rations, bottles of firewater, and alarming experiences with him over many years, and loved him dearly. No one, including me, ever called him Barend, by the way; in fact, it was only when I caught a glimpse of his passport one time that I knew that was his real name: Barend Schoombie Malan. Like everyone else, I called him 'Os', assuming his full name must be Oswald or Osbert or something similarly antique-sounding. It was only after a few years that someone told me – Os never would have – that it was a typical Afrikaans nickname, *os* meaning 'ox'. You only had to see him to understand why.

'Apologies, boss.'

He called me that because he thought I found it flattering. I did, of course.

'Bad news, though – something's happened to a mate of yours. That MP, Patrick Macready. The desk want me to head round to his flat. I thought you might like to come too. It's just off Sloane Square.'

He rolled his Rs as though he was clearing his throat.

'I know where it is.'

My irritation was instinctive, absent-minded; my heart had given a nasty jump at the news, and I was still trying to work things out.

'What's supposed to have happened to him?'

'No one seems to know. The cops are there. He's dead, I'm afraid.'

'I'll meet you outside his place,' I said, as though this was just any old piece of information he'd slipped me.

Despite the sharp sunshine, it was cold. When my taxi got me there, Os was sitting in his crew-car, illegally parked. He waved a large gloved hand at me and wound down the window. His hair stood up like a mopani tree in the African bush.

'Can we go in?'

'Got to wait a bit longer.'

I climbed into the passenger seat. His car stank of the snatched meals of years – mostly chicken nuggets and cold coffee, I would judge.

'So tell me.'

'His cleaner or someone came in early. He goes to work around seven thirty. Went. She let herself in, and found him.'

'What had happened?'

'Some sex thing, apparently.' He looked away from me, but I was relieved to see he wasn't grinning. 'The cops didn't say, but according to the desk that's the impression they gave.'

'I suppose everyone thought it was funny.'

'Well, you know how people are. But seeing as he was a friend of yours . . .'

'The best I had,' I said: that'd teach Os Malan to try being tactful. It was true, anyway.

I sat and thought about Patrick for a while, and Os said nothing. Afrikaners were mostly somewhere at the back of the queue when politeness was handed out, but Os had his finer moments. And anyway he liked me, almost as much as I liked him.

In the end a uniformed policeman appeared at the front door of Patrick's house and stood there, looking round.

'That's us,' Os said.

He jumped out, then reached back in and grabbed his camera from the back seat. A seat belt was buckled round it, as though it was a kid.

There was a stupid smile on the policeman's face as he waved us in through the front door: 'This way to the Folies Bergère.'

'I don't think that's at all appropriate,' I said in my most disapproving voice. The policeman went gratifyingly quiet; you can always embarrass the bloody English by accusing them of bad taste.

A couple of cameramen and some photographers appeared from somewhere and crowded through the door with us. We were shown into the flat, so familiar to me, and ended up standing round the long dining room table; genuine Chippendale, if I'm any judge. The place was as tidy and well furnished as ever, with that faint impersonality you usually find when a man of taste lives on his own.

His pictures gazed down as though they despised us for being there: an eighteenth-century admiral in front of his ship in an artistically choppy sea; a snooty magnifico from around 1880 in full hunting gear; an early nineteenth-century portrait of a dyspeptic grandee who looked as though he dined on quail and champagne while his tenants starved outside. Patrick's ancestors, you would suppose.

Wrong. His grandfather was an Irish tram driver from the County Mayo who ended up in Chester. But it's no wonder the characters in the paintings looked so disapproving: their owner had died right in front of them, on this very table. I'd sat here myself so many times, yet I couldn't imagine what had gone on

13

just a few hours earlier, any more than the people in the portraits could have: I suppose that, like them, I'd led a sheltered life.

I still felt weirdly dispassionate. I've seen a lot of death and destruction in my time, and it became clear to me long ago that getting worked up about it doesn't do anyone any good, least of all the people you most care about.

Thank God, they'd taken Patrick's body away, but his clothes were still rucked up on the floor, presumably where he'd shaken them off, and there were some canvas ties lying around, like the ones moving men use. Also an orange with bite marks in it. Everyone seemed to grin when they spotted that.

'Christ, look up there,' Os whispered to me.

On the wall, seven feet high, there was a spatter of colourless liquid. I didn't have to be a laboratory assistant to guess what it was.

'Respect,' Os added, but I glared at him.

The others had seen it by now, but no one took any pictures of it. There wasn't a newspaper or a television station in Britain which would use them; in spite of the efforts of a range of press barons, this still isn't Japan or Italy, after all.

'Amyl nitrate,' said one particular know-it-all, who in this case turned out to be right. 'They inject it into the orange with a needle, and they can go all night.'

Three

A lugubrious police inspector walked in and started addressing us as though we were medical students at an autopsy. Another character, in an elderly but well-cut suit, followed him in and stood with professional unobtrusiveness near the door. He didn't look like any policeman I'd ever seen.

'There was a call to the emergency services at seven fifty-two this morning from the cleaning lady who worked for the deceased, identified as Mr Patrick Macready MP,' he said. It sounded like a trial run of the evidence he'd be giving at the inquest. 'A cord was tied around the neck and feet of the deceased, and the head was covered.'

He glanced down at a plastic bag lying beside the leg of the table, on the floor. 'The neck', 'the feet', 'the head'; policemen and doctors and morticians never seem to use the possessive when they talk about dead people. I suppose it stops things getting too personal.

There was a pause, as if for effect, then the inspector hit the keynote: 'We removed an orange from the mouth. It contained a chemical substance, and a sample has gone to the lab for examination.'

One of the other policemen and several of the cameramen giggled like kids at the back of a sex education class. The inspector ignored them.

'Time of death is estimated at around eleven thirty last night. It looks as though the artery in his neck was constricted – that was the purpose of the exercise – and the accused must have fainted before he could free himself. This is an extremely hazardous practice,' the inspector added, as though we had to be warned not to try it at home.

There were a few questions, which the inspector fielded. I stood to one side, finding the whole thing utterly distasteful; Patrick had been rational, pious, and modest by nature. I wouldn't have thought that he'd even have heard about this kind of dodgy autoerotic game; I didn't know much about it myself, and I had always assumed that I was far more experienced in the ways of the world than Patrick was.

A shabby middle-aged character, a well-known crime reporter, waved his Bic pen in the inspector's direction.

'Can you tell us if you've found any pornography in the flat?'

The inspector looked irritated, in an 'are you trying to tell me my job?' kind of way.

'Not so far,' he said.

'I imagine you usually do, in cases like this?'

'Fortunately this sort of thing is a very rare occurrence.'

'But the kind of people who go in for this sort of thing would surely have plenty of —— reading matter about it?'

Up to that point the shabby character had had the inspector on the ropes. Now the sound of suppressed giggling returned.

'I'm not an expert in activity like this, I can assure you.'

The giggles became outright laughter, and the crime correspondent subsided.

'What about the woman who found him?' someone else asked. 'Is she all right?'

'She's had to be sedated. It was a big shock to her, obviously.'

'Never seen anything like it, I expect,' said a photographer, and everyone doubled up again. Not Os, though: he was too conscious of my angry glare.

'Time to get out,' I snarled at him.

The photographers started packing up. The inspector turned away and consulted his clipboard.

I wondered about the lack of porn myself. How would Patrick have known what to do, without some exemplar to guide him? Maybe he had downloaded the necessary stuff from the internet.

'Have you looked at his laptop?' I asked the inspector's back.

He turned round.

'Briefly.'

'Any porn there?'

'Not that we could see. But it'll be examined more carefully.'

He didn't like being asked.

The hacks were still grinning as they walked out. Os was finding it hard not to grin as well.

By the time I got to the office, half an hour later, the social media had smelled blood in the water and were already starting to swarm round. I've seen more thoughtful and generous piranhas in the Amazon. A couple of comments on Twitter annoyed me so much that I switched my phone off in fury:

They screw us, now screwing themselves.

Tory wankers – ha ha!!! Litarally!!!!

That afternoon in the Commons, the Leader of the House made a statement about it all. I watched it live on television, and could hear a couple of cackles from the nearby benches; one sounded as though it came from a woman. Sensitive types, these politicians.

Patrick, the most private and dignified of people, had become a crude public joke.

Four

You know me, by the way. Not like you know your auntie or your best friend or your dentist, but my face will be deeply familiar to you, every crease and expression and glance, because you've known me your entire life.

And yet you've never met me. You've just seen me year after year on television, standing in front of a dozen burning buildings, a hundred courthouses and parliament buildings, a thousand tanks and military vehicles, until it seems to you that I'm a figure in your life.

I'm like a picture on the mantelpiece of someone in sepia, standing stiff and proud in his new uniform before being shipped off to die at the Somme. You've known his expression, the set of his shoulders, the badges of rank on his tunic for as long as you can remember, yet you probably couldn't even put a name to him.

Same with me. And if, one day, you spot me in the flesh in a department store or down the other end of the saloon bar, you'll nudge the person you're with and say, 'Isn't that the chap off the telly? The one who does that stuff, you know.' And your friend will nod and proffer the name of another, different, television performer, and you'll nod too. But at the same time you'll be thinking, No, that's not the one.

This doesn't amount to fame; it's just a kind of accidental familiarity, like recognising a bit-part actor in a movie. It's a weird business, being not quite the person people think you are. 'You're much bigger than I expected,' they say, presumably because I've got a head the size of a pin. In fact, I'm built like the blind-side flanker I once was; only in those days, when rugby was still a game for amateurs and blokes of all sizes could find their natural position, we called my position 'wing forward'.

I was fast, rough, and didn't feel I'd been in a game unless my jersey had blood on it. Once I was given a trial for Leinster, but there was someone better than me in the other team who went on to play for Ireland and the Lions. Now I'm carrying quite a bit more weight, but even at sixty-one I can still run moderately fast for short distances; especially if it's in Afghanistan or Syria and someone wants to disembowel me. Or down a street in Paris, of course.

I have the faintest of accents: a rounding of the vowels, a softening of the consonants, the occasional intrusive *r*. It comes from being born, raised, and educated in southern Ireland. Because, you see, I'm not one of your curds-and-whey English types: I'm Anglo-Irish. My people's history is blood-drenched, whether we were fighting the Irish or the king's enemies abroad; our church is Anglican, our drink is Jameson. It was a quarter-century after the break with Britain before my prep school on the southern edge of Dublin stopped singing 'God Save The King' each morning. And on the eleventh of November we would troop to church in Blackrock for Remembrance Day, ignoring the catcalls, and sometimes the stones, of the local kids. As the old saying has it, we're English in Ireland and Irish in England; and neither country likes us much. If, that is, it even remembers who we are.

Mind you, the Irish are happy enough to claim our accomplishments as their own. Plenty of Ireland's Nobel prizes, which you hear so much about, were won by the Anglo-Irish; my own ancestor, Dean Swift, would certainly have won one if Alfred Nobel had been around to dish out prizes for literature in the eighteenth century.

Actually, the Dean didn't have any children, so he can't really be my ancestor. But small details like that never deterred my father, Henry Swift, who was a bullshitter of majestic proportions and talked loud and often about our family history. Against my mother's strong wishes, he named me Jonathan, she being too weak to go with him into Drogheda to register the birth. All she could register was her objections afterwards.

At St Andrew's in Dublin, where I went to school, I had to endure being called Jonathan Swift and listening to people laugh; but when I started at Oxford (Brasenose, to be precise), where I read Russian, I announced to everyone that my name was Jon. Jon Swift; there's a jauntiness to that which I've always tried to live up to. But my passports, British and Irish, reveal the awkward reality: 'Name: Jonathan Henry Lysaght Swift. Date of birth: 15.7.1957'.

My elder brother William still lives in the family house outside Drogheda, a handsome Queen Anne place with the original panelling, a magnificent oak staircase, peacocks screaming in the grounds, and buckets scattered around the top floor to catch the rain. He hunts every day, and you have to shove his smelly dogs off the armchairs whenever you want to sit down.

As for me, I became a television journalist. Some of my university contemporaries have written shelf-loads of books, or designed buildings, or founded successful companies; my career has been parcelled out in two-minute segments, which have been squirted electronically, God knows how, through the earth's atmosphere, up to the satellites they were aimed at, and on into the immensity of space.

My small collection of seventeenth-century Muscovite icons (picked up in the last years of Communism, when a few dollars bought almost anything, including KGB generals) tends to impress visitors, and one or two items from my Stalin memorabilia are moderately spectacular. I've got some nice old first editions of Irish authors, including my putative relation the Dean, a couple of plaster busts of Roman emperors (Septimius Severus took a nasty hit to the forehead from a mug of tea the day my second wife left, but the stain on his left cheek gives him a phoney air of antiquity), and some pleasant but unremarkable early Victorian watercolours by an Anglo-Irish artist whose name I can never remember: Augustus someone?

In my pleasantly messy sitting room is an excellent ten-sided Irish dining table in walnut from the 1780s, with six chairs to match. My aunt from County Wicklow left them to me. In a sideboard drawer, enclosed in a padded leather box and nestling in a bed of faded mauve silk, is a pair of 1750s duelling pistols, beautifully engraved, made for a bloodthirsty Swift ancestor who was also called Jonathan. My antique-dealing grandfather from County Meath gave them to me in an uncharacteristic fit of generosity, then tried to reclaim them three weeks later, the thieving old bastard.

And that's the lot. My last ex-wife got everything else: the furniture (minus the table and chairs, which everyone seemed to forget), the family silver (not much of that), and the money (even less). For some reason the judge at the divorce court, a lady, let me keep the flat; maybe she took a bit of a shine to me.

Sure, I've had an exciting and enjoyable life; but there's plenty missing. I am, you see, Yesterday. The Way We Were. Unregenerate, unreconstructed, unattractive, utterly without excuse. I make jokes about things I ought to take seriously, I still wear ties, I drink at lunchtime, and have a hankering for a cigar whenever I can afford one. I hold doors open for women, call some of them 'my dear', and make eye contact with them for longer than the maximum six seconds which American and some British companies now specify. In the court of present-day society I'll soon be found guilty of old-think, and sentenced to be ostracised by the neck until dead.

I've never been able to hang on to cash. Being a journalist is one of the most insubstantial ways of earning a living you can imagine, except perhaps for being a professional poker player. Or a backbench politician.

I am one that gathers Samphire – dreadful trade.

It is possible to amass good money in television, true, but only if you're one of the bosses or the top creative talent. The toiling masses, people like me, get zip – regardless of what you read in the right-wing press. And it's hard and not always very enjoyable work.

Umpteen friends and colleagues of mine have given up the fight and the inadequate salary and the unnecessary bureaucracy, and gone off into PR or management or death by early retirement. Not me: I'm a lifer. I love the fact that I'm free to travel the world and do the things I want to. And I enjoy the feeling that I don't have to come back to the office more than three or four times a year to endure the moaning of my colleagues and fill in the required forms. The rest of the time I communicate with them by mobile phone, and the bastards can't even tell what country I'm in.

The trouble is, my boss is trying to get rid of me. It's this fascism, which says that only people under fifty can hack it. A few years ago the sodding age-Nazis threw me out of the grand outfit I used to work for, and I managed to land a job with a sharper, smaller company you'll definitely have heard of. I'm sure you'll have watched it, too. But now they're at it as well, asking for letters from my doctor and stopping me from going to places where I might need to run around.

The outfit's founder is old enough, in all conscience: a raddled ancient with a neck like a Galapagos tortoise and a red lump for a chin which seems to have an existence of its own. His portrait hangs in the newsroom in the spot where Stalin would have hung in Radio Moscow. God help you if you report something detrimental to one of the other companies he owns. He doesn't seem to object to hostile stories about the politicians he backs, but if you cost him money you're in trouble. I know, because that's exactly what I did once. Maybe I'll write about it some time. But ever since that happened, the atmosphere in the office has been very different: no more beaming smiles, just a variety of leaks to *Private Eye* about how crap I am.

Eventually, of course, the company death squad will catch up with me. I'll be shot in the back of the neck and buried in a shallow grave somewhere outside the premises, with the voice of some friend and colleague of mine whispering in my ear that it wasn't his idea to do this, but you know how it is. And without a doubt I will know. In other words, I'm just like every other employee of a big outfit who has managed to linger on past his or her sell-by date, and expects to get the Black Spot every time the internal post hits the in-tray. I won't go on about this any more: you've got your own problems.

Oh – one more thing, though. When I talk of company death squads, I'm speaking entirely figuratively. What separates me from you and every other superannuated employee of a large, brutal organisation is that someone really is out to get me. It isn't my boss. Sure, he'd like to sack me, but he hasn't so far done it, either from lethargy, or maybe an attenuated sense of guilt because I've been injured in the company's service. (In Iraq, a bullet fired by some moron who was celebrating Saddam Hussein's birthday passed through the radius and ulnar bones of my forearm, clipping them both and giving me an odd-looking scar. I'll never play for Ireland now, but at the age of sixty-one my chances are fading anyway.)

The fact is, most of the people who run my outfit are decent enough: arts graduates, usually, who got into television because it sounded like fun, and stayed on for decades after it proved not to be. I'm not scared of them in any way. No – the ones I'm scared of don't want to hand me a P45 form, they want to blow me away. Literally. And when I say 'literally', I'm not just using the word to add a bit of emphasis, like people do nowadays.

By now, I expect, you're thinking that I've inherited an adult-sized dose of my father's bullshit, plus lashings of Slavic gloom from my Russian studies. But just because I'm gloomy, it doesn't mean they're not out to get me. I'm writing this narrative with the precise intention of persuading you that these things aren't just the fantasies of an elderly gent with too much Jameson under his belt.

The fact is, I'm terrified nowadays that I'll be murdered in my bed.

Five

The last time I saw Patrick was a couple of months before his weird and inexplicable death. There wasn't any coolness between us; it was just that we'd both been really busy. Especially him. As an up-and-coming backbencher, he took an interest in the business of selling weaponry to foreign countries; the kind of thing they write editorials about in the *Guardian*. He seemed to have a mild disapproval of this kind of trade, which I always thought was a bit odd for a Tory. But then, of course, he was also strongly against Brexit.

One dark, rainy night I found myself standing on the doorstep of the building near Sloane Square Tube station where his flat was, with the wind whistling down the narrow canyons with cutting force. The place was red brick, five stories high, dark and frowning: Jack the Ripper might have lived there, if he was the toff some of the conspiracy theorists make out. The obligatory bunch of flowers and bottle of wine were lodged in the crook of my left arm; with my right forefinger I pressed the third button from the bottom. 'Macready', said the label in fading blue biro.

Nothing happened for a bit. Then the light went on in the hall, there was a creaking noise, and a tall, thin, stooping figure appeared in front of me.

'Greetings,' said the figure warmly. Well, quite warmly, though given the stuff I was carrying and the drenching I'd received outside he might have been a little more effusive. As he stood aside to let me in, the light shone on him.

There are some people who simply keep the same features for most of their life and just add wrinkles. Others change but are recognisably the person you knew at twenty. A few seem to abandon everything about themselves, and turn into someone completely different. Patrick Macready, MP, from somewhere in the Midlands, was starting to be one of those: more serious, more dominant, more severe.

Yet he had the same broad face and covering of dark hair that looked as though nothing could penetrate it, the same heavy horn-rimmed specs and the same charming smile that appeared and then disappeared quickly. I remembered, as I always did when I was with him, the moment we first encountered each other: standing side by side, brand new arrivals, alone and lonely, at the bar of a ratty old pub close to our college in Oxford. We'd always stayed friends after that.

This time, though, Patrick seemed faintly, uncharacteristically distant, and I couldn't think why. He stood there a half-second too long, then said gruffly and with a surprising lack of his habitual smoothness, 'Well, you'd better come up.'

He led the way to the narrow, boxed-off communal stairs, past the descent to the basement and the entrance to the ground-floor flat. The unmistakeable sound of someone middle class laying down the law on Radio 4 filtered out from underneath the door. Quite good prints of Roberts' watercolours of Egypt and Sinai were screwed to the walls in the hall and up the stairs, as though the people who lived in these flats might have taste and money but couldn't entirely be trusted.

'You've come on your own?'

We had established a few days earlier that I would, when he'd phoned me out of the blue. My most recent squeeze had evaporated: was he trying to rub it in? He must certainly have known about it: some spiteful bastard at work had sent the details to the papers. 'Now TV Jon's Ladyfriend Goes Out With His Colleague', said one gossip-column headline.

What a silly, outmoded phrase that is, by the way: who nowadays wants to go out, when staying in and going to bed is the real objective? 'Dating', 'going with', 'seeing' – the American equivalents – are just as vapid and inadequate. They refer to a time, long dead, when you invited a girl to the pictures or the park. I actually rather preferred it that way, but nowadays, in the relatively rare times when I get lucky, I realise it's necessary to join the general rush to the bedroom. If you hold back, you run the risk of seeming reluctant, possibly lacking in sexual self-confidence: there are few desire killers more effective than that.

But as I get older, I find it increasingly hard to bother with all the fuss of tidying myself up, pretending to be thoughtful and generous, spending too much money at a restaurant or the movies in time-honoured fashion, trying to lure someone into bed, when all I really want to do is lounge around in front of the telly or read an improving book beside the fire. Well, that's what I tell myself.

The door to Patrick's flat was open, and in the golden light that flooded out on to the landing stood a slender, dark-haired woman, a good twenty years younger than Macready and me. It suddenly came to me why Patrick had seemed on edge: he was worried about the way I would interact with this young woman. Maybe he thought I would feel she was absurdly young for him. And never mind me; what about all those disapproving *Daily Mail* readers he needed to vote him in?

She had looked attractive enough out in the passage, but she looked even better when we re-formed in his sitting room. Polish? Russian? Possibly, but British-educated, I thought in the quarter-second before I shook her hand, after hearing her say the single word 'Hello'. *Ex pede Herculem*; from one small detail we can get an idea of the whole. The whole in this case being a degree from a British university in something, maybe economics, I would hazard. But the dark, razored hair, the discreetly covered flat chest, the small tattoo of some unrecognisable bird which roosted in the crook of her neck: might she be batting for the other side?

I've historically gone for soft, rounded, jokey blondes with a tendency to giggle and nudge me hard in the ribs, but this androgynous, serious, pale-featured young woman with the penetrating dark blue eyes was something utterly different. She made everyone else seem dull – Patrick and me included.

Like a forest creature, escaping from the hunt.

Who wrote that? Pasternak? Blok?

'Hello. I'm Barbara Kuznetsov.'

'*Privet, Varvara. Menya zovut Djon. Djon Swift.*'

She coloured pleasantly. She was Russian, yet she introduced herself with a Westernised version of her name; she even pronounced her first name as though the Vs were Bs. She must have been in England a long time.

Willowy was definitely the word for her: her back was as straight as a guardsman's and her short hair was glossy and orientally black. Her face had an irregularity that was highly intriguing, and her high cheekbones and slanted eyes hinted at Mongolian ancestry; like dear old Vladimir Ilych, I thought with a touch of spite. A knockout, but a completely unconventional one. Patrick had landed himself a Marxist–Leninist stunner.

'Vara read fine art at St John's. The Cambridge one,' he said, as though either of us cared about all that Oxbridge crap nowadays.

He didn't explain their relationship, but the way she moved around the flat made it clear she was fully at home there. Yet she didn't actually seem to live in it; perhaps it was the fur-collared coat draped over the back of the armchair, instead of hanging where it would have belonged. Or maybe it was just the lack of women's magazines. Have you ever been to a flat where a woman lives and not found magazines about clothes and makeovers strewn around everywhere?

For some reason, in spite of my admiration, or maybe because of it, I found myself reacting to her rather frostily.

'So what do you do, work in a gallery?'

I only start my sentence with 'so', I've noticed, when I'm being hostile to someone. Though nowadays every bore who's answering questions on the radio does it.

'Oh yes – that's precisely what I do.'

Hmm; so she didn't like me either. It usually takes people a bit of time to see through me and decide I'm not their type; this girl was quick off the mark. She tilted her head in a way which, although she was a good four inches shorter than my six foot, managed to give the impression she was looking down on me.

Patrick moved in, ever the smooth politician. 'It's the best. That vast great one in Cork Street. Postmodernist stuff, mostly.'

I could see now why he'd been nervous when he opened the door to me: it wasn't so much my reaction to her that worried him, but hers to me.

'So where did you grow up?'

'In Petersburg.'

'But you must have gone to school here.'

29

Silence for a moment; then, grudgingly, 'St Paul's Girls School.' As though she was under orders to give name, rank and number only, but had been tricked into disobeying.

'Deputy head girl,' Patrick said quietly and confidentially, with a distinct touch of amusement.

'I would have expected nothing less.'

By now I disliked her intensely.

So I turned to Patrick as though we had finished with her for the time being. I suppose that wasn't very nice of me.

'And how is the jolly old Party getting along?'

'Not very jolly at the moment. All this Brexit stuff makes everything pretty poisonous.'

'Whoever would have thought such a thing?'

I'm a lifelong, if discreet, Liberal, you see; my great-grandfather won County Wexford for Gladstone and Home Rule in the 1880s, and my grandfather was lucky to survive an ambush by an IRA murder gang when he went canvassing there in 1919. Whenever I put my X in the polling station box nowadays it seems a bit dull in comparison.

Still, my political views never got in the way of my friendship with Patrick. Both of us were scrupulous about not pushing a party political line with each other: it was a sort of mutual non-aggression pact.

We had a shared past, of course, but I often thought the real link that kept us close was that his family was from Ireland, just like mine was. If you're Irish, even residually, there's always something in you that never quite slots into the British conventions of class, politics, family, accent. You feel an outsider, and that makes you closer to other originally Irish people than to the pure-bred Brits.

This applies equally whether or not you're an Anglo-Irish Prod from a family long decayed by drink and falling off horses, like I am, or a true son of the bog, like Patrick; though in our case Patrick had turned out to be a smoothie, and I hadn't. Standing there with a glass in my hand, I found a bit of verse was working away in my head:

Sing the peasantry, and then
Hard-riding country gentlemen,
The holiness of monks, and after
Porter-drinkers' randy laughter.

Not that I really like Yeats all that much; a willy wetleg of a man, forever mooning after that awful bony harridan Maud Gonne who wasn't even Irish – she came from Surrey, for God's sake.

Anyway, Patrick was from the porter-drinking side of the house, but he looked, sounded, and *felt* like one of the hard riders. Please don't think I'm saying this with any kind of prejudice. Irish people are mostly born without the snobbishness gene; that's one of the many things that separates us from the English, thank God.

Patrick wasn't even a Catholic, though he had the thick, blue-black hair, brushed back from his forehead, which you see in lots of towns and villages in the West of Ireland. His peasant ancestors had been soupers during the Great Hunger, meaning they'd agreed to become Prods in exchange for a regular supply of cabbage boiled in water. Great people, my lot: like firemen who make the people they're rescuing sign a cheque before they'll carry them to safety.

And yet turning Protestant was the best thing that could have happened to Patrick's family. Instead of going steerage to America and lying in vomit the whole way, they got a decent education, moved to Dublin, became lawyers, and eventually lived in a big red-brick house in Rathgar. Them's my principles, Patrick's family thought, and if you don't like them I've got others.

And now, generations on, here he was in a thoroughly *Country Life* flat in Chelsea. It gave an impression of solidity and breeding. Patrick possessed excellent taste, refined and understated, and everything was beautifully organised.

There were half a dozen shelves filled with small, finely bound eighteenth- and nineteenth-century books in good bindings; I know, because I'd been with him when he bought some of them. Nothing much else: no garish modern dust jackets, and certainly no paperbacks like you find in my gaff. He kept a few in the guest lavatory – his idea of a joke, I imagine – but even then they were serious ones. Nothing racier than Patrick O'Brian on the fiction side, and mostly well-thumbed biographies of nineteenth- and early twentieth-century politicians. That way there was no temptation for guests to settle down in the loo and take root.

It was the kind of household where the owner would never need to say 'I wonder where I left such and such?' A place for everything and everything in its place, as my judgemental old County Louth grandma used to say. It wasn't just that he had money, and that he'd used it to buy wisely; it was that he'd spent it with precision. He didn't have a single, solitary thing too many.

'Boss treating you nicely, is she?'

'Not too bad.'

He said it with a self-congratulatory lowering of the head that showed he was conscious of doing well as an up-and-coming backbencher. But I also noticed that he didn't reprove me for the reference.

'And how about Macclesfield?' It was the next by-election.

'Piece of cake.'

'Not what I read in the fish wrappers.'

Vara was bored. I was deliberately excluding her from the conversation, which annoyed her in much the same way she had annoyed me. But I could sense her presence, and the curve of her neck, even though I wasn't looking in her direction. If externals were anything to go by, and in my experience they often are, Patrick was a lucky bastard. His only saving grace was that he knew he was a lucky bastard.

He went over to fix our drinks, which left her stranded with me. She was pretty devastating when she looked at you face on and those slanted, dark blue eyes zeroed in on yours.

'Good chap, Patrick.'

'I think so,' she said, and there was an unexpected ceasefire in the atmosphere.

'One of my oldest friends.'

'So he told me.'

'Anything else?'

I was on thin ice in asking this, but I skated on.

'He says you could have done a lot more with your life, and not just been a TV reporter.'

'Senior news correspondent.'

Her superb eyes switched from me to an early nineteenth-century print of Nevsky Prospekt on the walls. Plainly, professional titles meant nothing to this daughter of Bolshevism. It pissed me off.

'So I'd have done better if I'd sold fifth-rate daubings to the ignorant rich?'

That should have brought our relationship to a full stop, of course. But Patrick came over with the dry sherry, and because he could see that something had gone wrong he was particularly emollient.

33

'We thought we'd go for dinner round the corner,' he said, looking at her but speaking to me. 'Is that OK with you?'

The restaurant round the corner was full of the kind of people who would knowingly eat in a place where the house wine got a 250 per cent mark-up. I'd actually liked it a lot, on the few occasions I'd been there, but on a salary like mine, with all the deductions for maintenance and National Insurance, it was out of my range. There were posters from 1950s French films on the wall, and a great racket of conversation and the odd shriek of laughter. In here out of the rain and wind it was pleasantly warm, and I soon needed to take my jacket off. What makes dimly lit restaurants with steamed-up windows so attractive? Maybe it's a chance for us to pop back into the womb for a couple of hours.

It was only after I'd ordered a dozen Carlingford Lough oysters and drunk a glass of decent white that it dawned on me why, precisely, Vara had been so hostile. It was rather flattering, I now realised: Patrick was a straight down the line politico with, potentially, a tremendous future, which meant he would never be able to put a foot wrong. I, on the other hand, wore outdated clothes, used bad language, and did exactly what I wanted. She regarded me as the mistress of a great house might regard the leader of a troupe of gypsies who've come to call. I represented liberty, anarchy, adventure; God knows what trouble I might lure her man into if she left us alone together for too long. I was the raggle-taggle gypsy, come to Patrick's door.

He ordered a bottle of 2006 Gigondas without pronouncing the S on the end; that gave me something to feel superior about, at long last, though the sommelier, a Frenchman, ignored it politely. He'd have heard worse every day in England. But it showed that even successful politicians sometimes got things wrong. I might only be a humble hack who could have done a lot more with his life, but at least I know the correct way of saying the name of one of the finest products of the Côtes-du-Rhône.

I couldn't prevent myself showing off to both of them (well, mostly Vara, I suppose) by telling them that the name came from the Latin *jocunditas*, meaning 'jollity'; the original town was founded by the Roman army as a place for the soldiers to spend their R & R. Stick with me and you'll learn a wealth of entirely useless rubbish.

All right, this was merely the petty rivalry of someone less successful. I loved old Patrick, and admired him too. He'd had to swallow a great deal of crap in the process of swimming with the political tide, but he'd done it with dignity. He was decent and clever and straight-dealing, and if, as some people were beginning to forecast, he would soon be a junior minister, he was likely to be better than most of his colleagues.

He'd stuck by me, too. His Whips office would have known about our long friendship, because they know everything potentially damaging, and they can't have liked it; they hated MPs associating too much with journalists. That didn't seem to matter to him. After all, here we were, eating in public, in a place which was known to be infested by politicos and top civil servants. He and Vara could simply have given me a takeaway at the flat and kept me under wraps.

I could also tell from the proprietorial way he wielded the menu that he was going to pick up the bill when things came to their logical conclusion here. That was a relief on a purely practical level, since I had twenty-five quid and a bit of change in my pocket, and close to zero on my debit card.

The conversation languished briefly, in a way it never would have if the two of us had been alone. It felt like trying to light a turf fire on a wet night in the Mountains of Mourne, and I chose a distinctly unimaginative way of starting it up again.

'So how did you come to meet the gorgeous Vara?'

It was nothing serious, and I tossed it out pretty much without thinking. But it had a surprising effect. From being first cold and then hostile, the girl positively started to glow. For me, referring to her beauty involved nothing more personal than if I'd said it was a cold night, or that she'd just ordered half a dozen *fines de claires*: it was a matter of observable fact. Still, I've never yet met a woman who didn't like being complimented on her looks; Margaret Thatcher certainly enjoyed it, and so (I found on one occasion) did Angela Merkel, though with both of them it took a serious effort of will for me to get the words out.

Patrick liked it, too, in a proprietorial kind of way, as if I'd complimented him on something he owned: that super-delicate Northern Sung bowl, for instance, which he'd shown me back in the flat. He possessed it in the same way that he possessed Vara's beauty. Or, to put it more crudely, he had the use of it. Anyway, my chance remark got us all talking in a much more friendly way. The turf fire was starting to put out smoke, and even the odd lick of flame.

It turned out that Patrick had known Vara's father, a top civil servant, when he was based in St Petersburg, immediately after the collapse of Communism in Russia. She was fifteen at the time, and Patrick would have been, what, thirty-four, just as I was. He put the idea into the commissar's head that she should go to school in England, something that was still a big novelty for Russians then, and mildly daring, not to mention hugely expensive for someone on a Sov salary – no matter how much the old boy had been squirrelling away on the side; he was in the oil trade, apparently.

It had all worked out rather well. Patrick had kept a paternal eye on her when Vara lived in London with her mother, who never learned to speak English. That the eye was never anything more than paternal at that stage, I wholeheartedly believe. Yet even the most honourable and restrained of men aren't immune to the divine passion in the long term. As best I could work out, they'd been together for three years; and though I'm maybe not the greatest judge of these things, they seemed to be pretty comfortable and affectionate.

'Well, congratulations to you both for doing the right thing, anyway.'

Again, the definite glow in her fine eyes, and the faint preening in his straightforward ones.

'But don't those bastards at Five worry about it? Especially since you're now starting to go up the ladder?'

MI5 must have watched the two of them pretty carefully. It was fine to have a relationship like this in the old Yeltsin years, when the only problem was Russian corruption. But when the Putin era dawned, the problems grew and grew: corruption, sure, but mixed in with espionage, blackmail, murder, drugs, and God knows what.

The eyes – both sets – became instantly wary.

'Varvara has a British passport,' Patrick said stiffly. 'She knows more about British culture than you do. She's a Brit through and through.'

'I could get a South African passport, but it wouldn't make me a bloody Zulu.'

'Ha ha.' He wasn't amused, but Vara was visibly stirred up.

'You see, Russia doesn't mean anything to me.'

She leaned across the table with a sudden, unguarded frankness which completely won me over. 'My whole life is here.'

'Well, here and in Harrods.'

Patrick's quip cleared the air again, and we had become rather noisily jolly by the time the oysters arrived.

It was only afterwards, when we went back to his flat and Vara disappeared into the kitchen to make coffee and pour the brandies, that Patrick and I had a moment to speak privately.

'You're quite right. I've had my problems, yes.'

'I wondered if you might have. Those bastards have no romance in their souls.'

'It's nothing to do with Vara. There's still stuff left over from the past, you see.'

'What sort of stuff?'

'Well, slightly disturbing stuff, to be honest. I've been a bit worried recently.'

But at that moment she pushed the door open with the coffee tray, and we didn't have another opportunity to talk about it in private between us.

'Are you ever free for lunch?' I asked him as I struggled into my ancient overcoat, avoiding the rip in the lining.

'Not for another couple of months, if it's for work. If it's for pleasure, Mondays are usually good.'

We fixed on the following Monday.

'Thanks for being nice to Vara,' he whispered as he showed me downstairs to the front door.

'I didn't think I had been, particularly.'

Monday came and went without our meeting up, and so did another, more half-hearted effort to make a lunch date. Patrick was my dearest and oldest friend, but I never saw him again. All I saw was the sordid aftermath of a sex game gone badly wrong.

Six

Without consulting me, the boss had decided that I should be the one who did the reporting on Patrick's death. Maybe, knowing that we had been friends, he was trying to make life extra-specially nasty for me, with the aim of getting me to throw up the job and storm out in rage and despair. That's the kind of outfit they were: as much fun as a tea party at Berchtesgaden. The senior producer on the desk rang shortly after I'd got back to the flat that afternoon and told me the bad news. Naturally he wouldn't listen to anything I might have to say about the idea.

'Sorry, Daniel's decision. Take it up with him if you don't like it.'

Daniel Porchester was the news department's ultimate boss, the *capo di tutti capi*: as sensitive a character as ever wielded a beheading knife. Head of Factual Output was his title; only people tended to say 'FO' instead. He was the one who'd decided I was too old to be employable, and was looking for ways to get rid of me. To give you some idea of how ghastly he was, he went round with his shirt collar turned up. And he was famously difficult to speak to, guarded by a deputy who copied all Daniel's attitudes and superiority, plus a male assistant with no observable qualities except a pale spotty face and a habit of reading *The*

Spectator, and two tall, grandly dressed secretaries. I either stormed into his office and resigned, or I caved in.

I caved in.

'Oh yes, and Alyssa Roberts will be working with you as producer. She'll be ringing you.'

Putting Alyssa Roberts and me together was another refined form of torture; they really did want to get rid of me. Until now, my permanent producers had always been male, inclined to drink, and something approaching my own age. Alyssa was in her late thirties, clever, tough, feminist, and black. Something told me that privately educated old boys with a couple of wives to their account and a habit of quoting nineteenth-century poetry weren't entirely her thing.

My mobile vibrated in my pocket. An acidulous voice at the other end said 'Jon.'

She didn't feel the necessity to announce herself.

'Hello Alyssa. I'm just in the King's Road,' I said, as though I felt some explanation was due.

Judging from the way she replied, the King's Road wasn't her thing either.

'Yes, well, we've got to meet up and talk about the story. I'll be round there to meet up with you. Where's the nearest Starbucks?'

Starbucks are blessedly thin on the ground in SW3, and I explained this tactfully. It didn't seem to make her think more highly of SW3. There was a *gemütlich* café near Sloane Square which I suggested to her as a place to meet, though I didn't use the word *gemütlich*. I do have some idea of self-preservation.

This pairing has clearly been organised so as not to work, I thought: I'm old-fashioned, and I like an atmosphere of pleasant-ness and amusement when I'm working with people. Especially when I was being forced to report on the apparently self-induced death of a man I'd been close to all my adult life. At the same time, I was buggered if I was going to surrender to this awful woman too easily.

As it happened, my regular producer had just been promoted, so I didn't have anyone to work with at present. Producers and reporters make an odd couple. They live side by side in the closest intimacy, each knowing all the other's weaknesses of character and susceptibilities. They know precisely what their wives and husbands and lovers are like, the many failings of their children, and what goes wrong with their cars and dishwashers. My producers and I have had to pay for each other when we've run short of cash, endure each other's snoring (especially mine) in shared rooms in rotten hotels in horrible places, cleaned each other up after a bad bout of food poisoning, and – worst of all – laughed at each other's jokes, no matter how feeble and how often repeated.

I've had to break the news of a family death to one producer, and to another the fact that he'd been sacked. I've had to abase myself to a boss I hated, in order to save the job of a third. My producers, male and female, tend to work with me for four or five years, and I've usually stayed good friends with them afterwards – even the ones I'd slept with. The women, I mean.

It didn't sound to me as though I was going to stay good friends with Alyssa. Or indeed become friendly with her in the first place. As for sleeping with her – *Absit omen.* Or do I mean *Eheu fugaces?*

'I'll see you there at – what – eleven o'clock?' I ventured.

She couldn't agree to that, because she wasn't the agreeing type. Eleven thirty was the earliest she could manage.

'So be it,' I said with a certain darkness of tone, and ended the call.

41

I made sure of getting there at twenty past, and brought a book to read. If she was clever, I could show that I was too; and because I imagined she was something of a leftie, I brought a book with me to read which could act as a sign that I came in peace: Orwell's essays. We might as well start on as good a footing as possible.

Nowadays (I feel I've got to make this clear) I'm getting too old to run after women. If they want to run after me, excellent: but, as my grandfather used to say, a chance would be a fine thing. Even so, I confess the old Adam stirred momentarily in me when Alyssa came through the door. One of my ex-wives used to say bitterly that I liked the look of every woman I saw, and maybe there is something to that. Alyssa certainly wasn't beautiful in the conventional sense: she was too tough-looking for that. She reminded me a bit of the bust of Nefertiti which the Neues Museum in Berlin nicked from Amarna: grand and assertive, with sticking-out ears. I didn't like the look she directed at me when she spotted me. Yet there was something about her, all the same . . .

'I do have work to do, you know. It took me ages to get here.'

I didn't retaliate, though I felt like it.

'Well, it's very good of you to take the time. Can I get you a coffee, or maybe a tea?'

'Tea?' It sounded as though there was something morally wrong with tea. She ordered an Americano, I asked for a pot of Darjeeling. She looked down her distinctly fine nose at that.

'I don't know what your relationship was with this Macready man, and to be honest it's none of my business.'

She made it sound as though we were lovers; maybe she thought we were. 'But we've got to do an honest, straightforward job on this story.'

It was good of her to explain this to me; I might otherwise have been tempted to do a dishonest, convoluted job on it. Still, I

42

continued to keep my temper: working closely with other people isn't easy, and even if she had no concept of tact or understanding, that didn't give me a licence to respond in kind. Not yet, anyway.

'Fine,' I said noncommittally. 'How much of the sex stuff do you reckon we should talk about?'

'The orange is the key element,' she said, as though she was teaching a twelve-year-old the facts of life.

I assume she thought Patrick and I were part of some ultra-dodgy sex cult. Maybe she believed that everyone whose parents paid for their education and who went to Oxford was that way inclined. Well, if she needed any evidence, there were plenty of names I could give her.

'We've got a shot of that,' I said. Then, getting irritated, 'But I told the cameraman not to film the cum on the wall.'

That shut her up good and proper. She went entirely quiet for a few moments, too embarrassed to speak. It felt like an important point to me. In fact it was pretty clear she didn't want us to say anything at all explicit in our report about what had happened. Well, I knew my place; in this organisation, unlike the grand old outfit I'd been lured away from, the producers ran things. Here, we reporters were just – what was it one of them had once said to me? – 'a gob on a stick'. How charming.

We talked the story through. I didn't like the way she switched from censoriousness towards me to a kind of public tweeness about Patrick's death, but the Brits are a sanctimonious bunch, and they were our primary audience.

After our agreeable little Boston tea party we met up with Os Malan, the cameraman, in order to film the exteriors of various buildings in ways that would look faintly sinister. This, after all, was going to be a story about the sickness at the heart of the

British political system. Upper-class politicians who preached morality to the rest of society were themselves deeply corrupt: that seemed to be the extent of Alyssa's political analysis. It was no good trying to explain to her how buttoned-up and straight poor old Patrick had been. For her, he was a symbol of everything she disapproved of: Tory, upper-middle class, public school, and Oxbridge. Oh yes, and male.

Os's attitude towards her was a study in complexity. He disliked her intensely, of course: not because he was an unreconstructed white South African racist (I knew he wasn't that, because during the bad times of the 1980s I'd seen the warm relationships he'd developed with his black sound recordists, each saving the other's life time and again) but because she was so bloody bossy. At the same time he felt as insecure in his job as I did in mine, and he was less aware of the power structure at the Centre than I was. For all he knew, she could sack him on a whim.

Back in the edit room at the Centre, after we'd done all the filming, Alyssa and I had a Homeric battle across Os's large but self-effacing body as we sat in front of the editing equipment. In the end, because I was older and nastier and had loved Patrick like a brother, I succeeded in my refusal to write a script which followed her views. What I did write was a bit bland, I suppose, but I stuck to the basic facts and refused to stick in any hints about corrupt toffs.

At the end of the day, after our report had gone out, we said goodbye.

'Quite an experience, working with you,' was the formula she came up with.

'Thanks,' I said as noncommittal as I could possibly force myself to be. May this be the only time we have to do it, was what I was thinking.

I assume she felt the same, but we both reckoned without the people on the desk, who seemed to want an excuse to push me as close and as fast to the cliff edge as was humanly possible.

As it turned out, this was to be only the start of our partnership.

Seven

Patrick's funeral took place seventeen days later, at three fifteen in the afternoon. It had been slotted in between a two forty-five and a three forty-five. Nowadays even the disposal of the dead is just a matter of scheduling.

The police and the coroner's office had dealt with the case quickly – no doubt after pressure from Downing Street. Patrick's death had been bad for the government, with journalists and various politicians competing to dig out further details of moral lapses in the Tory party; not difficult to find, of course, but there was no shortage in other parties either, or anywhere else in society, for that matter. The fact is, though, the rest of us don't preach about the need for uprightness and decency.

The desk rang to say that Alyssa and I were down to cover the inquest, so I felt obliged to read all the detailed accounts of Patrick's death in the press in case I missed something. It was noticeable that the more moralistic a newspaper was about him, the more likely it was to linger on the sordid details of the way he'd died. Bloody Brits.

Vara was called to give evidence, but said nothing of significance. The coroner didn't quite like to ask her if she thought Patrick had dodgy habits. The closest he came was to ask if the manner of his death had surprised her.

'Yes, sir,' she said quietly. 'He was always so gentle.'

At the end the coroner shook his head and declared that a first-class career had been brought to an untimely close by misadventure. You could say that again. But the inquest did nothing to change the general perception that poor Patrick had been trying to get his rocks off in a particularly outlandish fashion.

The funeral took place a week later, and our wonderful news desk decided that it wasn't of any interest to its viewers. A Premier League footballer had been discovered by a newspaper to be involved in a love triangle – actually a love quadrilateral, if you chose to be pedantic – and for us, and the newspapers, all the prurience and moral disapproval that Patrick's death had aroused was diverted into a different channel.

I went to the funeral, of course. There was a service at a church near his flat: a rather dull place which he'd attended. If I lived near Sloane Square, I'd have gone to the excessively Arts and Crafts church at the end of Sloane Street. But no, he had to go to a smallish, dully mid-Victorian place a bit of a walk away. I think it appealed to him because it wasn't glamorous or classy. He must have thought it was the kind of place God would approve of.

If so, God was just about the only one. John Betjeman, who saved Holy Trinity from being knocked down, made no mention of St Eligius, Pimlico, in his book on English churches. Quite right, I thought as I sat on a tubular steel chair and stared up at the puke-making 1950s stained glass. The vicar's braying tone set my teeth on edge as he went on and on about duty and service: and of course 'service' drew a faint hiss of amused breath from the two rows of hacks at the back of the church.

An elderly couple sat in the front row, all on their own and holding hands, looking utterly devastated. When he stood up and held his hymn book, the old man's veiny, parchment-coloured hands shook perceptibly. A few distant relatives sat behind them, not saying anything to anyone and looking as though they wished they'd never come. The Whips' Office had sent someone junior whom I didn't recognise to represent the government. Patrick's constituency party sent a crappy, cheap-looking wreath, as though it was anxious not to call attention to the connection with him.

A couple of men in dark suits sat near the side door. One jiggled his crossed leg continually; the other leant across and whispered to him from time to time during the proceedings. They looked very official. Vara was a few empty rows behind them, dressed in a mannish black jacket and trousers and looking pretty good in spite of her pallor and puffed eyes. Poor kid: she'd taken the whole thing really badly.

As for me, I sat on my own at the end of a line of chairs, with the cheaply printed order of service on my knee and my mind wandering. There was a photo of poor old Patrick on the front of it, smiling at the camera. My camera, as it happens. I remembered precisely where and when the picture was taken: we'd been having dinner with our partners at the time (this was before Vara) in a pleasant little Lebanese place not far from my flat, and we were both in such a good mood that I decided to fix it in our memories by getting a shot of him on my mobile. When Vara put together the order of service I dug the picture out and sent it to her. We never know how the snaps we take will end up, do we?

We sang the usual guff – 'Dear Lord and Father of Mankind', and the 23rd Psalm, and ended with 'Onward Christian Soldiers' in the hope that it would cheer everyone up. It didn't; how could it? I meant to go and say something to the old couple in the front row, but as I was on my way to speak to them I was ambushed by one of Patrick's more boring political friends, who was clearly angling for me to interview him on camera; and by the time I'd managed to shake him off, they'd slipped away in humiliation and sorrow.

Afterwards, at a nearby gastropub, the hacks did their loathsome job of chivvying the subdued mourners into corners and trying to get a bit of scandal out of them. One trio (print reporters like to hunt in twos and threes – it's safer, and they have to think even less) tried it on me, and I told them to fuck off loudly enough for everyone round me to hear. Once I would have worried that they might take some sort of revenge on me in print, but now I simply didn't care.

I stuck to Irish whiskey, in memory of Patrick, and stayed on at the pub till I thought everyone else had left, propping myself up morosely in a corner of the bar. But not everyone had gone after all. It was half of the pair of dark suits. He had the kind of face that suited confidential work: pleasant, understanding, with a voice to match.

'You're pretty cut up about it all, aren't you?'

I looked up at him with a snarl. 'Whatever would give you an idea like that?'

'No, I agree.'

'With what?'

'I mean I'd be upset myself in the circumstances.'

Slight accent: Liverpudlian? Glaswegian? No, Belfast. *Prod* Belfast, though not from some side street down the Shankill. One of those big, expensive red-brick houses in the Malone Road, I'd say. That might mean a progression from the Army or the Royal Ulster Constabulary to MI5.

I grunted while I thought this through, and that gave him just enough purchase to have another go.

'He was a close friend of yours, I assume?'

'It's not entirely clear to me what it's got to do with you.'

'No, nothing at all. Nothing.' He smiled blandly. 'It's just that, like you, I'd feel angry in the circumstances.'

'What fucking circumstances? He topped himself by accident during some dodgy sex game. Death by misadventure – and you can say that again.'

'You know what kind of person Macready was,' Malone Road went on. 'Decent, moral, honourable. Would he have behaved like that in secret?'

'No one can say. You could be rogering the male help after hours, for all I know. Right there on the Embankment.'

Half a bottle of best Jameson had passed down my throat by that time. Without that, I don't suppose I'd have shown that I knew who he worked for.

Malone Road grinned: good response.

'That's me. But Macready was a man who was in complete control of himself. And he led a completely normal life.'

Vara, he meant.

'So what are you saying?'

'Just that you shouldn't take everything at face value. Suppose someone wanted to get rid of Patrick Macready, and they did it in the kind of way that meant no one would ever take his death seriously.'

'You're saying someone murdered him?'

The whiskey had certainly slowed my reactions down.

'Maybe.'

He sounded more Belfast than ever now.

'But who?'

'That's for us to find out. You too, maybe.'

I looked at him, the clouds of alcohol parting a little. He was tallish, stooped, dark, forty plus, and the pleasant smile didn't really match the jutting nose and long chin. His suit was neither very new or very neat, and the striped blue and silver tie could have come from a Poundshop.

'Any ideas?'

'You always have to look at people's backgrounds,' he said patiently, as though he was giving an induction lecture to a bunch of brand new MI5 recruits. 'Macready was interested in checking out the sale of weapons systems to some quite dodgy places: Turkey, some Arab countries, you know. Maybe someone took against him. Think about it, anyway.'

I did think about it. Not just when I settled up with the pub manager, but on the Tube on the way home, and lying in the bath, and sitting in front of the television chat shows and not registering what the boring brain donors were saying, and getting into bed, and trying to go to sleep and not succeeding, and waking up at three in the morning. I thought about it so much that eventually nothing else made any sense. It all came down to this: MI5 thought someone had murdered my best friend, and in a way that made him a laughing stock of the entire world.

Eight

I was still a bit shell-shocked two days later, when I eased open the door of the glass pod and insinuated my sizeable form inside.

There were too many people in there.

It was the weekly editorial meeting, and everyone wanted to show how keen they were. Most of us had to stand up, pressed to the sides of this overheated bubble. Posters emphasising the positive aspect of our activities hung on the walls, as though we needed to be perpetually cheered up and reindoctrinated. It had all the mental freedom of a local Communist Party office in, say, Minsk, circa 1975.

The room was getting hot. Also, I felt, smelly. Not with BO, of course – everyone here was too bourgeois for that – but with the odour of earnestness. People seem so serious nowadays: the modern world has banned facetiousness along with smoking and patting girls' bottoms. Soon, very soon, they'll ban booze.

O brave new world, That has such people in't!

In the old days, everyone had a fag stuck to their lower lip and took two hours off for lunch round at the pub: but it's probably illegal to suggest that you might once have enjoyed that kind of thing. Unless of course you don't mind sounding like a paid-up member of the Nigel Farage Remembrance Society.

What had happened to the monsters of ego we used to employ, always on the point of erupting with volcanic ire, whom I had to confront at meetings like this? God, they were awful. The one who stapled his secretary's braids to the chair, and taunted her with her virginity. Or the one who fell to the floor, laughing and crying, when she heard that her report was going to be the lead on that night's news and started to chew the carpet; something I thought had only happened in the *Reichskanzlerei*.

Or the one who threatened to fly his light aircraft into the editor's quiet, suburban home. 'Right into your fucking bedroom window, you cunt, just when you're fucking your fucking wife. Assuming you still can, which I sincerely doubt.'

All paid off, all sacked, all gone. Yet things seemed so bloody pastel-shaded now, by contrast. Everyone's horribly enthusiastic, as if they're involved in work of national importance. Even in a dump like this.

Not that they're actually dressed in pastels. Nowadays, science and the garment industry can give us anything – *anything* – and yet all we seem to ask for is prison clothes in black or dark grey. As a result the group here looked like off-duty undertakers, in pre-emptive mourning for something they hadn't yet received an office memo about.

Not me. I was wearing a creased linen suit with an unfeasibly tight waistband, a pink shirt on which one button in the region of my straining navel insisted on gaping open, and a floral tie with a couple of ghostly lunch stains on it. When I'd glanced at myself briefly and reluctantly in the mirror before leaving for work that morning, I looked like a large, affronted fish being held up by a proud angler in a brownish pub photo. Possibly a pike.

Both women and men, I noticed – not for the first time – were wearing a kind of uniform: jeans but jackets, trainers but no laces, collared shirts but no ties. The women were as brutally shod as the blokes. When did that start to happen?

Once, I reflected, still determined to keep my mind off Patrick, people at a meeting like this would have been exclusively male and would have worn striped ties, chestnut-coloured brogues, and greenish tweed jackets with or occasionally without elbow patches.

Among all these night moths I seem to belong to a different species altogether: a tattered elderly butterfly, caught in a spider's web. I'm a revenant from another age. For the rest of these people whose breath was starting to fog the windows of the pod, the twentieth century is something they have problems recollecting; for me, it's an ever-present reality from which I haven't entirely escaped yet.

I find myself referring to politicians, to political alliances, to *countries* for God's sake, which no longer exist. My colleagues, by contrast, seem to have problems understanding that the past once seemed exactly like the present, and that it existed in colour, not in black and white.

At my age, in an organisation like this, you can be cantankerous and difficult, you can have a wide range of outside interests, you can wear clothes unlike those of anyone else in the entire building; but you must never seem vague or forgetful. 'Waning powers' is television's equivalent of an execution warrant: they can top you for it.

Some of my powers might well be on the wane, had indeed perceptibly waned, as a recent encounter with a generously built and fortunately forgiving public relations lady from an oil company had shown. But it would be suicide in this polite snake pit to show it.

Of course, they'd feel guilty if the management got rid of me. Guilt was the medium we all swam in here, like spermatozoa in the seminal fluid. Yet no one, I'd noticed, actually stopped swimming or tried to do a U-turn back down the fallopian tube.

All this reflection was dangerous, though; it disarmed you when you most needed protection. Before I'd dipped out mentally, some minutes earlier, they'd been talking about the latest Russian activist who'd just been murdered in the streets of Moscow. Now there was a silence. From the way everyone was behaving, I realised that someone must have asked me a question. I spoke at random.

'Maybe I should go to Moscow and sort out an interview with the President,' I said finally.

They all seemed surprised. Oh Christ, I thought, I've screwed up big time. Why hadn't I listened more to what they were jabbering on about? Could these people, hunting as they did in packs, sense instinctively that my powers were waning, just as great white sharks can smell a billionth part of blood in the water? (Or whatever. On scientific subjects, about which I have zero knowledge, I tend to make my statistics up. No one seems to realise.)

I smiled round at the dishlike, oestrogenic faces. There was nastiness here all right, but it was carefully disguised. And it was a different kind of nastiness compared with the past. You never heard any suggestion of braid-stapling nowadays, no threat of bedroom crashing, no carpet gnawing. No one even seemed to use the word 'fuck' any more, except for me and the younger women. All these things had been quietly and efficiently trimmed away, like unsightly nose hair.

Better to seem amused, careless, superior, than not to have the faintest idea of what they have been talking about. Best of all, though, to show you have secret, powerful contacts.

'That'd be wonderful, if we could get it,' said one of the women editors.

'But do you really think it's possible?'

Make no promises; be modest, I thought.

'It won't be easy, but I've got someone who just might be able to fix it up.'

Yuri: his contacts were legendary, and he had all sorts of links, probably questionable, with the Kremlin. An image of that handsome, wolfish face floated across my frontal lobe.

'I'll have to go there, though.'

They hated spending money, but if I could half promise them an interview they'd probably agree to let me make the necessary soundings.

'Seems like a good plan.'

I'd managed to score an important if admittedly small victory: I'd established myself as the one person in the entire organisation who might be able to secure an interview with the Russian president. So of course I couldn't leave it there. I had to screw it up big time.

'There's another thing. Patrick Macready, the MP who died. I've been hearing suggestions that his death might not have been accidental – that someone could have killed him.'

'Brilliant,' said a prematurely middle-aged deputy editor acidly. He was sitting at the far end of the table. 'Just the kind of story we ought to be diverting our meagre resources to.'

He'd done this to me a couple of times before: a clean-nose specialist who never took the slightest risk. Every outfit has its share of them, but we seemed to have more than the adult dose. The fact that he had identified me as his target showed how little influence I had in this place nowadays; if my position had been stronger he'd never have dared to take me on.

Now he grinned round at the other faces.

'How long have you been planning to write fiction for a living?'

A few people laughed out loud. Others – the attractive woman editor, for instance – looked away in embarrassment.

'That presupposes I haven't spent my entire career doing it.'

Not too bad for the spur of the moment, I suppose, but I wish I'd said something really witty in reply: 'Fuck off, you stupid twat', possibly.

I ploughed on. 'Macready was particularly interested in the sale of weapons to the Middle East. Maybe he put someone's nose out of joint.'

It didn't sound strong, even to me.

'I really don't think we need to get into any of this,' said the wiseacre down at the other end of the table in a plonking sort of voice. He fancied himself an expert on foreign affairs, and often countered the things I said at meetings as a kind of preening exercise.

I was just going to reply when there was a small eruption in my pocket. The phone which weighed it down in an unsightly way was vibrating: a particularly odd sensation for a man of my age. I raised the palm of my hand in an 'I come in peace' kind of way.

'Sorry.'

I hit the button.

'Yes?' I said judiciously, conscious that everyone round the table was listening.

The voice at the other end was Varvara's pleasant contralto. She didn't say her name, but the faint accent was identification enough.

'Can you speak?'

I couldn't: not here. But something in her tone showed me that she needed help. With my hand over the mouthpiece, I looked round at the faces.

'Sorry about this – one of my Russian contacts.'

Well, in a way, so she was.

'Actually, I think we're pretty much finished here anyway,' said my friend, the woman at the far end of the pod, with the tact I'd always associated with her. Everyone headed obediently for the door.

I followed after them and flopped down into the chair which the annoying bloke who liked to contradict me had just occupied. It still had a distasteful warmth.

'I'm so sorry, Vara. I was having a rather awkward meeting.'

'I really need to see you. I'm at Patrick's flat. Someone's been here.'

She didn't say who, and asking her didn't seem to be an option.

'All right, stay there. I'll get a cab round right away. Don't worry, I'll sort everything out.'

I'd turned fatherly because I realised that was what she needed. But I didn't feel fatherly at all. I felt lost.

Nine

Patrick had been preternaturally tidy. Whether Vara was or not, I had no idea. Various Russian girls of my acquaintance had been pretty careless around the house: those little figure-of-eights that knickers make if they're whipped off in a hurry scattered around the sitting room and bedroom, bras in all states and conditions, usually grubby. Vara seemed the cool type, and cool types are often neat and clean. Still, it was impossible to be sure.

Now, though, when she opened the door of Patrick's flat, I realised that none of this sort of speculation mattered. The room behind her looked as though a fork-lift truck had been through it. I've seen tidier car-bombings.

She was still crying. She had been crying ever since Patrick died. It didn't make her look any better, though she was weird-looking anyway. Her reddened and congested eyes worked on my sympathies far more than if she'd been calm and collected.

'I don't know what to do. What should I be doing?'

'Calling the cops.'

'But that could lead to problems.'

'For you, or for Patrick?'

'I don't know,' she moaned, 'I just don't know.' She sounded exhausted.

I put my arm round her, with no intention except to comfort her; this self-possessed, attractive, rather mannish young woman was suddenly just a kid, alone in the world. She yielded to the pressure.

'Look, we can't just ignore all this. Stuff may have been stolen.'

We were still standing in the passageway, but I could clearly see what had been done to Patrick's sitting room.

'And the insurance will never pay up unless the police have been called in.'

She sniffed, then nodded. I pulled out my mobile, and dialled 999.

The first operator put me through to a refreshingly calm second one, who took the details and suggested I should leave everything exactly as it was.

'No worries about that,' I said, glancing at the disaster zone.

Nothing that should have been upright was; everything that shouldn't have been was propped up crazily in the mess. There were shards of glass and bits of crockery everywhere. They must have dumped the stuff from the kitchen in the sitting-room. Many of the books seemed to have been ripped open, and loose pages were everywhere. For some reason the carpet was sopping wet. Then I spotted the drinks trolley, and saw why.

Some of the paintings lay on the heap. One hung at a crazy angle, which intensified the sitter's look of general disapproval.

The police arrived commendably quickly; they usually do in Chelsea. But right from the start I could see they didn't like it. Not the damage, I mean, but the set-up. Who was I, with my half-remembered face, and why was I here in the daytime with an attractive girl? And who was she, anyway?

I tried to explain, but they went on not liking it till they realised that Varvara was Russian. In Chelsea that put her into a particular slot. The British police don't like foreigners, by and large, but they do approve of people with money; and most of the Russians they would have come across were absurdly, filthily rich.

After a while, too, they paid more attention to me and started realising they had watched me on television since they were teenagers. I would have thought that might have worried them. But no – on the contrary, it calmed them down. It meant I was reliable, you see; they could trust me, and believe what I said. Which only goes to show what an extraordinarily dangerous medium television is.

It didn't take them long, either, to realise who had recently died in the flat.

'Here, wasn't this where that MP was? The one who did the —— You know, with the orange.'

'Yes.'

At any moment, I thought, they would start grinning. I broke in, 'He was a close friend of mine. And of Miss Kuznetsova here.'

Gratifyingly, the potential grins didn't break surface.

'Doesn't look like kids,' said one policeman to the other, gazing round at the chaos.

He was dark-haired, with a curiously long head.

'Kids do most of the break-ins in London nowadays,' he explained to me.

'You don't say.'

The other policeman, a nondescript character with the kind of fair hair that turns to early-onset baldness, nodded. He wouldn't know irony if he trod in it.

Light and dark, tough and gentle, nasty and nice: policemen tend to run along tram-lines, just like journalists do. And, I suppose, everyone else. It's just a question of who lays down the tram-lines in the first place.

'Kids would never have gone to so much trouble,' he said.

That, it seemed, finally disposed of kids.

Glancing round, it was perfectly obvious that whoever had done this must have been physically strong and determined, and that there must have been at least a couple of them. A sizeable cupboard had been up-ended on one side of the room. That, in particular, would have been a heavy job for a couple of grown men.

'Searching for something,' Longhead said to the other quietly.

They both glanced at me again, and at Vara: what did we know, and why were we here?

'Can you see if anything's missing?'

Tears sprang to Vara's violet eyes all over again, but she didn't say anything. I knew, though: what was missing for her was Patrick.

'TV's still here, and all the hi-fi stuff. Smashed, though, which is funny.'

Patrick had spent a lot of money on electronics, and bits of expensive gear were lying round everywhere.

'They didn't come through the window,' said the older police-man, after he'd looked through the two bedrooms and the kitchen, and had clambered awkwardly over the debris on the sitting-room floor.

'Must have had come through the door somehow.'

Vara said, in a quiet voice, 'They were here before, you see – that's how they murdered him.'

I shook my head at her: it wasn't a good idea to start suggesting that Patrick had died a different death from the one they had been grinning about earlier.

The policemen chose to regard this as the excitability of some-one who had been through a hard time. But they examined the door, all the same.

'Yes – could very possibly have been opened,' said the dark one. He straightened up, and told us he was calling in the technical.

'Make sure you don't touch anything else. And I'd be grateful if you didn't even set foot in there.' He nodded his strangely pointed head at the mess in the sitting room.

We both nodded. Who would want to, anyway?

Vara and I sat silently in the hall on Patrick's neat little chairs, facing each other and waiting for the technical people to come and take our fingerprints, and for someone to write down our statements. Neither of us said a word.

Ten

Surprisingly, Susannah on the news desk thought there was enough in the idea that Patrick might have been murdered for me to spend a few days in London looking into it. Unsurprisingly, Alyssa Roberts, who now seemed to have been teamed up with me on a semi-permanent basis, didn't agree. I felt all her old suspicions about Patrick and me bubbling up again.

'I'm sorry, I just don't see why we should be interested in any of this,' was her opening gambit.

We were in the awful cafeteria at the Centre, and as part of my campaign to contract type 2 diabetes I was grappling with a KitKat and heaping a couple of teaspoonfuls into my builder's tea. Someone else's coffee had left a dried brown ring on the table. Alyssa sipped her lemon and water disdainfully.

'No, well, I don't suppose it's particularly likely either,' I ventured diplomatically. No point in working with someone if all you do is disagree. 'But given the remotest possibility that it might have happened like that, it's worth taking a look at.'

She sniffed disapprovingly and turned away from me.

'Don't you think?' I said, determined to excavate some opinion from her.

She turned back and looked at me full on.

'Listen, I don't like any of this, and I don't like what happened to your friend. And now he's dead I don't think we can do any good by reminding people of what happened to him.'

Well, that showed some kind of feeling, at any rate. It was the most I was likely to get from her.

'What would you rather be doing?'

'Something to do with social policy. Or pensions. Something positive.'

'And instead you're knocking around with someone you disapprove of, on a story you don't believe in.'

'You could put it like that.'

'All right, we know where we are, then. But let me tell you something: you can't always get the stories you want, and you can't always work with the people you like. It's a test of character, and yours is being tested to destruction by working with me.'

She gave me a look from which every particle of humour or sympathy had been extracted.

'Let's get on with it, then.'

I hadn't intended to tell her about Malone Road, the MI5 man. But now that I was distinctly short of any kind of support for my theory, I did. She didn't like it – more old boys' stuff, I suppose she thought.

'So why should someone have killed him? I don't understand.'

Her tone was dismissive, rather than a request for more information.

'How do I know? Maybe the Turks thought he was getting too close to the kind of people they don't like in Syria. Maybe the Israelis thought it would stop Britain selling weapons to the Arabs. And of course there's always the Russians. How many murders have they pulled? I've got no idea who did it, honestly. But it's a dodgy area, weapons procurement, and a lot of bad things have happened to people who were involved in it. And anyway, the last time I saw him, Patrick said he was worried about something that had come up from the past.'

If only that final lunch had happened: it might have cleared everything up.

'And please don't think there was anything dodgy about Patrick, however he died. He's got a very attractive girlfriend.'

'I told you – you should have put that in our piece when he died. But you didn't want to. "No point in dragging her into it", you said.'

You'd make someone a wonderful wife, I thought: this was precisely the tone one of mine had habitually used, though possibly with less acidulousness. I've always believed that if you experience the same thing twice, it's your fault rather than the other person's, but this didn't help me deal with Alyssa now. I shut up resentfully.

'Anyway, how do we go about trying to find something like this? I've never done a story like this before.'

'We could start with my mate at MI5.'

But he was no good. When I rang him, he said he didn't think there was anything else he could tell me. Alyssa seemed rather pleased when she heard that, as though it confirmed everything she'd thought about my contacts.

I rang a friend of mine, an investigative reporter called Tim Baxter, who specialised in this kind of story. He agreed to meet up for a drink at our old watering hole, the Chelsea Arts Club. I didn't invite Alyssa: at the very word 'club' she'd have frozen the beer.

I always used to think Tim was a bit susceptible to conspiracy theories. Me, I prefer to take the Occam's Razor approach: cut away the complexity and you usually find a perfectly natural, simple answer to the strangest problems. There was, for instance, the odd disappearance of . . . but no, I'd better not start wandering off into great stories of my past career.

I don't mean Tim was a fantasist. Far from it: he'd won all sorts of awards for the excellent stories he'd broken. But put it this way: if he saw a drunk fall over on an icy night in Rochdale, he'd look round for snipers. For Tim, the ordinary explanation always came second.

I told him what the Malone Road man had said about Patrick's death, and what Patrick himself had hinted to me about the past. Tim liked that kind of thing. We spent an hour talking it through, while largish artists and some distinctly attractive models yelled at each other all round us. Tim favoured a Middle Eastern explanation, and he reminded me of the odd, unexplained death of a British MI6 man whose body had been found in a duffel bag. He didn't need to; I'd reported on it.

At the end of an hour, sitting at a table near the bar and yelling at each other to be heard in the general racket, I didn't feel we'd got anywhere. Except to agree that quite a lot of people had died in strange places and questionable ways. From time to time one or other of the members, male or female, would overhear bits of our conversation as they passed with their hands full of glasses, and join in for a moment or two; that's the Chelsea Arts Club for you. Strangely, it didn't seem to worry Tim. He always was a social soul.

As we made our way out into Old Church Street I tried to sum it up.

'So you definitely think Patrick's death was suspicious?'

'Sure do.'

'And what should my next step be?'

Out here in the dark street, away from the cheery membership, he gave me three numbers to call: two linked to the Middle East, one to Serbia. He'd always thought that my friend, the lovely Jill Dando, had been murdered by Serbs. As it happened, I once did an investigative documentary about her which, although intriguing, only really proved that someone had shot her – which we were inclined to know already. Not my words, the words of the *Daily Mail*'s television reviewer.

I called all three numbers the following morning. The Lebanese thought the Israelis had killed Patrick as a warning to Britain not to sell any more weapons to Iran. The Israeli thought a Libyan, or maybe an Iraqi, had killed him as a warning not to sell any more weapons to Israel. I couldn't tell who the Serbian thought had killed him, just that it wasn't the Serbs.

Alyssa actually laughed when I told her all this the next morning. Maybe we're getting somewhere, I thought, but it became clear she just thought I was an idiot.

The only thing that seemed conclusive was the fact that someone had trashed Patrick's flat: that seemed to me to prove that he'd got some powerful enemies. And a man with powerful enemies who dies suddenly could easily, *ipso facto*, have been murdered.

To my surprise, Alyssa found this argument worth discussing.

'But why didn't the murderers, if he *was* murdered, which I'm not necessarily accepting, search the flat then and there for whatever they wanted? Why come back, and draw more attention to themselves?'

Good point. I could work with this woman, I thought, if only she wasn't so fucking unpleasant.

'I've no idea,' I said, and the look of contempt settled over her features again.

But she did agree to draw up a list of people we could interview on camera, if necessary. And she summoned up Os, the camera-man, to film inside Patrick's apartment – assuming we could get Vara's permission.

That she left to me.

Eleven

The idea of interviewing George Scales in the flat in Sloane Gardens, with all the chaos and destruction still uncleared around us, was mine. Vara couldn't bring herself to come back – I don't blame her – but she had no objection to our filming there.

'Anything you can do to sort this out,' she said, and the tears sprang to her eyes again, as she thought what 'this' meant.

I promised her in return that I'd get an industrial cleaning firm in, and that I'd oversee their work myself. She gripped my hand and clung on to it when I said that. I could see it meant a huge amount to her not to sort through Patrick's things, and not to have to go back to the flat ever again.

Maybe George Scales, ex-Special Branch, big and bluff and tweed-jacketed (he even smoked a pipe when he thought someone might be looking), and nowadays a writer of books about true life espionage, was the perfect interviewee; the kind of person that turns up on *Newsnight* on a regular basis and says that there is more to this – whatever 'this' happens to be – than everyone thinks. That was precisely the function I needed someone to perform, and old George was happy to do it. Kept him in the public eye, I suppose.

Alyssa disapproved. Predictably.

'I mean, even if he does say there was something funny about Macready's death, what does that show?'

'It shows that his death was open to question. And that's really the point, isn't it?'

'Well, I think Macready died because he was messing about in a particularly nasty way.'

Even so, she agreed we should get George to come and stand in Patrick's wrecked sitting room. He combed his hair carefully in a pocket mirror and smoothed down his eyebrows with a finger he'd licked. OK, that sounds a bit spiteful, but I've known George for years: he's a professional who understands that people who appear on television with flyaway hair and mad eyebrows simply don't get listened to. Unless they're David Attenborough, of course.

Os set up his tripod in the doorway while I stood close to him. I winced as my shoes grated on the broken glass from a black-and-white photograph of Patrick's parents. The photo had been half ripped out of the frame, to make sure nothing had been hidden behind it. I bent down and picked it up; it was the least I could do. George backed into the room, with the scene of brutality and rapine behind him, until Os said, 'That's it just there. Now hold it.'

I hadn't prepared any questions, because I hadn't needed to. The key thing was to get George to say there was something dodgy about Patrick's death, and I knew that was what he thought anyway. Was he a rent-a-mouth? Well, maybe a bit, but he'd had a very successful career, and being able to put his previous title under him on the screen would give the whole interview a big boost.

Os moved his head back from the eyepiece marginally and gave me a nod.

'Mr Scales, from your knowledge of so many political crimes over the years, do you feel there might have been something questionable about Patrick Macready's death?'

'Well, I have to say I think it's very strange that if Mr Macready died as a result of his own actions, someone should come and search for something in his flat afterwards like this. For me, this is a clear sign that there was something distinctly suspicious about his death.'

Succinct, seventeen seconds long, and decisively phrased: television news could ask for nothing better than this. He deserved his usual £250, but because we were filming him on location rather than in a studio, he wouldn't get anything. Wholly unfair, of course, but television news is a mean industry; and anyway George had already been told he wouldn't get anything except his travel expenses. The cheap bastard had come by a number 19 bus and would charge for a taxi. He'd be happy just getting his face on television; it was good for business.

I might have told Os to stop running then and there, on the grounds that we'd got everything we wanted, but I knew that each of the others, in their different ways, would have a sense of getting short measure if we ended after just a single question. So I ploughed on.

'How can you tell that someone was searching for something?'

'Because this scene is entirely characteristic of a crime committed by a person or persons with a precise object in mind. Look at this,' he said, and gestured in a practised way at the drawers left hanging out of their slots or lying on the floor, the papers strewn everywhere, the books ripped apart for any sign that something might be hidden in them.

Os, just as confident in his own way, turned the camera in the direction of George's pointing finger to the wreckage that was lying everywhere. It's great to work with people who know what they're doing, I thought, and glanced towards Alyssa. Those stern features of hers were also relaxed approvingly, though she started looking serious again when she felt my eyes on her.

'And' – this was the money shot – 'who do you think could have been behind it?'

'In my professional opinion, this could have been done by any one of a number of foreign clients using a team of British criminals.'

As a cop, he'd have stopped there. But as a retiree who wanted future work on television he plunged on. 'It could have been someone from a Middle Eastern country. Or it could have been Chinese, Russians, even someone from Central Asia.'

'Why?'

'Because Mr Macready was an MP with a particular interest in weapons sales. He may have upset someone, some foreign government, which wanted to make an example of him.'

'But isn't it easier to assume that his death here was just a sex game that went wrong?'

I found it hard to get these words out, but the question had to be asked.

'Let me put it a different way to you and your viewers: what better way to distract attention from a murder than by giving the impression there was something sexually bizarre about how a person dies. I mean, who would take it seriously and investigate?'

Bull's-eye, I thought, and snatched another glimpse at Alyssa. She was nodding slightly, and her eyes were shining. Rather fine eyes.

'You're hooked,' I said to myself; there's nothing as addictive as a good conspiracy theory.

Afterwards, when George had left and Os was packing his stuff away, I risked a question to Alyssa. How did she think the interview had gone?

'Not too bad.' I could see that a layer of toughness and experience had now covered over her initial enthusiasm, like the sudden arrival of a bank of cumulonimbus. 'But all we've got is shots of the mess in this flat and the interview with Scales.'

'Well, I think it makes a really good and intriguing piece.'

'We must let the desk be the judge of that,' she said in a plonking tone.

I detest put-downs, so I refused to say another word to her until we got back to the Centre. Fortunately, Os was in oratorical mode and told a long story about his time in the Congo, which kept me entertained for the entire car journey. Not Alyssa, though I don't think her objection was on the grounds of racism. Os wasn't any sort of white supremacist, but he was incontestably big and male. That was all Alyssa needed to find him guilty.

Our report ran that night.

'Really interesting,' said the charming woman who fronted the news and introduced our piece.

If only I could have people like that on my team.

'A bit theoretical,' opined one of the other producers, without realising I could hear him.

But a fellow foreign correspondent, a woman called Janine whom I had a lot of time for, came up with the best response.

'Fascinating. I love stories that mean you've got to make your own mind up about something that's happened.'

The following morning, the boss of news made an unusual appearance at the nine o'clock meeting. Standing at the head of the editorial table with the picture of our glorious though wrinkled founder on the wall behind him, he gave his verdict. I wasn't there – much too chicken – but I got at least three versions from other people which more or less agreed.

'We're in the business of news, not speculation,' he said.

Daniel Porchester was a grandee who'd ever so slightly come down in the world. He was amazingly clever, with an education

74

to match, and his analysis of the morning's news was as good as anything I'd ever heard at our editorial meetings. But he seemed to float slightly above the level of the rest of us, without quite realising it. There were teachers like that at my old school, people who thought they were our mates when we just found them embarrassing. Altogether, Porchester pissed me off. I mean, there was the way he went round with his shirt collar turned up: I've told you about that already. It made him look like something out of a Dickens illustration, and was incontestably wanky. Worse, he loved drawing attention to his infuriating skinniness. When he stood there at the end of the table he'd rest his hands on his belt, with the fingers pointing downwards in the general direction of his private parts. Have you ever seen a bloke with a waist bigger than thirty inches do that?

I'm being spiteful, of course. This is my book, and I'll do what I like in it. But I suppose I'd better admit it: the real reason I didn't like him was that he'd sussed me out and was trying to get rid of me on the grounds of my advanced age.

'Daniel doesn't like people much older than him,' said a friend of mine who'd worked with him in another incarnation. 'You'd better watch yourself, Swiftie.'

I did, but watching wasn't any good; it just meant I was more aware of the process leading to my downfall than I would probably have been if I hadn't understood what was happening. Daniel did everything he could to bring what passed for my career to an end, and smiled as he did it. As a result I wasn't getting nearly as much work as I'd had in the past, and he was able to cut my pay down to derisory levels in order to force me out. Bastard.

But there was no doubt that he was remarkably brainy. Handsome too, though it pains me to say so. Also the thirty-inch waist. So there were three reproaches to me, aside from the fact that he was making me even poorer and more paranoid than ever. When he spoke, it was a lot better if you agreed – unless you wanted him to turn forensic on you and humiliate you in front of everyone. It was like having a combination of Robert Redford and Leon Trotsky as your boss.

Anyway, now he'd handed down his judgement.

All the brown-nosers in the room – and there were several of them – nodded their enthusiastic agreement.

But not Alyssa. The dear, if tough, girl was standing at the back while bloody Porchester announced his verdict.

'Wouldn't you say, Daniel,' she called out, 'that the possibility that a British MP had been murdered by foreign interests was news? Because I certainly would.'

No one agreed out loud with her, naturally, but she told me later she sensed a kind of anonymous, subterranean rumbling of agreement from different parts of the room. 'Collective borborygmi,' I suggested, to annoy her. But she grinned instead. 'Possibilities don't come under the heading of hard facts in my book,' Porchester had apparently grated.

But he was at least a gent and an intellectual, so he didn't do what his predecessor, a nasty piece of work called Doug, would have done, and tell her she was a useless cunt: so I suppose the organisation had evolved slightly, from Tabloid Man to Christ Church Man.

'You little beauty,' I shouted down the phone line later, when she told me what had happened at the meeting.

'That's exactly the kind of thing Doug would have said. Really, you're just the same.'

Nevertheless something in her voice told me that even if she wasn't chuffed by what I said, she wasn't totally unchuffed. (Good line, don't you think? Adapted from P. G. Wodehouse, of course.)

'Doug would have given me a double cunting if I'd said that,' I ventured carefully, testing out this possible way forward. It felt like negotiating one of those terrifying rope bridges in the Andes.

Alyssa said something in reply which I'd never have expected. 'Yes, but let's face it – you're not exactly a black feminist from Lewisham, are you?'

And from the other end of the line there came a dry, crackling sound like somebody scrunching brown paper. It went on for ages. Until that moment I'd assumed she was physically incapable of laughter.

'Good girl,' I thought, but a well-developed sense of self-preservation prevented me from saying it out loud.

Twelve

Although I'd talked and thought about little else since the morning when Os woke me up, it had taken a surprisingly long time for the reality of Patrick's death to get through my defences. Slowly, I was starting to realise I would never see him again, never hear his quiet, mild voice or smile at his caustic jokes. During the first week or so it felt as though he was away, or just not answering his emails. The feeling had even lingered after I'd seen his coffin being carried out of the church on its way to a dreary suburban crematorium. Now, though, the penny had dropped. That was it: Patrick had been blotted out of my life forever. My memories of him, and the odd photograph, were all that I had left. There wouldn't be any more.

Plus, asleep or awake I couldn't get the thought that he'd been murdered out of my mind. His face kept swimming into my dreams, like Richard III's victims the night before Bosworth. At one point I even dreamed that he was speaking to me directly and earnestly, and telling me something of huge importance. Only, as so often happens with dreams, I couldn't remember afterwards what the hell he'd been going on about.

One night, when it was worse than usual, I got up three times in all, twice to go to the loo and once to make myself a hot Bushmills and lemon. (Bushmills is the stuff if you're not feeling well or can't sleep, by the way; Jameson works for everything else. Any well-ordered Irish household should have both.)

But each time when I lay down again all I could think about was that earnest look of his, and the way he used to speak, and the sheer inconceivability of the notion that he had tied himself up and bitten on an orange injected with amyl nitrate and died of asphyxiation with an Olympic hard-on.

And I felt really lonely. Like most of us, I take it personally when close friends and relations die: who's going to look after me now? Who'll keep me company? Just like a kid, I suppose.

Patrick was the best friend I'd ever had, and maybe that was the reason why, for once in my life, I found myself even more concerned about someone other than myself. Two people, in fact. I was overwhelmed with pity and sorrow for his poor parents; they had clearly believed he'd be prime minister one day – and instead this. The shame of it all was unthinkable. And whatever must Varvara be feeling?

In the end, when the Bushmills and lemon was finished, I broke the resolve of several years, and went into my chaotic bathroom to dig out some sleeping tablets. I'd been through a bad patch after I'd covered George W. Bush's crazed invasion of Iraq in 2003, and my doctor had prescribed them to help me over the after-effects. There was a soldier burning alive and screaming whose memory I particularly didn't want to come across in the night watches any longer.

The pills were quite effective, genuine knock-out drops. But the quack, who was a particular friend of mine, must have had serious second thoughts about prescribing them for me, because he rang up a couple of times over the weeks that followed, asking whether I was still using them. I lied, naturally, and said I wasn't; what else are you supposed to say to your doctor? I could tell he didn't believe me, but he wasn't going to come round and do a citizen's arrest.

Over the months that followed, the screams and the images of the burning soldier began to fade. The stench too; I'd never previously realised you could smell things in dreams, but I promise you, you can. In the end, though, I stopped taking the pills, and hid the ones that were left at the back of the bathroom cupboard. But I didn't chuck them away, in case the burning soldier came back. He didn't, but Patrick did, and Patrick was worse than any nightmare because I loved him, and the pain of losing him was sharper than the simple horror of watching a stranger die.

Anyway, that night the tiny little pill worked. A dozen of them, swallowed all at once, would probably have solved my every worldly problem, though I've never been the suicidal type. I duly took one at four o'clock in the morning, with a glass of Writers' Tears and water to wash it down, like they say you shouldn't do. You'll probably have guessed that my drinks cupboard is as stocked with Irish whiskeys as an O'Connell Street bar.

It was shortly after midday that I swam near enough to consciousness to hear the doorbell ringing. Even then, groggy though I was, I felt I could detect an edge of frustration in the sound. But maybe all doorbells are like that.

I hurried downstairs in my disreputable towelling bathrobe, which I'd nicked from a hotel in Baghdad; it had a garish monogram over the breast, where my heart would be if I had one. I opened the hall door and peered out into the late morning air.

A woman I'd never seen before stood there in a severe outfit with a glittery brooch of some sort on the lapel, a packet under her arm. She looked as shocked as I felt, and it wasn't the monogram that did it.

'Sorry,' I mumbled. 'Took a sleeping pill.'

That, curiously, seemed to reassure her. She was in her late fifties, a bit younger than me and a spinster if ever I saw one: sharp of feature and conservative of dress. She was wearing a dark overcoat of a cut I thought had vanished from the world.

'I wonder if I could just . . .'

She made a nodding gesture with her head to the inside of the building, as though willing me to say yes.

I stepped aside to let her in, of course. The Royal Hospital Road is a tolerant sort of area, but standing on your doorstep in a dodgy dressing gown and not a stitch else is probably pushing it. Especially at – I checked with the clock across the way – twelve twenty-four in the afternoon.

She took off her coat, revealing a severe office-like outfit of white shirt and dark skirt, and plumped down in my untidy sitting room, pushing aside a stack of old *New Statesmen*, and shook her head when I asked her if I could get her anything. That was a relief, so gripping the front of my dressing gown I sank down into my leather armchair, the one I do my reading in, and remembered to keep my knees together.

I was feeling more myself now, and apologised for the way I looked. 'A good friend of mine died recently, and I took it a bit hard,' I said.

She smiled a rather sweet, sympathetic smile. 'I know. That's why I'm here.'

She'd make a good therapist, I thought.

'My name is Hannah Jenkinson, and I work – well, I have been working – at the Palace of Westminster for Patrick Macready. As his PA.'

She looked straight at me, and her eyes glistened.

'I'm really, really sorry . . .' I started to say. But she wiped her eyes quickly and sat even straighter beside the pile of magazines.

81

'Yes, well, Mr Macready had a feeling that something bad might happen to him, and he said that if it did he wanted you to see this.'

She pulled out the big Manila envelope she'd been gripping under her arm the whole time, and thrust it towards me. I took it with one hand, still making sure with the other that the dressing gown stayed secure. The contents – of the envelope, I mean – felt like a book with a thin, hard spine. I opened the envelope and fished it out, and thought at first that it *was* a book – an eighteenth-century leather book, the kind of thing Patrick collected. But this was much thinner and taller than the stuff by Laurence Sterne and Henry Fielding that he liked. Plus the zip round the edges. It turned out to be an iPad cover, particularly classy and expensive. Typical of Patrick, I thought, to make a rather ordinary thing look like something altogether different, rare and attractive.

I gave Hannah Jenkinson a 'Yes, so what now?' look.

'It was Mr Macready's, as I say. I've never looked at it – I still haven't. I know it's locked, because Mr Macready said so. But he told me that when I gave it to you I was to say that you'd be able to guess the code because it was linked to the past.'

'Ah,' I said, the past being a rather long time. To give myself a chance to reflect on it all, I said I was going to make myself a cup of tea (I was pretty desperate by this stage) and would she like one too?

She nodded. My mind was still clouded – the sleeping pill, no doubt – and all I could think of was the year of Patrick's birth, 1957 – the same as my own. If it wasn't that, it could be anything from 0000 to 9999, so the odds against getting the right number were ten multiplied by ten multiplied by ten multiplied by ten. I'd better get down to some pretty intensive guessing instead, I thought.

I went out and made some strong Darjeeling. It tasted good, steaming from the pot. Hannah seemed to think so too. She even smiled, in a sad sort of way, then sniffed a little, and fooled around with a tiny patch of handkerchief. I suppose she'd had a thing for Patrick; she was just the kind of woman who would. I'm sorry if that sounds snide. What I mean is that she was the lonely, devoted sort, whose affections followed the direction of her work. But she was no emotional weakling.

'Yes,' she said reflectively, as though I'd spoken out loud. 'If you're wondering whether I . . . had feelings for Mr Macready, I suppose I did, a little. He was so gentle, so charming.'

Again, her eyes glistened.

I made 'such a thing never occurred to me' noises, but I don't suppose they did any good.

'He was a superb human being,' I said, and meant it.

But the subject was in serious need of changing.

'Why did Patrick think something bad might happen to him?'

'He never told me in as many words. But I had to organise quite a lot of research for him.'

I said I knew, meaning I knew Patrick had taken a critical interest in countries like Turkey, Pakistan, China, Russia, Ukraine – places where thinking the wrong thing could lead to a prison sentence.

'Mr Macready said he didn't really want to let me know what the problem could be, because it might be dangerous.'

'Do you think the iPad's got stuff on it about all this?'

'I'm certain it has. That's why he wanted me to make sure you got it.'

Mental arithmetic has never been my big thing, but ten thousand possibilities, each of which would take say fifteen seconds to try out, seemed to me to be in the order of two full days' work – if you didn't pause, rest or sleep. 'Tell me again what he said about the code.'

'That you'd be able to guess it because it's linked to the past.'

'My past? His past? Or just the past in general?'

'I'm just telling you what he said.'

She took her last sip of Darjeeling and stood up, still dabbing at her nose. Neither of us said anything except 'goodbye'. There didn't seem to be any need to.

I got dressed. I didn't feel up to shaving, but I brushed what was left of my hair and tried to think smart thoughts. There was a rather nice tapas place nearby, just off the King's Road, and a glass of very dry, very cold sherry was calling my name.

Ever since I'd read somewhere that no one drinks sherry any longer, I'd started asking for it in every restaurant and bar I went to, on principle, and I judged the places on the basis of whether they had it or not. This place had it, of course: what decent tapas bar doesn't? So within seven minutes of shutting the front door behind me I was sitting down, face to face with a glass of Manzanilla. The iPad, still in its elegant leather case, lay beside me on the upturned cask of the kind they used for tables in places like that.

I fished it out and tried our birthdays, and the birthdays of other people, and famous dates from history. I even tried the last four figures from our old, shared phone number in Oxford, which I'd never forgotten. 'It's linked to the past . . .' Well, aren't most things?

Patrick must have known I'd get it, if only I could rake it up from our shared past. That must mean Oxford.

After another glass of Sanlúcar de Barrameda's finest I tried the year we started and then the year we graduated. Neither worked. Regnal dates of kings and queens (he was a bloody royalist, after all)? No luck. The French Revolution, the American Revolution, the Cuban Revolution? Ireland, 1798, 1916? Surely not: he was a Tory, and Tories don't believe in revolutions, except when they start them themselves. Famous wars of the past? Not really Patrick's thing. Famous elections? I tried every single one I knew, which wasn't all that many: just back to 1945, essentially.

It was as I lifted the third Manzanilla to my lips that I knew what it must be.

'Idiot!' I said out loud, meaning myself. A couple of big office girls at a nearby cask looked over at me then back at each other meaningfully.

Patrick's big thing at Oxford had been the Second Reform Bill. I used to listen to him going on about it for hours on end. He thought it embodied all the greatness of the developing British political system; he adored Disraeli, naturally. And the Second Reform Act had been passed in . . .

I typed in 1867.

The much abused iPad, which had had to endure everything from 1066 to 2010, opened up instantly, and the contents lay there like an oyster on the half-shell.

It revealed a photograph of, yes, the Palace of Westminster in early spring, dotted around with various icons linked to Patrick's interests. Examining them one by one, I was glad to see that he'd downloaded a version of Solitaire; something linked him to the rest of humanity, at any rate.

It felt nastily intrusive, going through the things he'd kept in this private chest of drawers of the mind, and I confess I was scared of finding something indecent – something which might even link him to the auto-eroticism that had supposedly killed him. Well, I certainly wouldn't want anyone, friend or not, going through my iPad, and I've never had a relationship with an orange in my life.

Thank God, though, there was nothing of the sort; I'm not sure if I could have borne it.

It was easy enough to see what he had really been interested in: the material which he had instructed his Miss Prism to hand over to me. There was a folder on the iPad marked 'Russia', right at the top of the screen. I checked that no one was watching me or could see the iPad from some other part of the bar. No: everything seemed perfectly normal for an early lunchtime. People were talking loudly or clinking glasses or laughing, and the waiters were few and far between. When one made the briefest of appearances I ordered a few little dishes – chorizo, a chunk of tortilla, some grilled squid, plus another glass of Manzanilla – and tortured myself by waiting for them all to arrive before I finally clicked on 'Russia'.

This, I suppose, was the moment at which my life changed forever.

Thirteen

It was hard to know where I could meet Varvara. I didn't feel I should ask her to come to my flat, and I didn't want to suggest her place in Battersea, which I'd never been to. It seemed only right to maintain a proper distance between us. In the end I settled on the Café Colbert, the French restaurant in Sloane Square where we'd been with Patrick that first night, because it was neutral yet familiar territory. She agreed immediately.

I was early. There was a loud buzz of conversation, and the place was getting warm, though it still wasn't full. People looked up at me as I filtered between the tables, in the 'Who the hell is that bloke? I've seen him somewhere' manner that has followed me around for thirty years. The waitress led me to a table for two which had a clear view of the one where the three of us had sat, not so long ago, and I found I couldn't take my eyes off it. The same chairs, the same napkins and knives and forks, the same routine, even the same menu – and yet everything in the lives of the three people who had been there that night had each changed out of all imagining. And one of them was dead.

I couldn't help going back in my mind to the same old question – was it possible that Patrick had been attracted to the dodgier side of sexuality? I'm an *homme moyen sensuel* myself, and sometimes not all that *moyen*, but I'd never tried this self-strangulation lark and couldn't imagine I ever would. It seemed so unlikely, somehow, that a man like Patrick could have done it.

How could he have got hold of the amyl nitrate to inject the orange with, and give himself the amazing high which, together with the ligature round his neck, had killed him? And who could have taught him the whole procedure? It wasn't as though there were articles about it in the newspapers – well, not the ones people like Patrick and I read, anyway – and it certainly wasn't something you could practice again and again on your own until you finally got it right.

Gloomily, I swirled some dry white around in the glass and took a swig. I should have thought to ask for a Manzanilla.

I was still looking at Patrick's empty chair when Vara's contralto broke into my thoughts. I stumbled to my feet and put my hand out. She shook it firmly, like a bloke, and sat down opposite me. It was clear that she hadn't expected me to stand up – though Patrick always did, of course – and was pleasantly surprised when I did. She was wearing a black dress with a black plastic necklace and black earrings which hung down in a most unwidowlike fashion. Not, of course, that she and Patrick had been married, though they'd clearly thought about it.

'You see where we are,' I said, and she nodded.

For a time we talked about inessentials. I was mostly looking at the colour of her eyes, anyway, and trying to find a name for it. Her nose seemed rather long, but that only added to the strangeness of her face, which was one of the main parts of her – was it beauty? Or was it merely attractiveness? I couldn't work it out. God knows what she thought when she looked at me: 'rumpled old has-been', I suppose.

Maybe she could see my mind was wandering, because she asked, quite sharply, 'Did you bring it?'

I grunted assent and reached down by my feet to pull out the big buff envelope with Patrick's iPad in it. I held it on my lap for the moment and looked round, but no one seemed to be watching us. I had been careful not to make the reservation by phone or email; I'd dropped by that morning and booked the table in person, and I'd made sure I wasn't followed either then or when I came back. A lifetime of avoiding secret policemen around the world had taught me that.

As for Varvara, I had called her at her office from one of the public phone boxes outside the Centre, to tell her I'd got something important to show her. The phone box had been liberally used as a toilet, and there were a dozen postcards tucked into the frames advertising the bust sizes and general skills of tarts of various ages and colours. You can tell how preoccupied I was, because I scarcely even looked at them. Or registered the smell.

If anyone was really listening in to all the calls that go out from those phone boxes to bookies, massage parlours and divorce lawyers, they deserved to track me down, I felt. When I got through to Varvara I suggested she should be careful to make sure that no one knew where she was going, and she seemed to have taken my advice seriously enough. Mind you, seriously was how she did everything.

We ordered something to eat, and I noticed that each of us chose things that were different from what we had had that other night. No Gigondas, either; she had fizzy water, I had another glass of white. I waited till the food had arrived before putting the Manila envelope on the table between us and fishing the iPad out of it.

89

I'd been through the contents thoroughly by now. I like to give the impression that I'm an unreconstructed bundle of technophobias (or should it be 'technophobiae'?), but in fact I follow these things fairly carefully, if only out of self-defence. I don't want anyone citing computer inadequacy in order to get rid of me; that happened to a friend of mine. Mind you, he used to draft out his scripts on a typewriter.

'I'm not quite sure where to start,' I said to Vara, leaning across the tablecloth.

But it was only a form of speech. I knew exactly.

'As you'll recall,' I went on confidently, looking into her dark blue eyes, then looking away quickly because they were so disconcerting, 'people who question the system in your wonderful homeland often get killed. I've met quite a few of them: Politkovskaya, Magnitsky, Stanislav Markelov . . . I actually interviewed Litvinenko on his deathbed, you know.'

'It was Putin who put me here,' Litvinenko had said to me on camera as he lay there. Pretty dramatic stuff.

I broke off and took in a forkful of risotto for form's sake, wondering how many of these names Varvara knew. She nodded as though she knew them all.

'They died in a variety of ways, of course,' I went on. 'But other people have been killed too, and their deaths weren't so well reported, either in Russia or the West. This iPad of Patrick's lists fourteen people with some kind of anti-government involvement whose deaths scarcely got a mention outside Russia. The reason for that was that many of them seemed to have committed suicide, sometimes in very weird ways indeed.'

Her eyes were directed onto mine far too strongly now for me to be able to look away: it would have seemed shifty if I had. After a few seconds of that, I opened the file marked 'Russia' on the iPad. There they were: photographs of the fourteen who had died.

Two of them, both men, had been found naked, with their heads covered by a plastic bag and a cord of some kind round their necks. The pictures were disgusting and upsetting and ludicrous, all at the same time. I wasn't going to show her, but with a quick 'May I?' she turned the iPad round.

Then she looked up at me, her eyes filled with tears. 'You think they were murdered? Like Patrick was?'

I had wondered, until that moment, whether she had doubts about the cause of his death. Perhaps she had secretly been harbouring the fear that he really had been fooling around and it had all gone wrong, just as everyone else seemed to think.

'I don't have any doubt about it.' And, perhaps for the first time, I genuinely didn't.

She reached out and gripped my hand. Not in any affectionate sense; it was relief and fellow feeling that made her do it.

'So what do we do?'

I still wasn't exactly sure. Raising doubts in the public mind in a report for television was fine, but I would have trouble persuading my outfit to run anything more; pure speculation, the awful Daniel had called it. What was needed was clear, bankable evidence. Patrick's careful research, as detailed on the iPad, was good and pretty compelling, but it didn't in any way amount to proof. I have always believed devoutly – perhaps it's the only thing I *do* believe devoutly – that we have a duty to put difficult things into the public domain and allow people to make up their own minds about them. I suppose that was why I became a journalist.

But this wasn't a clear-cut case. Of course, a well-researched and well-argued article in the press or on television might make people wonder whether Patrick's death had actually been murder. But what was the point of their wondering if I couldn't point the finger at someone, with a serious degree of credibility?

Now I made up my mind. 'I think I've got to take this further,' I said.

'Please do,' she said. 'I'm counting on you.' She laid her hand on mine again.

That settled it.

Fourteen

After Patrick's funeral, something was different. I'm a moderately good observer – that's what I'm paid for, after all – and I had a feeling about it. You'll probably think I'm being fanciful, but I didn't seem to be alone any more. I had a constant sense of being watched.

Thinking back, it's hard to give you any solid, provable instances. But getting on buses or the underground or going to the shops seemed somehow different now. I started seeing the same people twice, sometimes three times, on my way to work, or to the shops: mostly men, but a couple of women on one occasion.

They never showed any interest in me, naturally, but that wasn't proof that I wasn't being followed. I know of course that really professional surveillance is pretty much undetectable, but it started to dawn on me that someone might want me to know that my movements were of interest.

I wasn't scared, but I was concerned. Much of it was bound to be pure imagination, of course – it always is. But some, even if just a small amount, was genuine.

And then, one morning, my suspicions turned into certainty. I was standing on the northbound Bakerloo Line platform at Embankment station just after ten o'clock, wrapped up in my own thoughts and listening to my ancient iPod on headphones: Shostakovich's Fifth, if it's of any interest, pretty noisy, with lots of percussion and energetic strings.

The platform was moderately crowded, but not so much that I was likely to be jostled. I was holding a copy of *The Times* and trying to read it one-handed; not easy if you're also carrying a briefcase full of books and research materials.

Was I aware of the young, mono-browed, dark-featured character in a grey hoodie who was standing near me? I suppose I was, vestigially. By that stage I was taking note of everyone I saw, in order to check them out. But he didn't look like any of the other people who might have been following me, so I dismissed him from my mind.

Still, there was something odd about him. He wasn't listening to music, or carrying anything. He just stood there, gazing intently across the line at a big advertisement for Cuban holidays on the far wall of the tunnel. That seemed weird; I mean, who actually reads the adverts on the Tube?

The train came in with the usual shattering metallic roar and high-pitched squealing. It was packed out, even in the coaches at the front and rear where there's usually a bit more room. I wasn't in any great hurry, since I was only going three stops and had a good half-hour in hand. The electronic board showed that another train was due in a minute, so I decided to wait for that. When there are two Tube trains close together, the first one skims off the crowd and the second usually has plenty of room.

One or two other people obviously decided to do the same thing, and I remember noticing that the young man in the grey hoodie was one of them. You wouldn't have thought someone like that would be so concerned about his personal space.

I did my best to carry on reading the editorials, and was just turning the paper over to get to the bit below the fold about giving Donald Trump the benefit of the doubt, when the next train came thundering in from the far end of the platform. I half turned to jam the folded paper into my pocket, and as I did so I felt a stunning blow on my right shoulder and, simultaneously, a grab at my briefcase.

My headphones fell off. I stumbled a step closer to the platform edge and turned even more to my right, still gripping the briefcase. That meant the young man who had charged into me didn't find the resistance he had expected. He gave an odd little yelp, and fell flat on his face. It hadn't been much of a face before, but the way he fell seemed likely to make it even worse.

A small crowd gathered, and someone turned him over into the recovery position. That revealed his face: not a good sight.

The kid's eyes sought me out in the crowd. He couldn't actually talk because his teeth were smashed, but I'm sure he wanted to.

Soon the driver was helped out of his cab, and after getting a look at the kid's face he was being quietly sick on a poster for a rubbish film. Someone in a uniform came running along the platform yelling 'For Christ's sake, what's going on? What's going on?'

And me? Well, there wasn't anything I could do to help. I bent down and picked up my headphones, and moved off before anyone could start asking me questions and telling me to come down to the police station to make a statement. I know, I know – it was a total betrayal of the duties of a conscientious citizen; you don't have to give me a lecture on that. But I was already starting to think that this had been an attempt to kill me, and getting my name and face in the papers wouldn't necessarily help me in my chief duty to myself, which was to carry on living.

Clearing out was easy. The uniformed characters who came thundering along the platform, or running down the escalator, weren't interested in a middle-aged gent in a Burberry trench coat walking away from the scene of the accident, as if in deep thought.

Actually I *was* in deep thought; I was thinking about who the hell had sent the kid to push me to my death under a Tube train, and why? Why being more important than who. I was shocked, of course; I'd come pretty close, and the aftermath had been distinctly ugly. But long experience of finding myself in unpleasant situations has taught me to suppress my reactions while the show is on; there'll be time enough later, I've always told myself, to follow through with the emotional stuff.

Out in the grey light and faint drizzle of the Embankment, heading up Villiers Street to the Strand, I tried to work it out. Had this been a warning which went wrong, or a deliberate attempt to kill me? I could still feel the pain of the blow where the kid – he can't have been older than twenty – had struck me.

That didn't seem like putting me on notice, the equivalent of an unsigned note through the letter box: it was the real thing, the full Monty, the final settlement. The force of the kid's forward lurch would have taken me over the platform edge. If it hadn't been for the fact that I was just turning a little out of his path to put the newspaper in my pocket, it would have been me with the 'What the fuck do you think you're doing?' look in my eyes. I must buy *The Times* more often, I thought.

Don't imagine the incident had left me as cool and collected as I'm pretending. I felt as physically sick as the poor old train driver, and my legs weren't entirely solid underneath me. But since I couldn't face a cup of coffee and the pubs weren't yet open for a stiff double I decided to keep on walking; and by the time I got to Trafalgar Square I felt steadier on my pins, and a lot stronger in the stomach. I thought I'd treat myself to a taxi: for some reason the Tube didn't seem so attractive any longer.

Obviously, I reflected as we rounded Piccadilly Circus and turned into Regent Street, this must all be connected with Patrick's death; it certainly hadn't been an accident, and it was impossible to think that I might have mortally pissed off some totally unconnected person or persons at almost the precise time when my best friend had apparently died in highly suspicious circumstances.

That iPad of Patrick's, carefully disguised as a book in its leather case and tucked away in the tired, baggy old leather briefcase I was carrying, contained a wealth of material that someone, surely, knew about and wanted to get their hands on. Hence, I assumed, the kid's twin efforts to grab hold of my briefcase and send me to meet my Maker courtesy of the Bakerloo Line.

We were getting near Oxford Circus by now, and I was still congratulating myself on my good luck at continuing to be alive.

The man recovered of the bite, The dog it was that died.

Oliver Goldsmith, by the way – yet another Irish Prod who came to London and failed to make money there.

Part of my luck, I realised, lay in my instinctive decision to get away from all the fuss which must have enveloped everyone else on the platform. I just hoped no one had given the police a description of a gent in a trench coat who had been there at the time.

On an impulse, I told the driver to stop near Liberty's. I paid him off, and went in. In the stationery department I bought one of those cheap German cartridge pens, and asked the girl behind the counter if she'd mind giving me one of their specially large shopping bags to carry it in: a showy purple number. Then I dodged into the gents, took off my raincoat, shoved it into the bag, and folded up the life-saving copy of *The Times* on top so the conspicuous beige of the coat was hidden.

After that, looking different, I trudged off to the Langham Hotel in Portland Place. And even though the faint drizzle had intensified, I was fully prepared to get wet. In an hour or so the *Evening Standard*'s noon edition would have the latest from platform whatever it was at the Embankment, and there might be something in it about a big bloke in a Burberry.

I liked the Langham even in the days when the BBC used it as an administrative block; maybe because someone in an office there had been misguided enough to give me my start in broadcasting. After that, years ago now, it was converted back into a hotel for well-heeled visitors to London. And because they seemed to like strange British customs, the huge room which had once served the BBC as the reception area was converted into a gigantic temple to afternoon tea.

The atmosphere was reverential, and the only people there seemed to be from China, Malaysia and the Gulf. No one was likely to listen in to the conversation of a couple of stray *gweilos*.

I was the first to arrive. I'd fixed this second meeting with Tim Baxter in order to move the investigation on a little. He wasn't the kind of person you would look to for sympathy if you had decided to give up on a story because it was getting too scary. By coming here, I was binding myself to carry on looking into Patrick's death. Tim's advice at the Chelsea Arts Club hadn't been particularly helpful, but now I knew quite a bit more. And there was the incident on the underground.

I caught sight of Tim's familiar questing look as he stood at the entrance to the lounge. He made no acknowledgement of me, but came over in my direction, pulling off his camouflage jacket. It wasn't his style to greet me or make light conversation about the weather, either. His eyes, intense and close together, locked on to mine.

'Look, I can't stay more than twenty minutes, OK?'

'Hello, Tim. Yes, I'm very well thank you, and I hope you are. Rather damp out there. How's Jenny? Would you like a coffee?'

'Well, I can't.'

With Tim Baxter, there was never any small talk. He had won all sorts of awards for his investigation into Litvinenko's murder by polonium poisoning, which included flying to Moscow early on to interview Luguvoy, the man everyone accused of being the murderer, and getting thoroughly thumped up by a crowd of Luguvoy's friends.

Earlier, Tim had carried out an investigation, together with Litvinenko himself, into who was responsible for the apartment bombs in Russia in September 1999, and came to the conclusion it was the FSB, the successor to the KGB. It was the kind of thing you could easily be killed for, but Tim was one of those people who didn't seem to be afraid of the consequences of what he did. His flat, he once told me, had been broken into and trashed five different times over the years.

Me, I'd rather investigate the five-star hotels of the French Riviera for *GQ* magazine: that's the kind of in-depth journalism I find satisfying. But Tim Baxter was a searcher after truth, a born campaigner, a dedicated crusader. Humourless? Well, perhaps a tad. But you can find funny men by the dozen in any newsroom; gutsy, determined reporters who are prepared to put their lives on the line are a lot rarer and more necessary. Poor old Tim: I haven't always been as patient with him, or as respectful of him, as I ought to have been.

I ordered coffee for two while he flicked through some photo-copies he'd brought with him.

'And biscuits?'

'Yes. What?'

'He'd like biscuits,' I told the waiter.

I hadn't intended to tell Tim about my experience on the Bakerloo Line that morning, partly perhaps because it seemed a bit meek and mild compared with some of the things that had happened to him, but in the end I decided to.

I went fairly briskly through it, and then we had to stop talking for a while because the coffee tray appeared. As soon as the waiter wandered off, Tim couldn't hold back any longer.

'Course it's linked. These guys use teenagers to do their dirty work all the time. It's just a question of cash payment.'

'They're Brits?'

'Of course they are – what do you think?' Tim was never very patient with slowness or stupidity. 'They're hired in from the larger gangs. The gang bosses make them available, and no one needs to know why, or who they're really working for. For the kids, it's a rite of passage – a way of showing if they're capable of doing bigger things.'

'And who does the hiring?'

'Oh for Christ's sake, don't you remember that series I did for the paper last year?'

I did, vaguely, but I couldn't remember anything much about it.

'Of course I do,' I said soothingly. 'Superb stuff it was, too. But just go over that bit again and update it for me.'

No one is entirely immune to flattery, of course, not even a scrawny obsessive like Tim Baxter. He allowed himself to be mollified, as I sat back and dipped my biscuit in the cooling coffee. His, naturally, remained untouched. For Tim, everything was secondary to the flow of information.

'The FSB used to have an enabler in London, Sergei Dolganev, who was mixed up in drugs in the nineties and got to know the British criminal scene then. As far as I know, he was the first real Russian link. He made the contacts with groups from Luton and Brighton who were thinking of moving into London at the time, and helped them by supplying them with guns and explosives.

'After I wrote my series about it last September, the Foreign Office quietly threw Dolganev out, but someone else took over from him almost immediately, and he's still here. Mikhail Mikhailovich Gronov. Nasty character, but quite smooth. I've met him.'

And asked him his date and place of birth, no doubt, I thought. Tim Baxter was an old-fashioned, straight up and down reporter.

'Gronov will have been the one who passed on the order to have you dealt with. Then the gang leaders will have put the job out to one of their hangers-on. And there'll have been someone else there, watching what happened, you know.'

That was a bit of a facer.

'Do you think I should go to the cops and make a clean breast of it?'

'No, actually I think you did the right thing by skipping out. The more public you are about all this, the nastier they'll get. But you'll need to be a lot more careful from now on.'

'Should I move?' My heart sank at the thought of packing my stuff up, little enough though there was of it.

'I think that's a bit drastic, so no. After all, this may have been meant as a warning, not a punishment. The kid may have been told to give you a shove and steal your briefcase, but not actually to go all the way and chuck you under the train. I had to move last year, because these bastards really wanted to sort me out big time. Maybe they still do. Jen wasn't exactly happy, though.'

'Did she come with you?'

'Wouldn't have been enough room.'

Poor loyal, brave Jenny: a believer in the rightness of everything Tim did, and invariably the first sacrifice in each new enterprise he got involved in.

'So do you think they'll come for me again?' I tried to make it gutsy and matter of fact, but it came out a bit querulous.

'Well, my sense of it is that this was probably just a warning to you to keep quiet about everything. They've done that now. They won't care about the kid – he is entirely expendable. The gang have got the money for the job off Gronov, and they won't be handing it back.'

'And Gronov?'

'Well, he's the one who wants to shut you up.'

His narrow, ascetic face gleamed with the pleasure of working the whole thing out. You could tell he just saw me as a part of the puzzle, no more important than any other part.

'And of course I've still got the thing they wanted, the briefcase.'

'Yes, there's that.'

'But you think I did the right thing by not staying to answer any questions.'

'Absolutely. Just put it out of your mind, is my advice.'

I wished I could, but the surprise and hostility in those reddened eyes would take a bit of time to get rid of.

'And now, if it's OK with you, I'd like to hear about Patrick Macready.'

That was me dealt with.

I told him the story of going to the ransacked flat after Patrick's death, but he knew all that already. To be honest, I was playing for time. I hadn't yet decided to show Tim the contents of Patrick's iPad, even though it was in the briefcase at my feet, resting on my right shoe so I would feel it if anyone tried to hook it off me.

'Bears all the hallmarks of an FSB hit,' he said decisively. Journalists are the only people apart from cops who use phrases like 'all the hallmarks'. I think it's because we're building up the story in our heads, and practising the phrases we'll be using.

'And why should they want to kill him?' I asked.

'Because he was going to do a number on them in the Commons. He was starting to shape up his speech. Got in touch with me about it.'

I felt a sharp pang of hurt and regret: why hadn't Patrick asked me for help as well?

'He didn't tell me he was going to make a speech about it,' I said. 'I knew he was interested in the whole thing, of course, but he didn't say anything about it at any point.'

I wasn't able to keep the hurt out of my voice. But there was nothing cold or spiteful about Tim; he was just a touch obsessive, that was all. He opened up to me immediately.

'Oh, he explained why he didn't want to say anything about it to you at that stage. He was worried that it might be dangerous if you found out too early. But he was going to give the text of the speech to you and me as an exclusive, to run the day before he made his statement in Parliament.'

I felt relieved – happy, almost. Maybe the incident on the Tube had shaken me up more than I'd realised. I still didn't pull out the iPad, though, but this time I can't say why. Instinct? The selfish desire to keep information to myself? A moment or two later, I was really glad about it. I'd just suggested to Tim that we should co-operate on the story of Patrick Macready's murder, when I realised that he didn't really want to share all of his material with me.

'Yes, good idea, but let's just keep cracking on independently for the time being. Then we can talk about pooling our resources closer to.'

You cold-hearted bugger, I thought, but I admired him all the same. Journalism's at its best when it's an individual enterprise. Sure, there's Woodward and Bernstein, but can you name any other couples? Gellhorn and Hemingway? They came to hate each other fast. The best journalists are loners, oddballs, obsessives like Tim Baxter.

We shook hands, and agreed to speak again soon.

'Maybe we should meet up here or at the Chelsea Arts Club,' I said. 'Nowadays you never know who's listening on the phone.'

That made him smile, at least.

I sat back in my comfortable armchair when he'd gone and ordered another pot of coffee. Talking to Tim about the Tube incident had made me feel better.

Then my mobile rang. It was awkward here, and the tune – 'Moscow Nights', as it happens – made people look round. The number that was displayed was a Russian one. I recognised the digits, or thought I did, but because of the delays on the line we talked over each other for a couple of moments.

'Yuri here.'

We got rid of the how are yous as quickly as we could. Yuri was the Mr Fix It I'd used a lot in Moscow over the years, to work on getting interviews: politicians, government people and dissidents alike. He didn't seem to make any distinction between them, and he almost always supplied me with the people I wanted.

'I've just heard from the boss's private office. It's going to happen. My friend says it'll be next week. Come over a few days before, and we can go out and get drunk.'

Typical Yuri: even when the Kremlin was being favourable to us and nobody could object to what he was saying, he was too circumspect to name names. He and Tim Baxter should get together, I thought.

Fifteen

I didn't tell Alyssa about the incident on the Underground. Why should I? Anyway, there were plenty of other things to talk about: how and when we should go to Russia, for instance. I decided to take Os the cameraman with us, even though Alyssa was audibly unenthusiastic.

'He attracts too much attention. And he's so—'

Her voice dropped away, but I could guess the adjectives she might have slotted into the gap: big, loud, assertive, male. For me, those were all marks of his value as a cameraman; in a physical, competitive business like ours, the 'after you, Claude' approach is a serious liability.

For her, no doubt, men like Os represented everything she disliked, identified and expected about the male sex: a manspreader if ever there was one. And an Afrikaner on top of everything else.

'I know what you mean,' I said emolliently; I didn't quite want a barney with her right now. 'But he's a good man to have on a difficult shoot. He never fails, you know; he always brings home the goods.'

She didn't actually sniff, but she might as well have done. For the sake of harmony, I pretended not to notice.

The following morning we were sitting on uncomfortable chairs in a soulless place on the rattier edge of the City, waiting for our number to come up. You have to apply in person for a visa to Russia, in order to give them your fingerprints, and if you're a journalist then someone in the country has to vouch for you: not some stray foreigner, but the head of a bona fide Russian organisation. And – surprise, surprise – the whole business is really expensive.

In other words, things aren't all that different from what they were in the old, unlamented Soviet days. True, most of the women who dish out the visas are moderately pleasant, even nice-looking – something you could never have accused their Sov predecessors of being. I have an abiding memory, dating back to the 1970s, of badly blonded hair, bristly chins and enormous, cantilevered chests that would have put your eye out if you'd made physical contact with them.

There weren't any of those here now: they were mostly willowy, and the blonding agents they used seemed milder and more natural. Ditto the chests.

Over and over again I read the posters that told me how vast the Russian Federation was in square kilometrage, how populous, how many writers and physicists it had produced, and what fun they all seemed to be having, while I kept an eye on the electronic board that told us how far off our number was.

Os didn't hold with Russians – no one seemed to have told him they weren't Communist any more – so he kept quiet. Alyssa was still annoyed with me for bringing him along, so she wasn't speaking to me either. I sat and digested some more figures about the number of Russians at university and the total lengths of Russian motorways, and watched the red electronic numbers creeping closer to 347.

We all went up together.

'Yes?' said an acid voice. Clearly, not every Russian official had got the message about being hospitable and friendly.

Alyssa, as the producer, was the boss of this kind of transaction. She explained in detail who we were, how we could prove it, and what needed to be done to help us. The acid one didn't approve of her, I could see. If you want to see real old-fashioned brutal racism, you should try being black in Russia. How Pushkin's Ethiopian great-granddad managed, I've no idea. It was obvious that the main question in this frosty cow's mind was why a black woman should be talking on behalf of two white blokes.

Still, it was all sorted out in the end. We handed over a ludicrous amount of money, and arranged to send a despatch rider to pick up the duly stamped passports the following morning. There'd just be enough time to get to Heathrow for the fifteen twenty flight to Moscow.

And so it proved. The moment I reached the end of the air bridge at Terminal 4 and was faced with a stewardess just inside the door of Aeroflot Airbus 319, I felt I'd arrived back in Mother Russia.

She stared at my boarding pass as though it was an official document; which I suppose it was, in a way. Then she pointed me down the plane to where the economy seats were. Mine was in the general direction of the toilets.

There were three stewardesses down that end, talking loudly and ignoring the passengers. I slid into number 18C, which was narrow, limited and uncomfortable, just like any economy seat on any other airline: all of them want to punish you for not paying to go business class. Alyssa and Os were allocated separate seats a few rows further forward; I like to be alone when I fly.

The plane filled up, and everything was ready for take-off. Except that nothing happened. We waited with the air bridge still attached for twenty minutes after the advertised take-off time; then, finally, an expensive-looking passenger came on board as though he had all the time in the world. His sprouting blondish hair and bulbous Russian-peasant nose looked like something you might see in the paintings of Ilya Repin, but his suit could only have been cut, expensively, in London: that made him a member of the Duma, maybe, or some uber-rich character who had diddled his fellow Russians out of millions. Now that he had finally got here, we were all free to leave. Nice of him not to have taken longer, I suppose.

Our plane started its bumpy chase down runway number two and eased up into the air. Four hours of doing nothing lay ahead of me, a pleasant stretch of time during which I would be entirely out of reach of the office and could just relax. Above all, I wouldn't give any thought to the big interview that lay ahead of me in Moscow: it was too complicated, and maybe too worrying.

I lowered my headphones over my ears, selected some Frank Bridge on my iPod, and took up a new biography of Edmund Burke; any Irishman who had skipped to London and told the bloody English what was what, had my admiration. After half an hour or so, with 'First Discoveries' still twiddling in my ears, I dozed off. I was happy.

We don't need to go into a long pre-history here, but during the 1980s I visited Russia loads of times, making discreet contacts and familiarising myself with the decaying patterns of Soviet life. Then, as relations warmed up a little, I went there openly as a reporter. Finally, from mid 1991 to 1994, I was based in Moscow full-time as a foreign correspondent, during and after the collapse of the old Soviet Union.

The way my life has turned out, Russia has been central to it. I love, admire, fear and despise the place in roughly equal proportions. I've devoted much of my existence to mastering its language and trying to understand its weird ways, and I acknowledge after all these years that I've had very little success. I've loved and usually despaired of its women, and in recent years I've pretty much forsworn them, much as another man might give up booze or cigarettes.

All this has left me with – well, not an awful lot. I can read *Moskovskiy Komsomolets* online every day in the original Russian, though I never know why I bother, and I can quote bits of Mayakovsky's poems by heart – sometimes in Russian, more often in inadequate English:

> *My most respected*
> > *comrades of the future!*
> *Rooting through*
> > *these days'*
> > > *petrified crap,*
> *exploring the twilight of our times,*
> *you,*
> > *possibly,*
> > > *will inquire about me too.*

He was a bit too Communist for Lenin's taste, and supposedly killed himself in 1921. The old joke used to be, 'What were Mayakovsky's last words before he committed suicide? "Don't shoot, comrades."'

I can sit on a number 19 bus on the King's Road in London and understand the disparaging remarks the Russians around me are making. And I can murmur a few choice erotic remarks in Russian to girls before, during and after love-making. That, I suspect, may well turn out to be my life's greatest achievement.

Sixteen

And there it was, waiting for us, the moment we stepped off the plane four and a half hours later: the old, pervasive, instantly identifiable smell of Soviet Russia. Thank God it still exists: the Duma ought to pass a law to preserve it, like the Siberian tiger. Most of the other laws they pass, making life nasty for gays and lavishing honours on the president, are a lot more reprehensible.

That smell: it's an acrid sweetness combining, I have always thought, sweat, some kind of officially supplied polish, cigarette smoke, unwashed clothes and damp overcoats. But in today's Russia fewer people smoke (though not that much fewer), and they rely on Western-made polish rather than the state-manufactured type they had in Marxist–Leninist times. A lot more personal hygiene seems to be going on, too; at any rate in the cities.

So the old Communist smell is dying out, just like the one aristos once identified with tsarist Russia: the scent of pine walls heated by big ceramic corner stoves. Will there be a new Russian smell, now that capitalism is back with a vengeance? The smell of money, perhaps – though as the emperor Vespasian once said to his snooty son Titus, '*Pecunia non olet.*' You must forgive me: my old-fashioned Irish education is turning into something of a burden. *Pecunia non olet* means 'money has no smell'; though of course it always does.

The next thing I noticed, as we queued up at passport control, was that in other essentials nothing had changed. We'd been unlucky enough to land at precisely the same time as a flight from Yerevan chock-full of Georgian peasants bringing supplies of sausage and dried meats to sell in the markets of Moscow. The smell of the sausage quickly drowned out the Russian smell; or maybe it was the smell of the Georgian peasants that did it.

I couldn't face talking to Alyssa and Os, and they didn't want to talk to each other, so we stood in the queue in uncompanionable silence. There was jostling farther down the line, and a woman feigning a serious headache, or maybe a fever, pushed her way in front of all of us and was then relentlessly shoved back to where she belonged.

After twenty minutes of waiting, it was my turn to step forward. A pimply nineteen-year-old in uniform went through every single page of my passport, looking at my past visas (that always irritates me). Then he stared at my hairline, my eyes, my ears and my chin, checking them against the passport photograph in front of him. After that he looked up at the angled mirror over my head – why? To see if I was bald? Or smuggling in a child? Or a machine-gun? I stared back at him in retaliation, noticing that there was a kind of pattern about his pimples: they erupted in groups on unlikely parts of his face and neck.

'*Spasibo*,' I said with heavy irony, when he handed back my passport. The watery blue eyes stared entirely through me now, as though the act of pushing the passport through the glass screen had wiped me out of his existence. He said nothing; after all, do you say goodbye to a word when you delete it on your laptop?

I waited for the two others to infiltrate the system, then we headed into the baggage hall and pulled our bags off the groaning carousel. No sign that they'd been tampered with: Sheremetyevo must be improving.

'Flight OK?' I asked.

They grunted, in their different ways, and Alyssa and I wandered after Os, who was pushing a trolley with one wonky wheel through the red channel. There was much flourishing of *carnets*, and then he was allowed through.

On the far side of the customs desk, out in the arrivals hall, a heaving crowd of Moscow-based Georgians was waiting to greet the sausage carriers. Behind and a little apart from them stood a tall, distinguished, grey-haired man in a dark suit. He was holding a board with my name in Roman letters on it. It looked as though the noise and the smell of so much Caucasian humanity pained him.

'Yuri, you old bastard,' I called out, and the distaste left his face in an instant. I introduced the others, but although he looked appraisingly at Alyssa's figure and at Os's general size and toughness, it was me he wanted to see.

It was twenty years or more since Yuri first drove me round Moscow and translated for me. That was when Boris Yeltsin called out the tanks to fire at the headquarters of the Moscow city government during a brief attempted coup. When you have been badly scared in someone's company, it generates a powerful bond between the two of you.

Nowadays Yuri looked like a senior male model, with his greying temples, his black suit (not Savile Row, as worn by the politico on the plane, but expensive off-the-peg stuff: Boss, possibly?) and his nicely tied red-and-gold Hermès tie. I don't know how he coaxes his hair into those elegant wings above his ears, by the way:

they're an art form. Still, none of this, the suit, the tie or the hair wings, inhibited him from aiming a punch at my solar plexus. He almost connected.

We put our arms round each other in a bear hug. It's not something a man of my age and background usually does, but I'd always been very fond of him. Os beamed, but not Alyssa. There must have been some type of male she found acceptable, I assumed, but I hadn't yet found it.

Yuri had started out as the office driver, but he knew more than any of the clever, dedicated young Russians who worked in the place, and soon rose within the system until he became more or less freelance. I always asked him to work with me when I visited Moscow, and was usually glad of it afterwards.

Did he work for someone other than us – the FSB, for example? Or Russian military intelligence? It's a question you often find yourself asking in Moscow nowadays, just as much as you did in the bad old Communist days. Yet once you have obtained a Russian's friendship and loyalty, in my experience, it doesn't matter who pays their wages: their heart and soul are yours.

At Yuri's unanswerable demand, the two others were despatched into the back of the car, while I sat beside him. We drove through the darkness in the direction of town, past the closest point the Germans reached to Moscow in 1941; past the place where my car was stopped at the point of a heavy tank gun in 1991, during the KGB's cack-handed attempt to topple Mikhail Gorbachev; past the place where, in 1983, my car broke down in the snow and a drunk stopped, donated the remaining contents of his home-made vodka bottle to me, and drove me to the nearest Metro station, all for nothing, because he came from Archangel and the Royal Navy had saved his family from starvation during the War; past the chemist's shop outside which my then girlfriend slapped my face, burst into tears, and told me she loved someone else (which was a relief, since I was trying to find the right moment to tell her something similar).

And, finally, past the shop where, in the days when the shortages of Marxism–Leninism finally seemed to be over, I bought myself an astrakhan-collared overcoat. It looked great in Russia, but it made me look like an Eastern European music impresario down on my luck when I wore it back in London.

In other words, I felt I was home.

The others looked out of the window as I listened to Yuri's sharply observed, amusingly delivered account in pretty good English of what was going on in Kremlin politics.

'Can I ask you something, Yuri?'

He paused in mid-anecdote, warily, and his eyes narrowed as he looked at the road ahead.

'Who else do you work for?'

'Sometimes for Canadian Broadcasting.'

'And . . . ?'

'Now for you.'

I grinned, and beside me in the darkness, with the headlights of oncoming cars shining into the interior of the Volvo, he grinned too, his teeth gleaming in the sudden beams like brand new gravestones. You could never get anything out of Yuri by asking him a direct question. I punched him on the arm. Not too hard, though: I didn't want him to crash. Os and Alyssa paid no attention.

They got more interested when Yuri started to talk about the arrangements for our coming interview with the president. It was the first time I'd asked Yuri to make the contacts, rather than one of the young office producers, and it had caused a bit of a fuss in the bureau. Complaints had been passed back to London, and dealt with in the usual indecisive fashion. Still, everything seemed to be working out disturbingly well, and I could see that Yuri was pleased – with himself, with me, and with life in general.

We pulled in at the hotel, and stood at the reception desk to check in. A dark-haired young woman smiled at us and asked in a pleasant, husky voice, 'Have you stayed here before?'

'Oh yes,' I replied. 'I certainly have.'

Seventeen

There were a number of things we had to do. We had to look in at our organisation's bureau to introduce Alyssa, find out what was happening and pay our respects. But it was Yuri who had made the arrangements for my interview, and Yuri didn't like the bureau any more than I did. Then we all had to go off to a nearby bar and have a drink, and I congratulated him on his success in landing the interview, and tried to find out how he'd managed it. I failed, of course. But it was great to sit and talk to him again, and listen to his grouses against everything: his colleagues, the government, the Americans. I never could quite understand why he had it in so heavily for the Americans; their cigarettes, their jazz and their movies seemed to suit him well enough.

Yuri headed off to whatever quarter of the city he lived in. I'd never been invited there, and I had no idea where it was. I think he preferred it that way. The three of us had a late, gloomy snack in the hotel dining room. The waiters talked to the waitresses and mostly ignored us. Alyssa was still annoyed with me and Os, and Os seemed to feel intimidated by Alyssa and the surroundings. I was just tired.

I lay on my hotel bed with one of those infuriatingly narrow duvets the Russians for some occult reason adopted from the Germans, and tried to sleep. All I could do was think about

Patrick. I heard his earnest voice and saw the frown he used to give before breaking into a smile; only in my half-dream the smile didn't come.

The duvet never seemed to cover the whole of me, and my room must have been the only one in the whole of Moscow that wasn't overheated. By the morning I felt as though I'd scarcely slept, though I suppose I must have. The three little bottles of Russian Standard Original which I liberated from the minibar must surely have had some effect, even if I wasn't altogether aware of it at the time.

The next morning I took Alyssa and Os to Red Square, which they'd never seen before, and left them there to wander round GUM as a punishment for being boring. I dropped in at an antiquarian bookshop I like in the Arbat, to see if they had anything interesting by Mayakovsky or Akhmatova. They didn't.

That brought my extra-curricular activities to an end, except for one last visit I was due to make that night. Before I left London I had made a discreet arrangement, through an old friend of mine, to see the most important of the Kremlin's critics, Boris Kulikov. You'll remember him: one night, a year or so later, someone shot him dead outside the front door of his flat.

Alyssa insisted on coming with me, and so did Os. But I thought that three people would be ultra-conspicuous, especially if a giant like Os was one of them. I tried to explain this tactfully; he was sensitive about his size.

'Just sounds to me as though you might be in need of a bit of back-up,' he said grumpily. You can see why I was so fond of him.

'All right,' I said, 'if you really want to, you can come. But don't walk with us. Travel in a different carriage on the Metro and follow us at a distance. I'll wait for you in the doorway of the block of flats.'

It was raining when Alyssa and I came out of the Metro station at around nine o'clock and turned left down the big, brightly lit street. Neither of us, naturally, looked round to see if Os was still there, carrying his little camera and his smallest lights in a holdall. We didn't need to, anyway: Os is just about the most reliable man I know.

Amazing how, even in these times of relative economic pain, there was so much in the shops to buy: I couldn't rid myself of the memory of all the shortages under Communism. This was a route I knew well, and a hundred yards or so down the road we turned left, as I had done at various times in the past. Away from the big, brash shops and the bright street lights, the architecture changed from grossly modern to early nineteenth century and it was darker down here. A car's headlights briefly picked out the buildings ahead of us. It was driving slowly. Maybe the driver was just trying to find the way.

I think I knew he wasn't doing anything of the sort. It wasn't just that my recent experiences in London had made me aware of such things; this had happened to me plenty of times in the past. The swine were trying to put the frighteners on me; it was their way of doing things. They had obviously been waiting for us outside the Metro station.

It was annoying, but not particularly something to worry about: this was simply their way of telling you that they knew all about you and what you were doing.

'Just to let you know, I think that car's following us.'

'Oh, Jon, you're always imagining things,' Alyssa laughed. 'Why would anyone want to follow us?'

'Because of who we're going to see.'

'Look, honestly, I'm sorry to say it, but I see this as a form of self-dramatisation. You're not in the Cold War any more, you know. So please . . .'

She meant belt up.

I grunted, rather than agree or apologise. Maybe she was right. You do dramatise things more as you get older, I've noticed. It's a way of assuring yourself and everyone around you that you still matter, I suppose.

The dark blue Mercedes behind us didn't suffer from any such feeling of self-effacement. Only one of the two men in it was looking where he was driving. As they drew alongside, going at maybe three miles an hour, the passenger stared at us without a touch of anger or threat in his expression: he could have been searching for somewhere to buy a carton of milk.

The Merc passed us, very slowly. Then, while it was still just moving, the expressionless character leapt out, and things started happening almost too fast to register. He raised a jack rod theatrically high above his head, and Alyssa yelled out something as a warning; even at that moment I was impressed by the way she reacted to the danger. Before I could move out of the way he brought the jack rod savagely down on my head.

But he reckoned without the protective power of astrakhan. I'd brought an old but still highly serviceable hat with me from London, one that I'd found in a shop just off the main ring road in Moscow years before. The ear-flaps were folded over on the top of my head, and I'd dutifully tied them up. Alyssa had disapproved of astrakhan when I'd put it on earlier, on account of its cruelty.

She may have been right, but that thick, curly black fur protected me from a whole world of cruelty now. Even so, I could feel the force of the blow travel right down my spine, and something that may have been bile came shooting up into my mouth and made me retch as I staggered into a doorway.

The man whacked me again and again with the jack rod, but he couldn't get a clear blow in, and my thick fleece-lined coat protected me. Still, as I curled up on the ground with my arms over my head, he gave me a couple of powerful kicks in the ribs. I hadn't been so comprehensively thumped up since the cops gave me a going-over in Soweto in the bad old days of apartheid.

The whole thing can only have lasted thirty seconds or so. Then Os caught up with us and waded in. The thug must have felt that Table Mountain had collapsed on him. In an instant there was blood everywhere, and it wasn't mine or Os's.

'Oi!' shouted someone further down the street, and the thug jumped back into the Merc and slammed the door. It drove off fast, disappearing into the darkness. I stayed in my doorway, hunched up like the foetus I had once been: it seemed the easiest and least painful thing to do, on the whole, and I didn't feel like stopping.

'Thanks, Os,' I managed to croak out.

'No problem, boss. Just wish I'd given him a proper *bliksem.*' *Bliksem* being the all-purpose Afrikaans word for sorting someone out, aggression, surprise, amazement, and other strong emotions.

By this stage whoever it was who'd called out further down the street had arrived.

'Are you OK?' he asked anxiously in English.

'Of course he's not.' Alyssa's crisp voice cut through the night air with the sharpness of a razor. 'He's been attacked by some maniac.'

'So what happened?'

Even then, with my ears at ground level, I thought the voice was familiar, but it seemed possible that something bad had happened to my brain and tricked it into making mistakes of perception. At this stage it didn't even hurt very much; I just had the feeling that I'd been quite badly damaged.

'It's me,' the voice said.

'Good God, Boris, you bugger,' I groaned from my position close to the ground, and realised I was saying it in Russian. Presumably, then, my brain was still in reasonable working order. That was a relief; my brain is my second favourite organ, as someone once said. Woody Allen, actually, but it seems to be illegal to mention his name nowadays.

'How did you find me?'

I suppose I was relieved, though the pain was starting in earnest and it didn't leave me with much scope for paying attention to anything else.

'I asked Gregoriy here to look out for you,' Boris said. 'He saw them attack you.'

'Who the fuck is Gregoriy?' It doesn't sound quite so bad in Russian. I was still lying on the ground, pretty foetal.

'You shouldn't be having conversation, you should be in hospital,' Boris said. 'Why don't you stand up and see what's wrong?'

Funnily enough, when I did what he suggested, there wasn't as much wrong as I'd thought. Some extraordinary colours lit up inside my head when they helped me to my feet, I was starting to entertain a headache like an erupting volcano, and the pain whenever I took a breath showed me that my notion about having a cracked rib probably wasn't far wrong. But I could stand, and walk, and even smile a bit at my rescuers.

'You remember where is my flat,' said Boris Kulikov in English, then 'You think you can walk there?' in Russian.

'If there's a bottle of vodka waiting I can run there, if necessary.'

As long as I could make a joke, I must be starting to feel better.

There was indeed a bottle of vodka in his flat. Many more than one. There was also one of Boris's latest gorgeous girlfriends, who fussed over me in a most satisfactory manner. My wounds – none of them in any way serious – were sponged and dressed, and my rib was clucked over sympathetically.

My headache began to yield to a couple of huge horse tablets the girlfriend fed me solicitously: Russians like their pills, like most other things, on the large side. I sat back in the atmosphere of warmth and affection, and grinned. Even Alyssa relaxed. I noticed, though, that she couldn't bring herself to apologise to me for having dismissed my fears of being followed.

Kulikov had been making tea in the small kitchen off the sitting room where I was being looked after. Now he brought the glasses in on a tray. I hadn't seen him for a year or so. He wasn't looking at all bad, and his handsome face gleamed with instinctive good temper.

Once upon a time, when he was a senior government minister, he'd been spoken of as the likeliest man to become president in the near future: not a good thing for your career in contemporary Russia. So he'd been threatened, hunted down, arrested, and imprisoned instead; and he'd responded (when he was released) by organising demonstration after demonstration against the leadership, and giving outspoken – I used to think, often foolhardy – interviews to the few Russian television stations which were prepared to run criticisms of the government.

As the years went by, those stations became fewer and fewer in number.

'I've got a feeling,' I said slowly, 'that what happened to us just now is more about you than it was about me.'

'Maybe. In which case I'm most humbly sorry.'

Kulikov's narrow eyes twinkled, and he bowed.

A lot of bad things had happened to him over the years, and he knew I was well aware of it. I was really fond of him; it was impossible not to be.

After a while I sat up and, when a bit more vodka had gone round, we started some serious talking. Out of common politeness I asked him about his own position first, but I was really keen to get him on to the subject of Patrick and the way he had died. He knew all about it, I found.

'I never met him, but I hear he was a good man. I'm really sorry for what happened.'

'Thank you, Boris. It was quite a loss to me.'

I looked away. Os was still caring for his bruised knuckles, but Alyssa was showing signs of impatience. She never liked being left out of things, and we'd been chatting away in Russian.

'And we can assume that no one in England is interested in investigating your friend's case, because they assume it was really just a case of self-strangulation, rather sordid in its details. Things like this are inclined to happen here as well, you know.'

I nodded, and switched to English for Alyssa's benefit. 'The thing about Patrick is that, as I've now discovered, he'd been doing a hell of a lot of research into FSB killings here and in Britain. He was planning to make a speech about it in the British Parliament.'

'People can also die here for doing that kind of thing.'

'So you think it's possible that Patrick was murdered to keep him quiet?'

'I would say it's quite likely. What was that expression you used here once before? "A racing certainty".'

With his accent, that sounded even better than when I'd said it.

'I'd like to do a programme about Patrick's death, you see, but for that I'll need proper slam-dunk evidence.'

' "Slam-dunk"?' Boris adored English slang. Word games were one of his great pleasures.

I tried to think of an exact Russian equivalent, but couldn't. 'Hard and fast. Ace. Incontrovertible,' I said at random. 'Without a shadow of a doubt.'

'Yes, I'm starting to get the idea,' Boris replied.

For a time he said nothing more, while I measured the strength of my headache and fingered my rib, wincing. But the horse tablets were now at their peak efficiency. The girlfriend had made herself scarce when we'd started talking about politics, I noticed.

'I'm trying to decide whether to give you the details of someone who's come to me recently. Someone who would almost certainly be able to tell you what you want to know. "Slam-dunk,"' he repeated to himself meditatively.

'Why not just give them to me now?'

'Because it would be dangerous for him, and quite dangerous for you too. Do you want to get another blow to the head like that?'

I didn't, of course, but I really wanted to get the proof I needed.

'The trouble is, you see, that this man, who's very senior, has come to me secretly with information about how the security people operate. It's quite extraordinary. And because he used to be so high up, using his name in one of your reports would have an explosive effect. And of course he too could be killed. I don't want the responsibility for that sort of thing. I'll have to think about it.'

'What shall we do?'

'I'll talk it over with him,' Boris Kulikov said. 'And it obviously can't be done by phone. There are dangers to that, as you have just found.'

I nodded, then wished I hadn't: the separate and distinct pains in my head and rib joined up and merged together for a bit.

125

'You know, there are plenty of people in our society who disapprove of the way our regime operates. Some of them come to me and give me information. This man is one of them, but the thing that makes him different is that he comes from within the system itself. High up.'

That, I thought, is my Russia; it's the aspect I love most about these people. They're ruled by the heart far more than by the head, and if they become convinced that the side they've been on is the wrong one, they'll change. Noisily and bravely. All I had to do now was wait to see if Boris would persuade this mystery character that he should talk to me on camera. Unless, of course, he was one of the ones who insisted on being ruled by the head.

My own head was throbbing unpleasantly now. How is it that painkillers stop acting after a couple of hours, but you're supposed to wait four hours before you're allowed to take the next ones? It doesn't seem a very sensible arrangement.

Eighteen

The antechamber was grander than most throne rooms, painted gold and white, and there were lots of nineteenth-century paintings of snow scenes and whiskery generals in magnificent cloaks on the walls. I paced down one side of the room. It took me a long time to turn round and pace back down the other.

'I'm sure everything will be OK,' said the local producer, a Russian from the bureau. She was a nicely brought up girl from Rostov-on-Don who'd worked for the Brits so long she'd become like one of us. What she meant was, for God's sake stop freaking us out and sit down; but she was too well polite to say this to someone of my advanced years.

The trouble was, you see, I had got this far with important interviews before, only for them to be called off. President Mobutu Sese Seko of Zaire, for instance: as slippery a character as you can imagine. When he sent a message cancelling at the very last minute, citing toothache as the reason, he was actually in the air, flying to Switzerland to get treatment for terminal cancer. And then there was Robert Mugabe. And Saddam Hussein. And Colonel Gaddafi. And Osama bin Laden. All no-shows at the very last minute, the bastards.

I did some more pacing.

Finally, a great gold and white door opened at the far end of the antechamber, so distant I couldn't recognise the face of the man who slipped in until he came a bit closer. The features finally resolved themselves into those of Pavel Zelinsky, the assistant to the assistant to the president's chief adviser, white-faced and cavernous, as though his mother had never fed him up or let him out into the street.

He was impossible to like, a smarmy little so and so, the kind of apparatchik who crawls to the senior people and barks at the ones lower down the batting order. We had enough of those in my own organisation at home.

I ignored him on principle, but he still brayed in my direction.

'His Excellency will be ready in a couple of minutes.'

I snorted with irritation: a century after they wiped out their royal family, Russians still grovel to their rulers with the same awe. How would the assistant to the assistant have spoken of Stalin in these very rooms, if I had come to interview him? Exactly the same.

Still, it was something to have an interview with today's Autocrat of All the Russias, and don't think I wasn't fully sensible of it. Also nervous. Recording an interview with someone as controversial as the Russian president is like a boxing match: it is essential that you land a few telling blows yourself if you are to go home with any dignity, but you can expect to receive plenty in return.

And you have to finish the whole thing in a way that won't have your interviewee knocking over his chair and shouting that he'll never think of doing an interview with you or anyone from your outfit ever again.

I'd had a couple of days to get over my beating. Fortunately – you can see I work for television – my face was unmarked. A top-notch Moscow doctor gave me a thorough going-over. He reckoned my head was all right and told one of his nurses how to tape up my not very cracked rib. It was fine now, except when I breathed. I tried not to.

Our cameras were all set up, and the others hung round it, waiting, while I stalked around still. The two cameramen, Os and a Russian who worked for the bureau, had put a couple of spindly-legged gold chairs in the middle of the room facing each other.

From the walls, Catherine the Great and Peter the Great and various other life-sized Greats stared disapprovingly down at us, some of them astride equally life-sized horses. The room was staggering, and the vast carpet, discreetly darned in places, was big enough for Chelsea to play Manchester United on. And valuable enough to pay off the national debt of Turkmenistan.

Our television cameras were ready on their tripods. One pointed at me, and one at the space where the President of Russia's face would soon be.

'OK,' said the local producer with a note of finality in her voice, 'I think we're ready.'

If I'd been twenty years younger I'd have found her distinctly fanciable. Nowadays, though, I have to rein myself in: after all, which thirty-year-old girl wants a sexagenarian panting after her? Unless of course the sexagenarian owns a large yacht and great swathes of Mayfair, or is called Donald Trump.

The presidential assistant's sidekick, who had been standing around as though to make sure we didn't chip the gold paint or steal the ashtrays, scurried off in a self-regarding kind of way, as though he was on a mission of national importance.

I grinned at the producer, which only showed her how nervous I was. The thing about these big interviews is that you could be moments away from the greatest disaster of your career: a possibility I've had to face plenty of times around the world. Sometimes, of course, you can see that the person you are about to interview feels the same way. That makes the odds rather better.

Down at one end of the throne room a door I hadn't previously noticed opened, and a slight figure slipped through it alone. Three more people came in through the great double doors at the same moment, but a glance showed that they were merely the backing group for the star soloist. It was the slight figure I had to concentrate on.

The temptation was to wait where I was and let him walk all the way towards me, like Stalin used to do. But that would be bad manners on my part, and he had at least had the decency to allow me to interview him. I walked thirty paces towards him down the carpet which could solve Turkmenistan's economic problems, and tried to think what I'd say. But I couldn't. All I was able to do was think about how small he was.

'Hello,' he said in good English, smiling nervously. I'd never actually seen him in the flesh before. Lesson number one about dealing with the famous men and women of the world: they are usually shorter and more nervous than you expect. And occasionally they can be almost human.

'I've watched some of your reports on television,' he went on, smiling. 'Very good.' He was being polite to me because I was older than he was, I realised. That's Russia for you.

'Well, it's a great pleasure to meet you.'

I was trying not to gush, but there is something about coming face to face with the famous that has that effect on us all. Would I have behaved like this to him if he'd still been a KGB colonel? Only if he was actually leaning over me with the electrodes in his hands, I suppose.

'You understand,' I went on, trying to establish my alibi, 'this will have to be a fairly combative interview.'

'Combative?' He somehow made it last for four syllables.

'You know – a bit, well, hostile.'

'That is the nature of your job.'

It occurred to me that instead of being hand-to-hand combat, as some top-level interviews were, this one was going to be like show wrestling, with phony falls and a lot of playing to the audience. So be it, I thought.

And that's how it turned out.

The first few questions were in the way of feints, to see how he'd react and where the points of real antagonism might lie. And he was really good.

'Why do you ask me if Russia wants to fight a war, when it is the NATO countries which are making all the warlike moves. "Warlike" is right?' he added disarmingly.

I had to bite my tongue not to compliment him on his English. Can you imagine what the *Daily Mail* would have said if I'd been nice to him? So I nodded and smiled, making a mental note that we mustn't use the shot of me doing so.

We moved to other topics. The allotted twenty minutes were running out fast, and I hadn't yet landed a glove on him.

Now was the time. I changed the subject abruptly, almost brutally.

'Why is it that so many people who criticise you end up dead?'

All round me there was silence. It buzzed so loudly in my ears that I could hear it. In it, I could hear an intake of breath from his spokesman, who was sitting close by, and I could imagine my producer's look of alarm even though I couldn't see her. This was the kind of thing that could turn into a major incident.

'Who told you that this is the case?'

'I read the Russian newspapers. And the British ones, for that matter.'

'Ah, so you believe everything you read?'

'No, but I do know that various people who have criticised you are no longer alive.' I recited three names.

A Saddam Hussein or an Idi Amin might have replied that I could find myself on the list as well, if I wasn't careful. But the president was a class act.

'I can't understand why you would make an allegation like that in this interview. I would have expected something better from you. Shall I say, something more sophisticated?'

'So it isn't true?' I persisted lamely.

'Of course it isn't true. Do you think the government of Russia is in the hands of thugs and murderers?'

As it happened, I rather did. But I couldn't say so, and he knew I wouldn't. Still, I did have one last name to put to him.

'And the British MP, Patrick Macready: he was a strong critic of yours, and he's now dead.'

'I'm sorry, but I haven't heard of this gentleman. I cannot answer questions about people I haven't heard of.'

There was a cough from his spokesman. I knew we had come to the end of our agreed time, and I'd managed to do precisely what I'd intended to avoid. One of the rules relating to interviews like this is to ask a series of easier, lighter questions to end with, after an awkward patch. It calms the interviewees down, and if you're lucky they'll forget the nasty questions and end up happy instead of stalking out when everything is over. But we didn't have the time.

I smiled at the president. The president didn't smile back at me.

'You ask difficult questions,' he said.

'My job,' I said with a shrug, as though it didn't really have anything to do with me. I once had an editor, a nice old boy, who when he needed to rewrite my copy would say 'I'll just pass this through the typewriter', as if it was a purely mechanical action. I found myself trying the same trick now. I was just part of the machinery.

'I understand,' said the president politely as he shook my hand.

But it hadn't worked: he was still angry. There was a yellowish gleam in his eyes, and his spokesman didn't even look at me as they took the long hike back to the exit.

'Phew,' said the Russian producer. 'Did you plan on asking him that?'

'Not really.'

But I had. A friend is a friend, and three of the four names I mentioned to the president had belonged to people I knew.

'You fucking idiot,' said Alyssa when we were in the car heading back to our hotel. 'You fucking, fucking idiot.'

Os Malan sat in the front seat, looking out at Gorky Street. I knew he wanted to wade in on my side, but he must have guessed I'd put him down if he did.

'So you think he doesn't kill people?'

'It's just—' She struggled, and her face grew longer and sharper. 'It's just so fucking unprofessional.'

I knew what she meant. Back in London, she'd get a sizeable share of the blame. I hadn't told her I'd be asking a question like that, so she wouldn't have had the chance to warn me off. But that didn't matter. She'd be tainted by my failure. It was like catching the Black Death: you might simply be part of the household where it struck, and certainly not the carrier, but you'd die just as surely as the person who brought it home.

Os too, only his years of friendship bound him to me.

'It's not unprofessional,' he said, his Rs making a particularly guttural Afrikaans sound. 'He's doing his job. If anyone's unprofessional . . .' His booming voice trailed away.

'Look, it's over,' I said. 'I'm to blame – except I think it was the right thing to ask him.'

But that didn't cover the danger of infection, and we all knew it.

'I'll ring the desk and warn them,' Alyssa said angrily.

Somehow, though, the desk knew already. Apparently it was the talk of the Centre by the time we reached our hotel. Presumably Yuri had told someone in the bureau, and they'd got on to London. People in an outfit like ours love being the bearers of bad news.

'How did you find out?' I asked the desk editor over the phone. He was a cold fish, and I'd never liked him.

'Never mind that, we've got to think about damage limitation.'

When did you ever think of anything else? I thought. Then I realised I'd said it out loud.

'Arnaud's been on already.'

Arnaud was the owner's younger son by his first, Belgian wife. He was also the favourite – his owner's implant, those of us who were less enthusiastic called him. He ran the television side of things for the owner. Sorry, The Owner; people in management always capitalised his title, even in speech. You could hear them slipping in a faint glottal stop between 'The' and 'O'.

'So?'

'So he's furious. Says it was—'

'Unprofessional.'

'Exactly.'

'Must have affected The Owner's financial interests, then.'

'I don't think that's—'

But I was already holding the indignant squawking away from my ear.

Across the hotel room Os grinned, but he knew that everything about this was bad.

'I still can't believe what you did,' Alyssa said, shaking her handsome head.

In a way, I felt sorry for her. It must be really hard to be in nominal control of an unruly character like me.

I even started to feel a bit ashamed of myself. After all, I was at the fag-end of a not very distinguished career, while she was still in the first third of hers. And I'd managed to screw things up for her.

'I suppose—'

But before I could get some form of apology out, she'd stormed off to her room.

Nineteen

'Were you happy with your interview?'

Your, you notice, not *the*, and certainly not *our*.

We were in one of the meeting pods back at the Centre in London, and five faces were turned towards me like dishes at a radio telescopy station zeroing in on an event in a distant galaxy. Be careful, I thought: these people are mostly pleasant enough as individuals, but their judgements will have consequences, and those consequences could include not getting my contract renewed. In my life, the difference between that and total financial catastrophe was so slight as to be completely negligible.

Some people, I knew, had been saying that my Moscow interview had been reckless, others that it had been self-indulgent. Not that anyone said these things to me, of course. I only knew because people passed the comments on to me: some in sympathy, others with a desire to stir things up. I tried to give the impression I wasn't upset by any of it, but I was.

There was a summing-up kind of voice from the far end of the table.

'Erm, HNP wondered a bit about your reference to that Tory MP who died in such weird circumstances.'

HNP? Mishearing, I thought for a moment she'd said 'HMP', as though we had become a branch of Her Majesty's Prison system. 'Head of News Projects', of course. It was a brand new title; they were being spawned all the time, each boss figure reproducing himself or herself in the corporate Petri dish by producing deputies and chief assistants exactly like themselves. And not a spine between them.

I started to say that that Tory MP happened to be a close friend of mine, but decided at the last instant that it might look as though I had been pursuing a personal vendetta. I had, of course, but I didn't want to confess it to all these creeps.

So I said in a voice which didn't allow much disagreement, 'I think we have to operate from a position of professional strength, don't you? Unless you ask the tough questions, people like the Russians and the Chinese will walk all over us. After all, we want to be a decent, respected news organisation, not a branch of PR.'

It was just grandstanding, of course, but there was a rustle of agreement from some of the younger characters. The older ones just looked glum. Once upon a time, they might have believed in something like that. Now, though, they just did what The Owner wanted, and tried to keep their noses clean. A great thing, corporate culture.

Still, the senior figure at the end of the table had to keep up the fiction that we were a strong, independent-minded outfit which didn't bow to pressure.

'No, absolutely – it's essential to stand up to these people.'

Then she turned to something else: a forthcoming trip to Beijing.

'Right – so you'll get on to the Chinese ambassador and try and persuade him to give us three extra visas?'

She looked me in the eyes for the first time since I'd stepped into this horrible pod, and did that annoying Australian thing of asking a question when she was actually making a statement.

'While Kevin concentrates on the Russian murders?'

This wasn't really a question at all: it was a sentence handed down from the bench. My punishment for asking a nasty question of the president was to be taken off the story of Patrick's murder and its link to other deaths. Kevin Braithwaite was a lacklustre character who could be relied on not to upset anyone.

'Wouldn't it make a lot more sense if I did that as well?'

Jeaned bottoms shifted and creaked. Someone tapped a pencil on the table: it was the new screaming.

'No, I don't really think so. In the circumstances.'

'And what circumstances might those be?'

I could feel the anger rising in my throat – not that this pleasant, rather feeble character was the right one to void it on. Anyway, up to now I'd always had the impression that she harboured a faint affection for me.

It's an incontestable fact that, when they reach their forties, some women develop a weakness for ramshackle old boys constructed somewhat along the lines of their fathers: I've started benefitting from that in recent years.

As we were filing out, she said quietly to me, 'HNP would like to see you now. He's pretty upset, I should warn you.'

'That makes two of us,' I said, but it was just bravura.

HNP was sitting in a different pod when I finally tracked him down. He obviously wanted to give me a bollocking in a place where he and I could be seen but not heard. The fact was, he was the kind of person who never said anything really unpleasant or threatening, and he wore a permanent smile, so you could never tell what he was actually doing to you.

People said that if he asked after your health when the

138

bollocking was over, that was a sign that it had been particularly tough. You wouldn't know otherwise.

He was a pleasant-faced man in his late forties, with the kind of wrinkles that made him look permanently anxious: which he probably was.

All his work had been done at a desk: he'd never heard a gun fired in anger, never been attacked by an angry crowd, and certainly never been subjected to a mock execution, as I had. Nor had he ever had to watch anyone burn to death.

I, on the other hand, had never had to sack someone after a lifetime's loyal service, or announce that the programme he or she had devoted their lives and sanity to was going to be closed down because its audience share had dropped. I wouldn't have swapped his experiences for mine, for all the money in the pension fund. If of course there was any of that left.

But I couldn't have much respect for him. He was a nervous, gutless waste of space.

Once, during a violent row, I'd shouted at him, 'If you'd been doing this job when the fucking Nazis marched in, you'd have called everyone together and said we all had to do what they wanted, for the sake of the fucking nation.'

I'd apologised, of course, because you have to in a civilised society. But he and I, and the three other people in the room when I'd said it, had all known it was true. Keeping his nose clean wasn't just an instinct, it was a religion.

'Good to see you – good to see you.' He usually said the nice things twice, and the nasty things once. 'Sit down, sit down. Interesting stuff in, er—'

'Moscow,' I said.

'Moscow, yes. Did you – not that I'm criticising in any way, of course – did you mean to ask that question about what's his name,

Patrick Macready? Sounded a bit, you know, spur of the moment. Off the cuff. As though it just slipped out.'

'Oh, really?' I said. 'Well, I wrote it down on my list of things to ask beforehand. I went there intending to ask it.'

'I see. I see. Hmm.' He made it sound as though premeditation was some kind of offence. 'You wrote it down.'

'Don't you think it'd be interesting if the president of Russia was responsible for murdering a British MP?'

'Well, if you put it that way, I suppose . . . But who's been suggesting it?'

'Me.'

'Any grounds, in particular?'

Sometimes he could be quite droll. When he wasn't trying to discipline me, that was one of the things I'd liked most about him.

I grinned, and he grinned back. At that moment, as it happened, two people were strolling past the interview pod and gawking at us. I was glad. One of them was an Olympic class gossip, and I didn't want the story going around that HND had given me a bollocking.

'Just a hunch. An idea of my own. A theory, I suppose.'

'A theory. Yes, I see. And you feel it was the right thing to put a theory to him?'

For HND, people in positions of power were special; even weirdos like Kim Jong-Un or Islam Karimov had to be treated with courtesy and respect; especially if The Owner had some dubious business deal going with them.

A few years earlier, when I'd come back from interviewing one particularly nasty dictator and revealed that he'd farted continually during our forty minutes together, HND gave me one of his most characteristic performances. He didn't tick me off, he just made me feel I'd behaved tastelessly and crudely.

After one of these sessions you could never quite pinpoint the wounds you'd received during the course of it, but they were pretty painful all the same.

'So I was wrong to ask about it?'

'Oh, I wouldn't say that. I just think we have to consider the wider picture.'

'What wider picture?'

'Well, you know, future plans. In Russia, apart from anywhere else. The Owner is thinking of expanding there.'

'So we mustn't upset the bastards.'

'That's not what I'm saying at all. I'm just saying, let's treat them politely, like we would treat everyone else.'

'Everyone else we want to do a deal with.'

He looked at me as though I'd hurt his feelings.

'How long did you know Patrick Macready for?'

'We were at Oxford together.'

'He was mixed up with intelligence at one point, wasn't he? Is that why you think the Russians may have killed him?'

'No, not for that. As I understand it, spooks usually have unwritten rules about not wiping each other out. Otherwise, I suppose, it'd all get a bit untidy.'

'But . . . ?'

'But I know he was involved with several people the Kremlin didn't like.'

'Can you tell me who they were?'

'Not really. If I did, I'd have to kill you.'

'Ha ha ha,' said HND, without doing any extra smiling.

As usually happened at meetings with him, it was impossible afterwards to work out precisely what the outcome had been; I suppose that's why he'd risen to such great administrative heights. He could say he'd ticked me off, but I could just as easily say he hadn't.

And yet at some stage, if required, the whole incident could be brought out and used against me, like ammunition issued to a firing squad. It was amazing how long, in a big organisation, these incidents remained in storage, available for use.

Twenty

I'm not much of a one for diplomatic receptions. Sure, you can occasionally find a new contact or a nugget of information by going to one, but for the most part all I do is stand around shifting from one foot to the other and trying to work out how soon I can decently leave. And because I turn so many invitations down, the supply has rather tended to dry up.

Not from the Czech embassy, however. I love the old Czechs, you see – they're like sane Russians. Once, long ago, I had a thing with a Czech girl who was a second secretary at their embassy in Paris. It ended badly, but I turn up at their dos just in case she's been promoted to London. She'd be deputy ambassador level by now, I suppose, and a size or two heavier.

The Czech embassy in London is a grisly Soviet-era slab of concrete in Notting Hill Gate, erected when Leonid Brezhnev was an aspiring apparatchik and could still go to the toilet by himself. In the 1980s I had some difficult experiences in this building – maybe I'll write about them some time – but nowadays a big black-and-white photo of my dear friend Václav Havel graces the main reception room of the embassy, and everything seems a hell of a lot brighter and nicer. No fiftyish female diplomats seemed to be around when I came into the room, though there were plenty of other good-looking women there; the Czech Republic seems to breed them.

William Hooper was standing near the fireplace, holding forth to a small crowd about Syria: not that William had ever risked his sizeable arse by actually going there, or anything energetic like that. William is the doyen of diplomatic correspondents in the London press corps. He reminds me of Mycroft Holmes, solving international problems from a capacious armchair in the Diogenes Club. I'm a bit in awe of his brain-power, I confess, and I compensate for it by being spiteful about him, as you'll have observed. But it's mutual.

'Well, well,' said William as I came up, 'it's television's own Jonathan Swift. Where have Gulliver's travels been taking you recently?'

The group of people around him tittered. What he was implying, of course, was that I was a retailer of tall stories.

We sparred a little. I've actually got a lot of admiration for William. Somewhere in that supersized body is a heart in more or less the right place.

'A word in your ear, dear boy,' he said, drawing me away. 'One of the Russkies has been asking me about you this evening. Wants to meet you. Be on your guard, is my advice.'

'Name?'

'Gronov. One of the top men on the information side at the embassy, but something else entirely, as you might expect.'

'Mikhail Mikhailovich Gronov?'

'The very man. Someone's been briefing you.'

'Even television hacks stumble across things occasionally, you know.'

William smiled like a Buddha in a Portobello Road junk shop, and for the first time I realised that I actually liked him. In small doses.

'Just watch out for him, that's all.'

It was another couple of Becherovkas and several diplomats later that my elbow was captured quite painfully by the thumb and forefinger of someone standing behind me. I turned round in mid conversation with a man from the EU Commission, so it was a blessed relief.

A tall character in a grey suit and grey tie was standing there, smiling.

'I thought you needed rescuing,' he said. 'Mikhail Gronov is my name.'

He had an accent, but it simply gave a pleasant colouring to his perfect English. I tried a little charm of my own.

'How on earth do you speak God's own language so beautifully?'

'You're very kind,' he said, but there was, I swear, a faint pinkness to his well-tended upper cheeks. It just goes to show that even unpleasant spymasters can be human. A smoothie, I thought: slim, good-looking, late forties, decent suit, with that spiky dark hair that Russians often have, combed straight back from the forehead, and a definite touch of T. S. Eliot:

A tough reasonableness beneath the slight lyric grace.

Characteristically, I can't remember who Eliot was talking about; Marvell, maybe? Gronov, anyway, was all the things I'm not.

'Been in London long?'

'Almost a year now.'

'And before that?'

'Questions, questions, Mr Swift. But isn't that what got you into trouble in Moscow recently?'

'I wasn't aware of being in trouble there.'

'I'm afraid I think you were rather insulting to our President.'

'Just doing my job. That's what journalists do in a free country.'

Watch it, I thought, you're getting into this a bit too deep. Looking away from Gronov's beautifully tended face I saw the

145

large shape of William Hooper a little way away. He was talking to a couple of young diplomats, but his eyes were on us.

'I'm not interested in debating society slogans. You disappoint me. I thought I could talk to you as one grown-up to another.'

'All right, talk to me like a grown-up.'

I took a swig from a third Becherovka which a waiter had put into my hand. Unwise, perhaps.

'I like you, Mr Swift, and funnily enough I heard that the President liked you before you were so rude to him.'

Something was coming, but I couldn't tell what. I let him talk.

'You know, right in the heart of your nice country, where everyone is so proud of their rights, all sorts of unpleasant things happen. People get maimed and killed for what they think, who they are, what they've done.'

I could feel the red mist rising.

'Listen, Mr Gronov, I've been threatened by experts. I don't need to listen to this.'

I probably said it a bit too loud; people moved away from us.

'No, no, no, you misunderstand me,' he said with consummate smoothness, 'no one's threatening you, Mr Swift. I'm just stating it as a fact. Nothing to do with your trip to Moscow. No, I was just going to suggest that you might like to find some way of making it up to us – to the president. Perhaps an interview with our prime minister? One in which no insults are traded?'

I have to say I was tempted. The prime minister was rumoured to be dissatisfied with the way he'd been sidelined. But if the quid pro quo was that I would have to agree to do a soft interview, I couldn't accept. Maybe the bosses in my organisation would like the idea, but I was trained in a different school.

'I could only agree if there were no preconditions.'

'The sole precondition would be that you treated the prime minister with politeness and your usual charm.'

What would Tim Baxter say to this? Not of course that he was much of an arbiter of politeness and charm, but I couldn't face coming back from Moscow with a soft, emollient interview, and hearing his reaction to it. Russia was doing things that needed to be talked about openly.

'Russia is doing things that need to be talked about openly,' I said out loud.

'You journalists are so sanctimonious. Do you think the British aren't doing things you'd be ashamed of – often at the request of their American masters? Yet I don't remember hearing you reporting about that.'

A list – short, admittedly – of things I'd reported on about British dirty practices internationally sprang to my mind, but it seemed a bit pathetic to try to persuade this smooth bastard that I behaved according to the rules he laid down.

'So where have we got to?'

'We haven't got anywhere, Mr Swift.'

He sounded like a villain in a Bond film.

'You sound like a villain in a Bond film,' I said.

Weirdly, he rather seemed to like that.

'Why don't we just have a drink together and talk about something more enjoyable. Look, we've driven everyone else away.'

It was true: at a diplomatic party, no one wants to get caught up in an argument. Not even me. For the next five minutes we talked about Chelsea's prospects of winning the Premiership, and then he said his goodbyes.

'I'm a great admirer of yours, Mr Swift,' he said. 'You always seem so wise and experienced. Let's hope that next time we meet we can agree about everything – and not just Chelsea.'

He really was smooth. Could I put my hand on my heart afterwards and say he'd threatened me? Of course not. Yet that's exactly what it felt like.

'So how was our Russian Talleyrand?' William Hooper asked before I left, looming over me.

'He offered me an interview with someone else.'

'But this time without asking about the subject of political assassination, I presume.'

'Something like that.'

'And you said no.'

'Correct.'

'Listen, Jon.' For a moment he dropped the air of superior badinage which he habitually carried round with him like an expensive aftershave. 'Just be really careful for a while. We don't want any more casualties in our profession, do we?'

And then the jokey superciliousness was back. 'After all, how could your admiring audience possibly do without you?'

Twenty-One

Then began a particularly nasty time in my life; a time I still look back on with pain and self-dislike.

It kicked off one evening quite soon after the episode at the Czech embassy, when I decided I'd been ignoring Vara too much. We'd arranged to go out for a drink, and I went to pick her up at her flat in Battersea. I was late getting there, so when I arrived she decided that if I headed round to the offy and picked up a couple of bottles, she would knock us up a bit of dinner.

'You can get an Uber home afterwards.'

By which I assumed she meant there was to be no hanky-panky.

Well, that suited me. Starting a thing with the recently bereaved girlfriend of my best friend didn't quite seem like something out of the guide to gentlemen's etiquette.

Anyway, Vara was labouring away on some eggs and ham when I got back, and trying to decide whether it was worth using up a whole tin of caviar, stored away in the back of the cupboard, just on me. Not that she put it that way, of course.

I put the bottles on the table: rather nice ones, which may just have swung the argument in favour of opening the caviar. And then there was a ring at the doorbell.

'Delivery,' said a voice over the intercom.

I assumed it was something extra she'd ordered; she assumed the same about me.

'Be a love and get it,' she said, with that faint accent that made the words sound even better.

A character in his twenties stood there with something the size of a shoebox and carefully gift-wrapped.

'Sign here,' he said gruffly, without looking at me.

'A present or something,' I said, going back to the kitchen and putting it on the table.

'Would you mind just opening it for me?'

Even before I'd got past the wrapping but hadn't yet opened the lid, I knew there was something wrong. The smell, I suppose. For some reason, though, I didn't stop when I ought to have. It's the story of my life.

Vara came over, asking what it was, and she got a good look.

It was a dead cat, and not recently dead either. It had a rather fetching red ribbon round its neck, with a label hanging from it. The writing was big and impossible not to read.

'Mr Jon Swift, RIP.'

I was still staring at it when I heard Vara throwing up in the lavatory next door.

So the Uber came rather earlier than I'd expected, and I had to take the shoebox with me, even though it stank to high heaven. I couldn't leave it with Vara, naturally, or even dump it in her rubbish bin; it was evidence – evidence of something as nasty as the smell of the dead cat. The Uber driver was as sensitive to the stench of decay as anyone else. I had to give him twenty quid before he'd agree to take me and my box.

I put it out in the tiny square of garden at the back of my flat, and dragged a handy tarpaulin over it to keep the smell in. I knew what I'd have to do: we'd have to film it, because it wasn't just disgusting, it was evidence. How it would fit into my eventual report I couldn't say; but if I didn't have any pictures of it, I knew I'd regret it.

So I called Os and told him I needed him to do a bit of work for me. He hummed and hawed for a moment, which irritated me. I'm not always at my most polite when I'm irritated.

'Look, sorry, boss. Something's happened.'

There was a strange note in his voice I don't think I'd ever heard before. It sounded like fear. I'd been with him in Sarajevo when they were firing phosphorous shells at us, which could have meant the nastiest deaths imaginable, and Os had just laughed. I'd been with him in Baghdad, driving down the most dangerous road in the world, and he'd sung some song about crossing the Drakensberg Mountains.

So now I went quiet.

'They've said I can't work with you any more. It was that little toad Lander. He said that if I took no notice of him they'd just sack me. You know how it is, boss – I've got the kids to look after, and things are a bit difficult.'

I could hear the embarrassment in his voice. Those disgusting, small-minded swine, I thought – that was the power they had over a man like this.

'My dear Os,' I said, trying to drown out his embarrassment with some artificial jollity. 'No problem at all. The family must come first. It's me they're trying to get at, anyway, and they're doing it through you.'

I told him about the dead cat. I could imagine his huge fists doubling up as though he wanted to hit someone.

'I've got the camera in the car – I can just come round and knock off some pictures of it now.'

'Suppose they find out?'

'Agh, man, they're not going to find out. Anyone can shoot a couple of statics like that. No fingerprints on the pics.'

I was relieved. I didn't want to have to explain everything to someone else – someone who had no idea what all this was about.

Os arrived half an hour later, and went out to inspect the box.

'You better watch yourself, boss. Next time it might not just be a cat.'

'What, it could be the old lady upstairs, you mean?'

He gave his great guffaw, which made me feel better. Then he fetched his camera, and filmed the box and its disgusting contents. The passage of time, though fairly brief, hadn't done the smell any good at all.

'I'll go and drop this off somewhere,' Os said when he'd finished, nodding towards the box.

'No, really,' I said weakly, but I knew it was his atonement for being forced to obey the orders of the management.

'I'll find a rubbish bin,' he said. 'Is there anyone you don't like round here?'

'I'd better take the label off its neck first.'

'Ha ha.'

I cut through the ribbon with a pair of scissors, trying to keep my head away while I did it. Even the scissors smelled bad afterwards. Os slipped the card out of his camera and handed it to me. Then, with the camera under his arm, which made it look small, he held the box out in front of him and went down the front steps.

'It was really good of you to come.'

'I'm just sorry.'

'Oh, fuck off, Os. We know each other better than that.'

It felt good, saying that – about the closest I'd ever got to talking to him with affection, though he knew perfectly well how I thought of him.

'*Totsiens.*'

I stood on the top step, watching him as he drove off. I probably stayed a moment longer than I normally would have done.

'Farewell,' I thought, and of course that brought out a bit of doggerel: Byron, if I'm not mistaken.

> *These lips are mute, these eyes are dry;*
> *But in my breast, and in my brain,*
> *Awake the pangs that pass not by,*
> *The thought that ne'er shall sleep again.*

Why the hell was I being so gloomy? I'd have understood it if I'd felt scared, but I didn't, really. The cat was a message to me, to let me know they were watching me and didn't like me. If they'd wanted to kill me they could have done it easily. No, I was mostly feeling bad that the bastards I worked for were determined to break me down by putting the frighteners on my close friends and allies. And I was really depressed at seeing a man as strong and gutsy as Os being forced to cave in to them.

Twenty-Two

We were back in the café at the Centre. There was the usual clatter of crockery being thrown around by people who didn't like the job and weren't paid enough to change their minds about it. The output from our channel blared out from a television screen on the wall, as bland and flavourless as the crap they were selling as food. A photo of The Owner hung on the wall, showing him twisting his face into a simper, with the elderly blonde he'd married grinning on his arm and trying to work out how much longer she'd have to put up with him. I stirred my tea.

'But I still don't understand why they should have done a thing like that. And how can you be sure it was intended for you?'

Alyssa was in her 'I'm just not convinced' mode. It didn't help that she was also a cat lover. When I first told her what had happened she was so upset I thought she was going to start blaming me for killing the bloody animal.

'Well, the fact that it had my name on a label round its neck may be something of a clue.'

At that, suddenly, she changed completely. The strong, gloomy lines of her face turned into something much more sympathetic.

'God, it must have been really horrible. You poor old thing.'

And she actually put her hand over mine and squeezed it. If I'd done that to you a few days ago, I thought, you'd have been off to

HR complaining about inappropriate conduct, and I'd have been on a sex offenders' register.

But thinking that made me feel really guilty. She'd made a human gesture of kindness and support, and I'd turned it into a skirmish in the sex war. I was just starting to say something friendly when she interrupted me sharply.

'Listen, I'm not allowed to work with you any more. I'm sorry, but they've given me written instructions.'

She pulled an official memo out of her bag and smoothed it out in front of me. I didn't need to look at it. Short of issuing me with a leper's bell, they couldn't have made the point clearer.

'It's not something I can fight.'

'No, no,' I said soothingly.

It was getting to be a habit.

'But I want you to know I'm really unhappy about it.'

That cheered me up a bit, anyway. I told her that I'd got some-one to film the dead cat – I didn't say who it was, but she must have guessed – and I handed her the camera card on which the shots had been recorded.

'I'm sure Kevin will be interested in this,' she said, but the tone she said it in showed me that she didn't expect him to be inter-ested in it all.

Kevin Braithwaite, who'd taken over the story of the murders from me, was pleasant enough, but calling him a plodder would make him sound a lot more inspired and energetic than he actu-ally was. And indeed, later in the day, Alyssa rang to tell me Kevin didn't think the cat pics worked. Saying something doesn't work is television speak for explaining that you're not interested in using it. I asked Alyssa to get the camera card back off Kevin and put it in the post to me. I'd have to look elsewhere if I wanted someone to report on what had happened to me.

That meant Tim Baxter, the investigations whiz. I went round to the offices of the *Guardian* – did I mention that he worked for the *Guardian*? Well, he did, anyway. We sat in a goldfish bowl a bit like ours at the Centre while I told him what had happened, and he jotted things down in an old-fashioned notebook. Then we had a coffee, and Tim wandered round the glassed-off cage muttering to himself and me, and finally he said, 'I'll have to put this up to Sarah.'

Sarah, it seemed, was the head of investigative reporting. She happened to be free, and came to the goldfish bowl to see me: fortyish with a strong face, she wore clothes that made her look as though something more important was on her mind when she'd bought them. She gave me an unexpectedly pleasant smile, and I liked her from the start. Why is it that other people's bosses invariably seem better than one's own?

She was a good listener, too, taking in the points I made and asking one or two questions that showed she was keeping up. Then Tim talked for a bit, giving his own view of what had happened to me. Given the way my own outfit had treated me, it was all rather flattering. Their instinct wasn't to talk my experiences down, it was to accept what I'd said and move on from there.

And yet, in the end, their view wasn't all that different from dear old plodding Kevin's: it was interesting, but the story wasn't quite there. The difference between their approach was that Tim and Sarah added the word 'yet'. Kevin had felt he should get on with a different subject altogether.

'All right,' I said, willing to accept their verdict as I hadn't been prepared to accept Kevin's. 'So what more do I need?'

There was a silence. Tim looked at Sarah.

'I'll tell you what, but I doubt if it'll be easy,' she said, brushing imaginary crumbs off her long grey skirt and looking up at me.

'You need proper, strong testimony. Someone serious, someone in the know. They've got to tell you what's really been going on. If you don't have that, you've just got a string of very suggestive, very disturbing occurrences.'

'I need a smoking gun, you mean.'

'That's an expression we tend not to use here,' she said, and gave me a comradely grin.

We talked for a bit longer about what the strong testimony might be, and where it might come from. And funnily enough I knew exactly where and what, though I didn't say so to them. That, I felt, was my business.

'When I've got it, I'll let you know.'

We shook hands. Sarah's handshake was even firmer than Tim's.

Twenty-Three

At this point I want to break off and explain something – something which, if I have to interrupt the flow of the story later, will just get in the way. So here it is, called up before its proper time, like a witness in a badly organised trial.

Back in 1982 I decided to get myself an Irish passport. The Falklands War had just started, and I wanted to report from Buenos Aires. It was a decision which was to bring me promotion, much greater visibility, a certain amount more money, and a broken collarbone. Shortly before I was to leave for Buenos Aires, the vicious yet pathetic Argentine junta announced that it would no longer accept British journalists.

Suddenly, the fact that I'd been born in Ireland took on a huge new significance. I flew to Dublin the same day and took a cab round to the magnificent old Custom House, where the passport application office still was in those days. One or two old relics were hanging round, reading the racing pages. On every table and desk there were application forms. I picked one up and read it through, including the fine print.

There in eight-point italics it said, in a tired kind of way that seemed to indicate that you'd be giving a lot of people a huge amount of unnecessary difficulty, that if you really insisted you could apply for a passport in the Irish version of your name. It's part of the wonderful looniness of my motherland that if your name is a perfectly easy and understandable one – Paddy Moloney, let's say, like the great performer on the pipes and the tin whistle – you can call yourself, for all official and unofficial purposes, by its Irish equivalent. In Paddy's case that would be 'Pádraig Ó Maoldhomhnaigh'; something which no one outside Ireland, or even inside it, will ever be able to spell properly. Especially down a bad phone line on a rainy night in the County Clare.

I had no idea what 'Jonathan Swift' might be in Irish; both forename and surname were rigorously Anglo.

'I'll bring this back in a bit,' I said to the chap behind the desk. He carried on doing the *Irish Press* crossword, and I had the impression that my comings and goings weren't of huge importance to him.

I hurried round to a lovely old second-hand bookseller, not far away: long since gone, of course. Three minutes of scrabbling through an ancient English-Irish/Irish-English dictionary on the shelves produced a couple of Irish equivalents for 'Jonathan': 'Ionatán' and 'Seánac', pronounced 'Shon-ac'. Ionatán was too obvious, so Seánac it would be.

Just about every English name has an Irish equivalent; well, perhaps not Giles Talbot-Ponsonby or Sir Ranulph Fiennes, but all the more usual ones. On a shelf around knee height was a copy of *Irish Names and Surnames* by the Reverend Patrick Woulfe, dated 1923. This learned Church of Ireland clergyman, who must have compiled the book while his Ireland fell to pieces around him, decided that the correct equivalent of Swift in Irish was 'Ó Fuada'. That sounded kosher enough to me.

Back at the passport office in Merrion Street I announced grandly, 'I'd like a passport in the Irish version of my name.' The effect was slightly spoiled by having to bend down to speak through a little hole in the glass.

'I'll get the form,' he said gloomily.

Under *Sloinne* I wrote Ó FUADA, and under *Aodh* I put SEÁNAC.

'You sure about this?' he asked, when I'd filled the whole thing in.

'It's been our name since the time of Strongbow,' I declaimed.

Which wasn't true in the slightest, by the way: the Swifts were middle-class grifters from Herefordshire who fled to Ireland after Cromwell confiscated their property in the 1640s, and immediately started battening on the natives of Counties Meath and Louth.

'OK, OK, no worries,' said the man behind the glass, anxious not to get into some ideologico-linguistic fight with a Gaeilge fanatic.

A week later my new Irish passport arrived in the post. I fished it out nervously at Heathrow when I checked in on my way to Buenos Aires, but everyone who inspected it seemed to find it perfectly unexceptionable.

And so for the purposes of infiltrating hostile territory I wasn't Jon Swift any more; my new name was Seánac Ó Fuada. I just had to remember to answer if someone called me by it.

Twenty-Four

I was at the Centre, sitting at my workstation – what we used to call a desk. It wasn't actually mine at all, of course. The bastards love to show you that there's nothing permanent about you or your job nowadays. Even the head of news had to hop round sometimes, looking for somewhere to sit. A sliver of ancient lettuce was stuck to the keyboard in front of me, and a couple of military aviation magazines lay in the top drawer, left by some previous user.

I thought I'd just check to see if there were any emails for me on an external address I sometimes used for contacting people I didn't want my employers to know about. Yes, sure, there were a couple of women I'd been talking to, but my ex-wives used it when they wanted something from me, and from time to time I contacted sensitive sources on it. It was private, and no one could easily trace it back to me.

That's what I thought, anyway.

Sometimes there would be a bit of junk mail on it. A year or so ago, famous African leaders or their representatives took to getting in touch with me, offering a remarkably large share of some financial windfall if I would only be kind enough to send them my bank details. Apparently loads of people did just that. Good luck trying to syphon anything much from my bank account: I've been trying for years.

Anyway, when I looked at the unread emails on this account, there was one which didn't look like spam. 'From Helen', it was entitled. Not 'Look at this' or 'Unrepeatable Offer!!' or any of the things you instinctively delete without opening. As it happens, there was a girl called Helen who had replied to me a couple of times on this email address, so I clicked on it.

A picture of such graphic disgustingness burst on to the full screen that I gasped, and made a couple of people turn round to look at me. Fortunately I managed to press 'delete' before anyone could get a proper view of it, but that merely spawned a dozen or so smaller pictures which all came up at once, followed by more and more and more. When I deleted them, others came. Worse, a loud cackle of laughter accompanied them, and during the moment or two before I could block the sound, new pictures exploded all over the screen.

I couldn't bring myself to look at them, but I can tell you that they all seemed to be of quite small children being tortured or hurt in some way. Real children. I may be no great fan of kids, but that doesn't mean I want to see them or even think of them being harmed. You've got to believe me about this, because it's central to everything that has happened to me since that first dreadful picture arrived. After months of wandering, I still haven't been able to cleanse my mind of those pictures, and I'm very much afraid I never will.

Of course I should have got on to our computer support team immediately and reported it. I should probably have rung the security people as well. Why didn't I? Partly because I was too deeply embarrassed, partly because in these horrible cheek-by-jowl workstations I didn't want the people around me knowing what had happened. Most of all, though, I assumed it was some kind of dreadful accident, and that I could just delete everything that had arrived. That, I accept, was the height of stupidity, and as a result I deserve to take some responsibility for the problems that were starting to arise. But I swear to you, my only fault lay in not telling the relevant authorities. And at the risk of protesting too much, let me say again that I don't have the faintest interest in any of this awful stuff, had never seen it before, and will never willingly look at it again.

The memory of it was still with me when I got home, when I went round to the nearby gastropub (what else in Chelsea?) and had a lonely bite and a glass or two of Laphroaig, and when I got back home and watched *Newsnight* in bed. Usually I'm well asleep before they've reached the third item, but not this time. So, with a certain degree of misgiving, I switched my laptop on again. A friend of mine from my university days had sent me an email, and I clicked on it.

'You unspeakable bastard,' it said. 'Whatever do you mean by sending me this disgusting, outrageous stuff? You belong in a mental institution.'

So the awful pictures were starting to do the rounds. Hastily, I sent an email out to everyone I could think of, saying that some really nasty material was being sent out in my name, but that it had nothing to do with me. Only then did I feel able to go to sleep.

Even before I was properly awake the following morning, I knew I had to tell Malone Road, the MI5 man, about it all. Directly I got up, I emailed him.

It was late morning by the time I heard back from him, and by that time I'd had three messages from people telling me what a swine I was; I'd forgotten to write to them the night before.

'Sorry to hear about your problem,' Malone Road said. 'All you can do is report it to your service provider and ask them to shut down your address. And it would probably be a good idea to report it to the police as well.'

Thanks a bundle.

I got on to the service provider, but they faffed around for ages, sending me from one person to another, so it was a long time before I could contact the cops. And before I got on to them, I thought I'd better tell the security department at the Centre. The woman there sounded really suspicious.

'But you have downloaded pornographic material in the past.'

It didn't sound like a question.

'Well, I . . .'

The fact is, dear reader, I live on my own nowadays and sometimes get lonely.

'Nothing remotely like that,' I finished up, stumbling.

For her, clearly, there was no difference between one type of porn and another.

'I'll have to report this,' she said, and I could imagine her mouth closing like a rat trap.

'Please do. That's why I rang you.'

That didn't seem to have any effect, either.

I stayed home that day, not feeling up to facing all the freaks at work who might have received this torrent of awfulness in my name. Shortly after five o'clock there was a ring at the door.

'Police,' said the voice on the security set-up. I buzzed them in.

A big, young, ebulliently pimpled detective stood on the doormat. Behind him, as far as I could see, were another plain-clothes man and a constable in uniform.

'Jonathan Henry Lysaght Swift, I have here a warrant enabling us to search your place of abode for any materials thought to be connected with a breach of the Obscene Publications Act 2003, as amended by Parliament.'

Actually, I've made that up. I don't have any memory of what he really said, because I was so appalled by the whole business. I let them in, and heard my voice quaveringly asking if they'd like a cup of tea. They shook their heads, as much as to say 'We don't accept cups of tea from perverts, you pervert.'

They took the place apart. They even ripped up the fitted carpet at a point where it felt as though there was something underneath it. And so it proved: the carpet layer had left his copy of the *Sun* there by mistake.

The pimpled one read me my rights, which didn't seem to be all that extensive, and announced that they were taking me in.

I tried to call a lawyer friend of mine, but by now he'd gone home. They didn't actually handcuff me, but they held my arms in a pretty obvious way, and of course a couple of neighbours happened to be on hand as I was shoved into the back of the police car. As we turned round in the street, the two old biddies were still shaking their heads. I started to understand now why people in old black-and-white movies used to shout out 'I'm innocent – innocent, do you hear?' But I didn't do it.

The thing is, that although to most British people being arrested is just about the worst thing that could conceivably happen to them, a television journalist who's spent most of his life nosing around in foreign countries in places where he's not wanted is thoroughly used to the whole process. I've been arrested on so many occasions over the years for the crime of filming the truth that it doesn't have any terrors for me, and certainly no shame.

The difference is, I would usually have a cameraman and a producer with me in the nick to help keep my spirits up, and an organisation back home which would put out angry or pained statements about the rights of journalists. Once, Amnesty

International even issued an appeal on my behalf, which (when at last I heard about it) made me feel I'd really arrived.

But here I was on my own. Big time.

Yet no one was unpleasant or threatening to me. The desk sergeant even made a joke about not expecting to see me out of my flak jacket. No one slammed the cell door shut on me or said they hoped I'd rot in hell; but they didn't ask me how I'd like my eggs done or what newspaper I'd like in the morning, either.

I'm glad about that, since it was all over the front of just about every paper in London, with headlines like TV JON: EVIL PICTURES SHOCK.

> Swift's colleagues were horrified. 'We never knew he went in for that kind of thing,' said Harry Wilkinson, 34, a producer. 'But he was slightly different from the rest of us, you know.' Another colleague, who did not want to be identified, said, 'We did wonder about him. He always seemed to be quoting poetry.'

How did the papers hear about it in the first place? God, you're slow. Pimple-face or one of his mates would have had the number of the *Sun* or the *Mail* on speed dial for just such a moment as this. It's a nice little earner, if an occasional one, and although every time there's an inquiry we're told the police will now make sure it won't happen any more, and editors solemnly swear they'll never source their news like this again, they're all at it after a couple of months, just like before. And don't think it's only the red tops that do it. In my experience the sole outfit that actually wouldn't be interested is the *Financial Times*, and I bet even they would ask which company board the arrested person sat on.

To be honest, being in a prison cell isn't too bad – no worse than, say, a hospital with all-male nurses. They've seen it all before: rape, murder, child abuse, TV licence fee evasion. In here, everyone's more or less equal, and more or less guilty. You sink into self-pitying silence, staring at the wall and trying not to notice the crudities scratched on it. Fortunately I'd brought something to read. I'd always promised myself to tackle *Tristram Shandy* if I had a couple of weeks with nothing to do, but the occasion had never previously arisen. I'd only got to chapter three before the sergeant on duty came and rapped on the door like a butler.

'Got a Maurice Browning to see you. Says he's your solicitor.'

So in a way he was. Maurice was the chap I'd tried to contact when the cops came for me. In fact he's more of a friend who happens to be a solicitor, though he did give some advice before I got divorced the second time. 'Just hand over half of everything you've got' about sums it up. He's very charming, though; apparently he's the poet Browning's great-great-grandson.

> *God's justice, tardy though it prove perchance,*
> *Rests never on the track until it reach*
> *Delinquincy.*

Actually, I can scarcely understand a word Browning wrote, and when Maurice gives me his legal opinions I feel the same.

'Well, Jon, this is a bit rough,' he said when I was brought in the room.

Still, he's a gent, and stood up to greet me. I could see the sergeant was impressed – policemen being the only truly class-conscious people left in Britain. Maurice's perfect lightweight grey suit helped.

I babbled on for a bit about being innocent. At first he struggled with that, but when I told him about the Russian side of things I thought I got through to him. People believe everything villainous they hear about the Russians nowadays; they perform the function the CIA used to, in the good old days of the Cold War, when liberal-minded people thought it was capable of any evil.

'Well, I know this sort of thing can happen,' he said. 'But how do you explain the stills they found at your flat?'

'Stills?' I felt my mouth go dry, just like they say in the thrillers.

'Apparently. Nasty ones.'

I felt I had to pull myself together and persuade at least one person of my innocence.

'Look, Maurice,' I said, summoning up all my powers of persuasion, 'you and I have known each other for thirty years. We've chased the same women, we've shared the same flat, we've even shared the same car. You must know that none of this can remotely be true, however bad it may look.'

I felt he was starting to turn.

'I can't explain any of it, except to say that it's got nothing whatever to do with me. It's all been planted. I promise you.'

He tried to avoid my eyes for a moment or two, but couldn't for long. At that moment I had him.

'Listen. Years ago, we got a bit pissed and I said you were the one person on earth that I felt I could tell about the very worst thing I'd done, and you would work out a way to help me. Remember that?'

He nodded.

'This is the moment – only I didn't do anything. Everyone else can believe what they like, but I'm absolutely depending on you to stand by me. Please.'

I was staking everything on this throw.

Whatever else Maurice was, he was an old-style, dyed-in-the-wool, sixteen-annas-to-the-rupee British gent. He didn't say anything, but he gripped my hand and held on to it a long time, like Donald Trump shaking hands with a fellow president. Tears came to my eyes, and I was touched to see that they came to his as well. At least I'd got one friend.

Not long afterwards, Maurice Browning had bailed me out and I was in a cab home. As I left, the sergeant called me 'Mr Swift', which seemed to show that my stock had risen a little.

Something nice was waiting for me beside my upstairs front door: a bunch of flowers with a message which read 'Don't worry – I know you're completely innocent. Much love, Barbara'.

And half an hour later things got even better. There was a ring at the door, and when I looked at the little grey-and-black television screen on the entry phone I saw Os's great head filling it.

'Can we come up, boss?' he asked.

I was so bloody grateful I didn't ask him who 'we' might be, but when I opened the door the first person on the doormat was Alyssa, my producer, with Os hovering and grinning in the background.

I was so gobsmacked I couldn't speak.

'Aren't you going to let us in?' she said, and I'll swear she was smiling.

'Of course it's obviously all a big set-up,' she said when we were sitting down.

To do them minimal credit, Spotface the cop and his colleagues hadn't messed the place up too much. According to the *Mail*, they'd found the 'explicit' pictures in the top drawer of my desk – a pretty dopey place for me to hide anything, but there you are.

'Do you honestly believe I'm not into child porn?'

Os nodded his great head vigorously, but loyalty is so built into him that he could have discovered me *in flagrante* and still denied it. It was Alyssa I was anxious about.

'Look, I'm not an expert in these things, but everyone knows you're always running after women, and you've obviously caught plenty in your life. And while I don't approve of that kind of behaviour very much' – she turned her long face away from me and pursed her lips – 'I can see it's not in any way consistent with – with – being a paederast.'

'A nonce,' Os volunteered, in case I might not understand these long words.

I went through much the same rigmarole with them that I had done with Maurice, promising them that none of it was in any way true.

'What are they saying about it at work?' I asked, not really wanting to know.

It turned out that no one was saying anything much in public. There'd certainly been no message of support from the bosses, but I didn't expect that.

'And the rest of them?'

I knew Os would be totally honest, so I directed the question at him.

'You know how people are,' he said.

He didn't need to say any more.

'Anyway,' Alyssa said, as though she was summing up the sense of the meeting, '*we're* a hundred per cent behind you, and anything we can do to help, we will.'

'I may hold you to that,' I replied, trying not to get emotional. 'And I thank you both from the bottom of my heart.'

I found the last couple of words quite difficult to get out.

There wasn't much to say after that, just a quick question about the adequacy or otherwise of the contents of the fridge, and a promise from Os to come back with some bread, milk and beer.

'I wouldn't go out there unless you have to, boss.'

As they stood up to leave, I glanced through the window. Twenty or so photographers and camera crews had collected on the pavement.

'I'll try not to speak to them,' said Alyssa, with a tough look on her face, 'but it may be unavoidable.'

I saw the results on television a couple of hours later.

'My name is Alyssa Roberts, and I've worked with Mr Swift as his close colleague. I can honestly tell you this is all absolute nonsense about him. What I can also say is that in the past he has done some reporting about people who are more than capable of setting some kind of trap for him.'

'Who are you talking about, Alice?'

'What sort of reporting?'

'Name some names!'

Then, characteristically, Os shouldered his way through the group. 'And when I find them, I'll knock their bloody heads off,' he roared.

You couldn't ask for better or more convincing backers, but of course the two of them had a hard time at the Centre as a result. Alyssa, as a black woman, was pretty much fire-proof, but she was certainly going to languish without work on the news desk for some time to come. By contrast poor old Os was easy meat: big, white, male, totally unreconstructed. They sent him home for a week as a punishment. 'Disciplinary lapses', they called it. Apparently you're required to get permission beforehand if you're going to speak to the media. Unless, of course, you want to praise the organisation, but they don't seem to find many people keen enough to do that.

As for the journalists outside my front door, words fail me. I'm one of those who defends the British press loudly and often, but I can't deny that when you come across packs of them in the wild, they're pretty loathsome.

After Os and Alyssa had left, it took the assembled hacks half an hour to tape down the bell to my flat with duct tape. That made it ring continuously. At first I put up with it, and tried to convince myself that it didn't really bother me. Within ten minutes, though, I was searching for the heavy-duty scissors and tracking down the wires; after which I got a bit of peace. Apart from ringing my number continuously until I took the phone off the hook and switched off my mobile – how had the bastards found the numbers? – there wasn't much else they could do except starve me out.

It took them thirty-six hours to tire of me, and even then they left a couple of representatives on the pavement outside. I don't suppose a single one of the group, even when it was at its strong-est, was actually a staff reporter for any of the papers there. They were freelances, hungry and distinctly lacking in the professional honour department. If they didn't get a story, they didn't eat. Guess what I thought about that.

Poor Mrs Atkinson from upstairs, large, shapeless and lonely, got heavied by them at some point, and said all the things neigh-bours always do say on these occasions: how I seemed like such a quiet person, and how she couldn't believe that disgusting things of that kind had gone on in a flat like mine. Quite a nice flat, she said, as though the rateable value of the place should have kept me on the straight and narrow. 'But you never really know with people, do you?'

Well, Mrs Atkinson, I thought as I read the varying accounts of what she'd said in the online versions of the newspapers the next morning, that's the last time I'll take your rubbish out when you're not feeling well. I noticed she hadn't mentioned that I'd done that.

Speaking of rubbish, the hacks had obviously been going through mine pretty thoroughly. A couple of firms I'd had mail from were quoted in the papers. I'd been a good payer, one of them said, while the other told the hacks that he couldn't possibly talk about the nature of my business with him over the phone. That made me sound unbelievably dodgy.

By the following day I was starting to get low on provisions. The loaf of packaged bread had tasted like putty even when the slices were soft; now they were harder, they resembled the plaster-board in a cheap hotel.

That evening I drank the whole of my last bottle of cham-pagne: really good stuff that someone had given me as a way of saying thanks for some favour I'd done at short notice. I'd hidden it away ages before in case of need. Now, I thought, my needs had never been greater. It was Pol Roger, Churchill's favourite, and it was beautiful on the palette of a deprived man. A purist might feel that baked beans and mackerel in brine weren't the perfect accompaniment, but I was getting really hungry. And anyway I beg to differ.

It was after my third glass of Pol Roger that I saw things as they really were. Whatever was I hanging around here for? The hacks would no doubt fade away when their attention span reached its limit – two days max – but the problem wouldn't. I rang Alyssa and Os for the third or fourth time, and thanked them again for supporting me, but I decided not to tell them anything about the plan which Pol Roger and I had worked out together. Alyssa, I said, should tell the bosses tomorrow morning that I'd decided to keep my head down for a week or so. The bosses, I knew, would be gratified. Their idea of a good problem was one that went away.

I looked at my watch: eight thirty. There'd be at least three trains to Paris still that evening, but I'd need to get out quite quickly. If I slipped out on to the landing, I could look down at the skeleton crew the hacks had left outside to guard the front door of the flats, from an angle they wouldn't be expecting.

Except they were. One of them happened to look up just as I peered out at them. He shouted, and two others came running over, and one of them was starting to make a phone call. Bugger.

Pol and I had another conference. Maybe I should call Ali, my taxi driver friend, and ask him to come and wait for me just round the corner, where the hacks wouldn't be able to see him.

Ali, I should explain, is a Hazara – an Afghan from a particular population group I've had a lot to do with over the years in places like Kabul and Bamiyan. They've got Mongolian features; supposedly Genghis Khan left a regiment of them behind to garrison Afghanistan when he left to rampage through the next country along, and they're treated like dirt back home. If you praise them and like them and trust them, as I did, they're yours for ever more.

I've no idea how Ali got to London: in modern Britain, it's not polite to ask. But there was a sizeable tribe of Hazaras here, anyway.

'Ali, old fruit,' I said, 'can I trouble you to be round the corner – (I specified where) – at three o'clock in the morning?'

'Ah, Mr Jon,' he said, and I could hear the grin down the line, 'I think you being naughty man.'

It was easier to let him think that. He hadn't read the papers, I was certain, and there'd been a time once before when I'd had to call him up urgently to help me out of someone's house when her husband came back unexpectedly. It was all starting to remind me of Richard Hannay dressing up in a milkman's white coat. I always found that a bit hard to believe in *The Thirty-Nine Steps*, but here I was proving that it was at least plausible.

I packed a few things into my ancient camel leather shoulder bag (made in Ali's home town, Kabul, as it happens), then lay down on the sofa for a few hours' kip. My alarm went off at two forty, and I had a taste in my mouth as though some creature of the night had died there – or is that a line I've copied from somewhere? God, I thought, I can't even have real-life escapades without acting out some book or other.

At a minute past three I rang Ali: he was, of course, ready and waiting with his engine turned off, just as I'd asked.

'Wait another two minutes, then switch on,' I told him, then slipped out through my front door and down the stairs. This was going to be the difficult bit.

The front door was big and heavy and slow-moving, a bit like me, and there were some steps down from it. If I was to be free to jump down the steps, I'd have to let the door slam behind me. I did. The hacks, three of them, were sitting dozing in a people carrier parked on the other side of the street, and it was only the slamming that woke them. I was off and past them while they were still struggling with their car door, and I reached the corner before they could clamber out and the photographer among them could work out which way round his camera was meant to point. There'd be no shots in tomorrow's red tops of my escaping backside.

'Superb, Ali,' I said as I sprawled across the back seat, breathing heavily. He drove off. The hacks were all too out of condition to get close enough for a look at Ali's number.

'Oh, Mr Jon,' he said when we reached Knightsbridge. 'Time to slow down, sir.'

I rather agreed with him.

We'd both forgotten that I hadn't told him where we were going.

'St Pancras station,' I said.

'But St Pancreas shut, sir.'

'Never mind, just take me there.'

Actually, between there and King's Cross, just across the road, I knew I'd find somewhere to slump down and wait for the first Paris train in a couple of hours or so. I might even get a cup of tea.

'And it's "St Pancras", Ali. The pancreas is a part of the body.'

I wasn't quite certain which part, actually.

'Sure, sir.'

When we arrived he said, 'Here St Pancreas, sir.'

I thrust lots of money into his hand.

I wasn't recognised or questioned. The lady I bought my ticket from at St Pancras didn't say, 'But you're not Seánac Ó Fuada, you're that one off TV,' maybe because she'd never watched British television news in her life. Nowadays you can watch anything from anywhere, no matter where you live, and presumably her viewing was rigorously Slovenian.

No problems, either, at the French passport desk. The sleepy character in his uniform glanced at the front of my passport, and may just have caught a glimpse of my photograph before he handed it back.

Don't worry – I won't be ripping off John Buchan or the various film versions of his book. No coppers chased after me as I climbed aboard the train, there were no beautiful girls to kiss in the corners of carriages, no jumping off the express train, no roaming over the moors with handcuffs on, and no blokes with dodgy eyes and missing fingers.

I got on the first train to Paris. I didn't work out what I was going to do when I got to the other end, because I was fast asleep even before the Eurostar pulled out of St Pancras. Not that it mattered, because I'd planned it all out beforehand. Well, I thought I had.

Twenty-Five

The news that I'd skipped out of my flat in Cheyne Place went the rounds quite quickly, and even the police found out about it later that morning. I assume they contacted the taxi services to see who had picked me up and where they'd taken me, but they didn't contact the Afghan Hazara network, and even if they had I don't suppose they'd have found Ali. Anyway, he was the kind who wouldn't have talked. I've seen Hazaras after they've gone several rounds with experts – Russians, and the old Afghan secret police, Khad – and rough treatment had as much effect on them as a sandstorm in Badghiz: they just waited till it was over.

So all there was, was the testimony of a couple of hardcore hacks, who'd seen me hightailing it down the road and heard a car's engine being gunned up out of sight. I could be anywhere. The papers went for the Old Bill, presenting them as clueless, which they were.

They came to interview Alyssa, though.

'Look, I haven't any idea where he is, and frankly I don't want to know. If he did the things you're accusing him of, I wouldn't want to have anything to do with him, ever again.'

Alyssa in full flow is a pretty alarming sight, and I imagine even the cops were convinced. She told me afterwards that everything she'd said was completely accurate; though it was all dependent on the one little word 'if'. Great girl.

They went round to Os's house in Wimbledon, too. Os had once been a military policeman himself, back in the bad old days in South Africa, so there was a certain degree of fellow-feeling there. The mistake the local flatfeet made was not to take advantage of this. They didn't like him because he had a foreign accent, and they didn't like him because he was big enough to throw them both out into the back garden. And most of all they didn't like him because our wonderful employers had told them that Os and I were good friends.

If they'd approached him right they might have wheedled something out of him. He knew, for instance, about my old flat in Paris, so they could at least have had a general direction to head in. But Os, the ox, goes very quiet if he's treated aggressively, and becomes very tense and dangerous. That's when you see how accurate his nickname is.

So no one had any idea where I'd gone. They probably wouldn't have cared too much, if the fish wrappers hadn't got on to them all the time. The vanishing of a moderately well-known television face, and the accusations against him, stirred the hacks to new heights of self-righteousness and pseudo-anger. 'Pervert TV Jon', they called me, plus 'child abuser', 'paedophile' and a variety of other epithets – though they mostly put them in inverted commas, just in case. But the longer I was away, the more careless they got, and the more they assumed I must be guilty. It wasn't long before the inverted commas dropped off the story. That meant I'd be able to get them good and proper, once I'd cleared my name.

Not that I knew about any of this, of course – I had no laptop and no mobile phone to check the newspapers' websites – but dear Alyssa went through the papers every day on my behalf, looking out for what they were saying about me and clipping the articles out. I don't want to give you the impression I was headline news after a couple of days, but every now and then the great editorial brains wondered what had happened to me, and saw a further opportunity to attack the police, the Home Office, and anyone else they didn't like.

As Alyssa realised, I was stacking up a fortune in libellous material. All that was needed was for me to come back and brief Carter-Ruck or some other piranha-like libel lawyers. But for that to happen, I'd need to break cover and come back to London. And I wouldn't be able to do that until I'd cleared the whole thing up.

Twenty-Six

So then I began the life I introduced you to at the start of this
account. I slept in the basement of my old apartment block for a
couple of weeks – I still had the passcode – and spent my days
sitting in cafés and perfecting the art of stealing the money left
behind for waiters. It may not sound much to you, but I was actually getting myself into a rather comforting routine: up and out
by six thirty, a cup of coffee and a croissant in some café, a wander
round the shops until lunchtime, then stealing a bit of cash. After
another few hours of drifting around I'd have dinner and then
steal a bit more.

Then one evening (I soon lost count of the days and nights, but
I assume it was about a fortnight after I started living in the cellar)
I got back to my street at around twelve. I was tired, and had
drunk more than usual. Even so, my senses seemed quite taut.

A car passed, and then another, and both slowed down as they
passed the front door. Each time the driver ducked his head to
look at the building.

Something was up. I turned swiftly into a side street and sat in
the doorway of a shoe shop, like a beggar. That way I could see
the front door of my building without being obvious.

Half an hour passed, then forty minutes: still no movement,
but I felt certain now that something was going on. And at one

o'clock on the dot a couple of plainclothes men arrived in an unmarked car, which dropped them at the door. One of them tapped on it gently and they were let in. Two minutes afterwards another pair came out. Policemen are civil servants, you see, and they work set hours. I was watching the night shift changing.

No point in staying any longer. I was tired and aching, and found to my surprise that my knees were shaking as I stood up. Being hunted didn't suit me, I suppose. It was odd how abandoned I felt; I longed for the security of my shake-down in the cellar.

I took a train to Belgium, changing several times, and ended up in Brussels. There my life became much worse. I had to sleep in the streets, on flattened cardboard boxes I took from outside supermarkets. One night, as I lay there sleeping, a heavy boot crashed into my ribs; the same ribs, as it happened, that the Russian cop had concentrated on.

A big character was leaning over me, shining a torch in my face. I put my arm up to shield my eyes from the light, and he booted me heavily again.

'What the fuck?' I shouted.

Bad choice of words. The figure leaning over me was, I came to realise, a cop. Belgian cops are rarely chosen from the top drawer, and this one spoke no English. But of course he recognised the word 'fuck'. Everyone does the world over. It drove him into a fury, and he kicked me again and again, mostly in the same place. It started to hurt right away, which is usually a sign that some serious damage is being done.

I groaned and turned over, trying to shield my stomach and especially my balls from that monstrous boot. Carefully, thoughtfully, the cop moved round to get me from a different angle. Once, twice, three times the boot smashed into my face. When I turned it down to the pavement he kicked the top of my head. There were some remarkable colours. I had a sense that terrible damage was being done to me.

Finally, it stopped. I lay there, breathing hard, until he pulled me up and propped me against the wall. There was quite a bit of blood coming down my forehead, but I could see his face. He was breathing hard and grinning.

With a practised twist of his arm he turned me round and held my hands together while he dug around in a pouch for a pair of metal handcuffs. I felt the cold of them on my wrists; it seemed sharper than the dull pains that were competing for attention in my head and chest and stomach and lower back. The small crowd which had been watching the show in silence began to move off. No one said anything still.

The walk to the police station was the worst bit. The bastard had kicked me in the knees, and they simply wouldn't work as fast as his pace demanded. Once I almost fell over, but he started kicking me again and I decided that anything was better than that. He never spoke, by the way: he just indicated everything he wanted me to do by hitting me.

I was pretty much out of it by the time we reached the station, but there was a kind of roar when we got inside and his mates saw what had happened to me. A sergeant shouted something at me, which I imagine meant 'don't bleed on my floor'. There didn't seem to be an awful lot I could do about that, but he thumped me for doing it anyway. By this time there were so many aches and pains in my body that one more didn't make much difference.

Still, my feeling of being badly damaged returned.

'Doctor,' I said experimentally, through lips that seemed absurdly big.

The cops looked at each other and laughed.

The one who had beaten me up pushed and pulled me into a small windowless room with a chair and a bucket in it, and some posters on the walls telling me in three different languages what I couldn't do. Then he slammed the door and left me to it.

I started a physical examination of myself, but quickly gave it up: it was too depressing. I mean, I'd never exactly thought I was a looker, but the amount of swelling and abrasion my probing fingers discovered around my face gave me the feeling I was going to look like Lon Chaney in *The Hunchback of Notre Dame* for the rest of my life.

And I ached. I ached more than I'd ever done. After a while I noticed that the aches moved in concert with one another, throbbing up to a kind of small-scale climax then moving down a few notches in the scale before starting to climb once again. It was like some kind of kid's game, except that it hurt. It was so awful that I found myself laughing; and that, I think, was when the fight-back began.

I crawled over to the door – not literally, but bowed over and moving inches at a time – and beat on it. Silence for a bit, then someone came and wrenched at the handle. He didn't seem to be full of the milk of human kindness.

'Look,' I said, 'I'm an Irish citizen and I need a doctor.'

The trouble was, I said it in French, and as a Fleming he didn't seem to hold with that. He looked at me as though I was a dog turd on the carpet and went out, slamming the door shut.

Twenty-Seven

Nothing happened for quite a long time afterwards. I sat slumped there, feeling the throbbing pain mounting in my head and body, then falling back in order to gather again. And then, if you can imagine such a thing, I started singing. Quietly at first, then louder and louder.

> *The pulse of an Irishman ever beats quicker*
> *When war is the story or love is the theme,*
> *And place him where bullets fly thicker and thicker . . .*

And that was the point when a man with some sort of silver braid came into the room.

'Shh,' he said.

You'll find him all cowardice scorning, I went on. And for good measure, *And though a ball should maim poor Darby, Light at the heart he carries on . . .*

It felt obscurely good. This man, I could see, was not as far down the scale of brutality as my original tormentor. He looked a bit concerned, and by the time I got to *Fortune is cruel, but Nora my jewel* he came over to me with his hands outstretched and said in a heavy accent:

'*Le médecin va arriver.*'

So you bastards do speak French after all, I thought. Time for a bit more singing, to speed up the process.

And how we will jig it and tug at the spigot, On Patrick's Day in the morning.

It worked. No need to give them both barrels. I'd scarcely got to the bit about *Blest be the isle in the wide western waters* when a fussy little man came in carrying an old-fashioned shiny leather bag and looking like Hercule Poirot without the moustache. He clicked his teeth sympathetically, and started speaking Poirot-type French.

'How badly have they hurt me?' I asked.

Then I felt this was a bit feeble.

'I am an Irish citizen and I demand to see my ambassador,' I added pompously.

In other places where I've tried this line, notably Rangoon, Kabul, and Chongqing, it has been the prelude to more beating. Poor old Hercule was worried, though. I expect he'd seen the results of plenty of punishment beatings before now, but the thought that there might be consequences got to him. He had the look of a man who was worried about quite a few things.

I can't quite remember the order things happened in, and at one point I must have gone into some kind of stupor or doze, because Hercule started shaking me nervously by the shoulder and making incomprehensible sounds. After a bit I realised they were an attempt to pronounce my Irish name.

'That's me,' I said, smiling though my lips were split and starting to swell up like small pinkish sausages. And, in case he needed help, '*C'est moi.*'

He cleaned my face up. Soon there were a lot of paper towels with blood on them piled up on the deal table. Then he checked me over. His fingers hurt, but it didn't seem to me that anything was actually broken.

After that, some offensive bastard came in and read something to me loudly in Dutch, which I couldn't understand. There was a bit of to and fro about whether I would sign it, but I pointed to my right hand, which his mate Heinrich Himmler had stamped on when he gave me the treatment, and basically refused.

'I want to make a phone call,' I said in French. Now it didn't seem likely they'd beat me up any more, I felt I should needle them as much as possible.

The trouble was, I couldn't remember anyone's number. And the only numbers I did remember, like the Centre and Patrick Macready and the weather forecast, all seemed a bit irrelevant. But, thinking it over, I realised I could just about reconstruct Os's number. God knows how – maybe it was because he'd managed to book himself a memorable one. It ended 2200, and I worked out the earlier part from all the times over the years I'd called him.

Speaking was getting harder as my injuries settled in, but I finally got them to understand what I wanted. It would have been easier to write it down, but I'd made that impossible. Someone handed me a mobile, and I dialled.

'Os, is that you?'

'Can't hear you. Who is it?'

I told him. It took a bit of time. Then I asked if he could come and get me out. Dear old Os: not a pause, not a 'Well, I've got an awful lot on'. Not a hint of reluctance, especially when I told him they'd beaten me up.

He needed more than a day to get there, though. Nothing much happened in that time: Poirot turned up looking even more nervous, and someone in silver braid looked in on me with a couple of minions and said nothing to me but muttered something to them. Were they worried about beating up a rate payer in the public streets? Or a foreigner? I couldn't work it out.

I was in a cell by this stage, and just lay dozing on my back on the smelly bed, shifting every now and then to try to get comfortable. I did a lot of staring at the wall, too – just white-painted bricks, but they seemed to have all sorts of features on their surface: maps, faces, animals, even a praying mantis. Did they mean anything, I wondered sleepily, before deciding they didn't. Nothing meant much, except the pain. The worst of the throbbing had faded, but I ached intolerably.

Three times a day they gave me something which masqueraded as food but tasted like wallpaper paste with some unrecognisable meat in it, plus a mug of coffee. Since they were Belgians, the coffee was rather good: strong and black, with a fierce kick, and a damn sight better than most of the coffee you get at those dreadful imitation Italian cafés in Britain.

Poor old Poirot – I felt sorry for him now because he seemed so anxious – came back and slipped me some kind of alcohol. I could tell he was breaking the rules, but he seemed to want to please me. I was definitely mending, he said, though my lips were more swollen than ever.

It was an hour or so after he'd left that I heard the booming sound of Os's voice, speaking Afrikaans. Flemish Dutch and Afrikaans are pretty close to each other, and don't require an interpreter; a bit like the French of Canada and the French of France. I could hear him raging at the cops outside. I've no idea what the Afrikaans for 'disgusting' is, but my guess is he used it. The door of my cell burst open, and there he was, as big and full of life and reassurance as ever.

'Hello boss,' he said.

'Os, you bastard,' I said feebly.

I could see he was upset.

'Jeez, you look bad, boss. They did you over pretty good.'

I didn't answer. To be honest, that side of things was completely finished now, and I was concentrating on getting better and getting out.

'They're very worried. They think they'll be in trouble for beating up a foreigner.'

'You didn't tell them who I was?'

'Oh come on, *baasjie*, I'm not that stupid.'

What happened after that is a bit unclear to me. They obviously let me out, and good old Os helped me down the steps and into a taxi. It hurt quite a lot, but I seem to have compensated for it by dozing most the time. We were on a train to London before I came properly awake.

'I'm worried they'll stop me at St Pancras.'

'You think they'll recognise you, eh?'

I felt my face, and guessed how swollen it must be. I might attract attention for my injuries, but no one would know it was me.

'But where am I going to go?'

I sounded like a kid.

'Don't worry – I've fixed all that.'

He felt a bit abashed, and it took me some moments to get it out of him. Os had married a rather tough English-speaking wife from Durban, a big rangey girl built along the same sort of lines as him, only a size or two smaller. They had a couple of boisterous kids. I obviously couldn't stay with them.

'I rang that Russian girl,' he said eventually, not looking me in the eyes.

'What, Vara?'

'She'll take care of you.'

So it was all fixed up, like a blind date. When we reached St Pancras there was no problem. We just got in a cab and went to Battersea.

Twenty-Eight

'Wow, they really did give you a rough time,' Vara said when she opened the door. Cool, factual, but welcoming.

For the first time I got a proper look at my face in her sitting-room mirror. I could have worked as a body double for the Elephant Man. So much swelling and laceration – I gasped. And now I realised how disgusting I was. After all, I'd been living rough on the streets for some time now.

'Do you want to sleep first, or clean up?'

'Clean up, I suppose.'

Os, strangely shy, said his farewells. I wasn't up to the job of thanking him for all he'd done, but I think he realised what I was feeling.

The sound of the bath running brought back to me how uncivilised my recent life had been.

'All ready,' said Vara. Then, casually, 'Do you need help?'

I probably did, but taking my stinking, blood-stained clothes off in front of this crisp, attractive young woman wasn't something I felt comfortable with.

'No, thanks.'

'OK. Call if you need anything. I'll bring you some tea in the bath.'

'You don't have whiskey?'

She didn't, and vodka with tea is a taste I don't feel like acquiring.

It took me an awfully long time to get my clothes off. I can't describe how disgusting they were, especially at the underwear level. I rolled them all into as tight a ball as I could, and jammed them into a corner where I hoped Vara wouldn't see them before I'd dealt with them. They weren't quite the thing a deputy head girl of St Paul's Girls' School should be expected to look at.

She'd done the bath to perfection: hot, but easy to slip straight into. God, it felt wonderful. The water seeped into every wound, wrapped around every painful bruise. I lay there for ages, my eyes closed, my senses dulled, and did a fair bit of groaning.

After a while there was a knock at the door, and there was Vara with a mug of tea. I didn't have time to cover my private parts, but I noticed her eyes didn't stray in that direction: which was a bit of a relief, since the cop had landed several pretty heavy kicks there and there was a general swelling and purple colouration which I didn't really want to be seen by anyone except me, or possibly a specialist in traumatised dicks. The normal everyday thing is bad enough.

'Shall I stay?' she asked, and when I nodded she sat down on the closed lid of the lavatory.

I put a large yellow sponge over the area in question, which made me feel a bit better. She behaved with exemplary politeness, and that was even more of an improvement.

'So what happened?'

I told her. In fact, I told her all about it – the Irish passport, my Ó Fuada identity, stealing money from cafés in Paris, getting thumped up by the cop in Brussels. She laughed at my jokes, which I liked, and sympathised with my troubles, which I liked even more.

She loved me for the dangers I had pass'd, And I loved her that she did pity them.

Actually there was no sign she did love me, or vice versa. But she was a good listener, and her eyes sparkled attractively when I told her about the various times I'd been pursued and had escaped. For once in my life I didn't bother to pretend I'd behaved better or with more intelligence that I actually had; that too was part of the effect she had on me.

She laughed and laughed as she sat on her lavatory seat, but she displayed genuine sympathy when I described how the cop had put the boot in. I didn't have to exaggerate that part: the extent of his target practice was displayed in the bath in front of her.

Merely lying there, dressed only in a sponge, increased the sense of intimacy. By the end, when I either had to climb out or put in more hot water, we had reached the point that old, successfully married couples spend years achieving. This isn't, I have to say, a sensation I have ever actively pursued, but now I found it warming and healing. When I chose the hot water option, she stood up and said she'd leave me now, but that I could stay in the bath as long as I wanted, and the bed was waiting next door.

And what I liked about that, after a lifetime of trying to get women to say words of this kind, was that it had the charming asexuality of true closeness. I wasn't in a state to take action anyway: every single bit of me ached and throbbed, especially around what you might call the *point d'appui*. For perhaps the first time in my entire life, I felt genuinely glad that nothing sexual was in any way expected of me.

Twenty-Nine

That was the start of quite possibly the most enjoyable ten days of my entire life. I slept and read and bathed and ate and talked and listened, then repeated the process. Vara had to go to work every morning, but she made me sandwiches or provided me with drinks and left the radio close to hand, and in the evening she'd come back to sit on the bed and talk and talk. The sense of peace, of safety, of sheer satisfaction was overwhelming; and after a few days I started crawling out of bed on my own with infinite care and watching television in her sitting room. Soon there was nothing about racing, antiques, old 1950s westerns and buying houses in Spain and Portugal which I didn't know. I even started reading *Portrait of a Lady* for the first time, and by the time I got a quarter of the way through could walk without any real discomfort.

But I was still a prisoner. We ventured out a couple of times at night-time and wandered along the river, but for me it was fraught with tension. Every time someone looked at my face for more than half a second I was certain I'd been spotted. Vara was much more sanguine about it.

'No one can tell it's you, Jon. You really mustn't worry. To be honest, your face is still pretty messed up. If that man was looking at you, it's because he was wondering how you'd got that way.'

'He probably thought I was the victim of domestic violence.'

'Yes, well, you will be if you don't calm down a bit. It's good for you to walk round, and no one's going to recognise you.'

She was right, of course, but that didn't make it easier or more believable.

There was absolutely nothing between us. I didn't try to hold her hand or indeed make any physical contact. At night, in her small flat, she closed my door and her own. She quite often smoothed my hair, and a couple of times she squeezed my shoulder, but it was in the most amicable of ways.

I didn't want it to be anything else – honest. There were photos of Patrick everywhere, and it would have felt pretty disloyal to him if I'd started to make moves on his girlfriend. Ungrateful to her, too: it would have been introducing an embarrassing note into an otherwise pleasant and healing process. Suppose she was horrified and reared away from me – and believe me, that has happened plenty of times in my life – whatever would we have done next?

No: the old Adam was locked away in his cupboard for the duration, and I was all the better as a result. Sex is, after all, a tremendous effort, and I simply wasn't sufficiently worked up for it. And there was all the ethical stuff as well.

Thirty

One evening, the tenth day after my arrival, the doorbell rang. The sound made my hands tremble, and I had to put my glass of wine down. During the few seconds it took for Vara to go over to the security panel and get a look at whoever was out there on the front step, half a dozen possibilities went through my mind, none of them particularly good. But my instincts were wrong.

'Oh, hello, Os. Yes, he's here. Just push the door and come up.'

When he came in I gave him a cautious bear hug, though we never normally showed any sign of affection. He smelled of edit suites and cars and cameras, or at least I assume that was it. It was certainly something professional.

'Hmm – bit of improvement there, boss,' he boomed, looking at my battered face. And indeed that morning I'd noticed that the swelling had finally gone down and the cuts had healed over, though the bruises were turning a startling yellow-green, the colour of young leaves in the springtime. Even if there hadn't been the possibility of being recognised and arrested, I couldn't conceivably have gone out into the street by daylight. Dogs would have barked at me.

Vara and Os had obviously agreed on this meeting a day or so earlier, only she hadn't told me. Maybe she didn't want me to get too excited. Os downed a couple of glasses of her red, and we talked in a desultory kind of way about the situation. I could tell there was something else coming, and tried to work out who would break it to me.

'The thing is, boss, we've got to do something. You can't stay here forever, and the police haven't forgotten about all that stuff.' He meant the child porn, of course.

I waited: there'd be more.

'So we talked about it.'

'We?'

'Vara here and me. And Alyssa.'

That worried me, and my hand jerked. Fortunately my glass was empty.

'Look, you can't just go round telling everybody what's happened and where I am.'

I could hear that my voice was sounding unnaturally shrill.

Vara stayed calm, as ever.

'He hasn't been telling anyone else, just this Alyssa person. He says he can trust her.'

'Yes, well, he's right,' I said. I felt a bit better, to be honest, and my instinct was that Alyssa was indeed trustworthy. 'So what are we going to do?'

'She'll be here in a few minutes.'

I felt manipulated. These people between them had decided everything about my life and future, and I was only finding out about it now.

'Anything else to tell me? Are we giving a press conference? Or some kind of party?'

'Hey, come on, boss. You've had it pretty rough, and we've had to do our best while you got better.'

In the usual way Os was such a fiery character, so quick to take offence, that this easy, natural tone of his shut me up completely.

And after all, these two people had run considerable risks in helping me – which they had done generously and well.

'Sorry,' I muttered, with my head down. It hadn't been one of my finer performances.

There was a short silence, and then Vara laughed, a pleasant, light, relaxed kind of sound. Os beamed, and when he does that no one around him can possibly help smiling too; it's like yawning.

'You two bastards,' I said, and they laughed again.

I was telling them about Hercule Poirot, the prison doctor, and the look on his face after I warned him I'd have him arrested as an accessory after the fact, when the doorbell rang again. This time I wasn't nervous.

Or so I thought. But when Alyssa came through the front door and I listened to the polite phrases, I was suddenly scared. Suppose she thought, like the deputy head of security had, that there must be something in this porn business after all?

'Hello Jon,' she said as she came into the room, and I could see it was all right, after all.

We shook hands. In the past, I'd have kissed a female producer I'd worked and travelled with, but things have changed a bit and you've got to be really careful nowadays. Our wonderful organisation has adopted some American ruling about having no more than six seconds' eye contact. Six seconds! In the past, I'd scarcely have got going in that time. 'Unwanted sexual advances', 'Inappropriate kissing', 'He made me feel uncomfortable': I really didn't need that kind of thing, especially with my new record as a child pornographer. But Alyssa didn't at all look as though that was what she thought. Instead, her long, handsome face was registering concern at the way I looked, and (I thought) relief that I was still alive.

'Thanks for looking after him,' she said to Vara, though I could see there was a certain something between them: not quite tension, perhaps, but unquestionably a lack of any kind of clicking.

Vara nodded coolly and went to fetch another bottle of her rather good Burgundy, together with a plate of cold meat and cheese, and we settled down around the place where the fire would have been, if they had fires in modern flats in Battersea. Eating still wasn't quite my thing, especially since I'd shed a tooth in the last few days, but there was nothing wrong with my drinking reflexes. Never has been.

'All right,' I said while a certain amount of chewing was going on around me and a silence had fallen, 'so what do you think I ought to do?'

Of the three others there, there was only one I was addressing myself to. Alyssa was the decision maker, no doubt about it; but because I had so many reasons to feel grateful to Vara and Os, I included them in the general approach.

'First of all,' I went on, 'I can't stay here. It's a flat, and the neighbours always get some idea what's going on. Secondly, I've got to take this thing forward in some way. I want my life back, I want my job back, and I want to be able to walk down the street without wondering if someone's going to do me in.'

Too much 'I'. Time to sit back and let the others talk.

Alyssa, inevitably, spoke first. And of course all I could do, instead of listening carefully, was to try to decide whether I fancied her or not. I hadn't decided by the time she came to an end, so I had to rerun her words in my mind like spooling back on a video.

'You – we – have got to clear your name. The only way to do that is to find some new material which will demonstrate that you're the victim of a much wider plot,' was what I decided she must have said.

'That means we'll have to get something together in Russia,' Vara put in.

I noticed the 'we', which made us a neat little foursome. For some reason, which I couldn't explain to myself, this made me feel uncomfortable. Too many people in the know, I suppose, without sufficient reason to bond us all together. Vara was, you could say, motivated by the death of her fiancé; Os was in because of personal loyalty; Alyssa, perhaps, because her association with me had damaged her own career and she had something to prove. All these reasons were good and right, but it didn't feel to me that they were strong enough to keep us all together if the going got tough.

Vara, we agreed, would make some careful soundings in Moscow on my behalf. If we could get Boris Kulikov's contact, the FSB general, to agree to speak on camera, then we'd work out how we were going to do it. In the meantime I'd stay on for a few more days in Vara's flat, in order to let the bruising fade even more and grow my beard to something that looked intentional rather than just the absence of water and a razor. Vara agreed to dye it for me, too, to make me harder to recognise.

After that I'd head out, and I didn't want anyone to know where I was going. That was the most painful bit, especially for Os. But I did promise to keep in occasional contact with all three of them. It seemed to calm them down a bit.

Why did I want to go, you may ask? If I were them, I'd have been only too delighted to shut down an awkward relationship which carried so much trouble with it. But that's why I'm an arsehole and they're all nice decent people in their different ways. I said my goodbyes to Alyssa and Os, and they headed off. The front door closed. Vara came back into the sitting room.

'Please don't start it all up again,' I said wearily.

'I've got no intention of doing that. I just wanted you know that none of us liked being told you didn't trust us enough to tell us where you'd be, in case we needed to help you.'

'Yes, well, it's for the better, believe me.'

'I don't believe you, you so and so,' she said, but there was a new warmth in her weird dark blue eyes and around her androgynous mouth.

Going to bed alone that night was distinctly harder, but I managed it eventually. Good thing I was moving out soon.

I knew exactly where I was going: it was the only place I'd ever lived for a long stretch of time, apart from London. A smallish city, with a big population that moved in and out like the tide in a rock pool, so that odd-looking strangers were a constant and wouldn't be noticed.

I got down to the detailed planning: what clothes to wear (an inconspicuous coat, tweeds to keep me warm and look reasonably good, thick dark-coloured shirts which wouldn't show the dirt, a few pairs of socks and underwear), enough cash to last me for bus fares and occasional meals, a backpack loaded with a whole bunch of books, a pen and notebook for writing, an MP3 player, a head-torch, an electric razor to keep my beard tidy, and my Afghan shoulder bag to put everything in. I would pass as one of those shy, slightly nutty academics you see wandering around a university city, whose pet subject could be anything from the sewer system of Abbasid Baghdad to the sex life of the vole.

Over the next few days Vara made some shrewd guesses about where I might be going, but she never got it right. Fine by me. She went out and bought all the things I needed from Peter Jones – where else for a girl like her? – and supplied me with a thousand pounds in tenners, plus one of those things that look like a truss to keep them in, strapped round my body under my shirt.

It got dark around five o'clock, so I started my detailed packing at three.

'Just give me a number which I can ring to see if you're all right.'

'Don't call us, we'll call you,' I said in my theatrical manager's voice.

'When will you get there?'

'That's a question I ask myself,' I answered.

'You're a real swine, you know – I give you everything, and you give me absolutely zilch.'

'You haven't given me everything,' I said, and dragged her close to me.

I'd never have done that before, but I felt it was safe now. Surprisingly, she let herself be clinched. And kissed on the lips. The closed lips.

'Yes, well, time to go,' I said.

'Stay and have a drink. Go on.'

She was delightful in this mood.

I jammed my beanie on my head and tweaked her beautifully formed ear.

'I'll ring you. Quite soon.'

Somehow, though, I knew it wouldn't be soon at all.

Thirty-One

I'm not actually going to tell you precisely whose mercy I threw myself on, because it'd just be a lot of unnecessary extra detail, and the person I stayed with would probably prefer I didn't give any hint about it. It was about an hour outside London, that's all, and I went there by road.

A week later I got off a coach at Victoria bus station at around three thirty: too late to go to a hotel for a few hours. The best I could do was stretch out on a bench at the coach station and wait for morning. I couldn't sleep – too much artificial light, too much noise – so by five thirty I was really desperate to go somewhere.

I knew that Vara would take me back, but I guessed that her flat might be watched and her phone bugged. Anyone who was familiar with my old pattern of life would be also checking Os's phone and house. That left Alyssa; would she be under some kind of surveillance too?

Oh, come off it, I'm sure you're saying to yourself, surely someone with a lifetime of friends, lovers, acquaintances, and ex-wives would have plenty of people to go to. You ought to be absolutely right, but somehow there wasn't anyone I felt I could dump myself on at this time of the morning. And for all my drinking buddies and all my alimony payments, I didn't have that many real friends. I used to blame my peripatetic existence for it, but actually I think it was because of my character: I'm one of those unfortunates who needs people yet insists on pushing them away.

I found a workman's caff that stayed open all night, and sat hunched over a bacon butty and a cup of something described as coffee. And then it occurred to me: I must call Alyssa when she got to the Centre. With all that hot-desking and hot-phoning, no one would be able to keep track of a short phone call. She'd be in by nine, I assumed; just over three more hours to wait.

I moved from caff to caff, spending a couple of quid in each. Fortunately I still had plenty of cash left in my flesh-coloured truss, and I'd exfiltrated some tens and twenties from it and put them in my pocket for just such a wait as this; so I hadn't been entirely without some forethought, after all.

God knows how the time passed, but it did. At Victoria railway station I found a line of phone boxes, chinked my pile of carefully prepared coins, and silently practised my Glaswegian accent. It took me a few minutes to discover a box which worked and which hadn't been used copiously as a urinal during the night.

'Cuid a speak tae Muss Roberts, please? Muss Alussa Roberts?'

The telephonist was outsourced and sounded as if she worked in Manila, so the accent was wasted on her; she had a stronger one herself. Still, the number rang.

'Yes?' An aggressive, put upon male.

'Cuid a speak tae—' I started.

'For fuck's sake speak English,' said the male, and put the phone down.

I waited for him to go and pick on someone his own size, then rang back. I still put on an accent, but not such a thick one.

'Yes? Alyssa speaking.'

'It's your long-lost friend,' I said in my own voice.

'Oh Christ,' was all she could answer at first. I could imagine her looking round desperately, but it seemed to me she must be working out, as I had, that it was moderately safe to talk. 'Give me your number and I'll call you back.'

She had a lot more practical sense than I did. Fortunately I could still just read the number on the phone, and a few seconds later her voice was in my ear again. A nice voice, I decided now that I was listening to it after a bit of a break.

'Remember that place we first met up?'

'Do I ever?' How, after all, could I forget that icy encounter in the King's Road.

'Then be there at eleven on the dot.'

She rang off. I've always had a soft spot for masterful women, though it doesn't often seem to have been reciprocated.

Thirty-Two

If you're old and scruffy, no one looks at you. They don't want to make eye contact, you see, in case it might embolden you to ask them for money. Actually, I think there's more to it than that: by looking you in the eyes, they might be obliged to connect with you, to listen to your depressing story, to have to come up with some excuse why they can't take you in and look after you. Whatever the opposite of the Good Samaritan is, that's what they are. Don't think I'm being judgemental: when I'm scrubbed up and have somewhere decent to spend the night, that's exactly how I behave too.

Anyway, being old and mad was my protection. I played it up, dragging one foot behind me and muttering occasionally to myself. If there's anything most people dread more than someone who's old and scruffy, it's someone who's old, scruffy and a nutter.

> *Sweep on, you fat and greasy citizens;*
> *'Tis just the fashion: wherefore do you look*
> *Upon that poor and broken bankrupt there?*

As You Like It, by the way – I wouldn't want to put you to the pain and difficulty of looking it up. At eleven o'clock I wandered along the King's Road, dragging my left foot, my head down, muttering these lines to myself and replacing 'there' with 'here'. They scattered before me like hares in a meadow.

I had to reconfigure myself quickly when I stepped into the coffee shop. This was somewhere I'd been before, in a different life, and I didn't want to draw attention to myself. If acting like a harmless lunatic had served me in the street, my best protection in the coffee shop would be silence and unobtrusiveness. Fortunately she was there already.

'Thanks,' I said as I sat down.

'Don't mention it. How are you?'

I didn't feel like telling her, even though she'd chosen a table where no one could overhear us, so I just shrugged. There wasn't much time, and if I got started on all the things that had happened to me I might find it hard to stop.

Even so, we must have spent more than an hour and a half there. The coffee people gave way to the lunch people, and we felt obliged to have a sandwich in order not to attract attention.

'I've thought it over,' Alyssa said. 'You've only got one chance, and you've got to do it right. I'll help you, and we can bring several other people in as well. You know, Os and Jo, and maybe one or two others.'

Jo was a picture editor we'd both worked with – a tough, unemotional type who was inclined to wear dungarees. She was excellent at her job, but she was also loyal. In a way, she and Os had their similarities. I knew both of them would stick by us if they believed in the project.

'You've got to get absolute, total proof that everything that's happened has been set up by the Russians. Your friend's death, all the stuff that's been happening . . . You know.'

I did indeed. I'd thought of little else since I'd been on the run. What surprised me was that she was so committed to seeing it from my point of view. I would have thought she'd be the one who would point out the inadequacies of my story, not back it wholeheartedly. It just shows how wrong you can sometimes be.

But if I'm absolutely honest, this willing agreement made me wonder about her motives. Might she just be sounding my plans out so that she could pass them on to someone else? The management at the Centre? The police? Even the people who had been following me around?

'Who'd broadcast something like this? The bulletins? *In Depth*? *Tonight*?' These were the main outlets we worked for.

'I think we should just get the material together and then approach them all. If we can prove that there's been a big conspiracy – really prove it, not just make the accusation – then we've got something that everyone will want.'

Something pessimistic inside me needed to get out.

'We can easily get lots of people to say there's been a conspiracy, but when you talk about proof, what would you think could actually prove it?'

There was a silence. We both thought about it while a waitress came and put a couple of toasted sandwiches in front of us.

'Didn't you tell me there was some chance of getting an FSB general to talk?'

'Do you think that'd be enough?'

'Depends what he says, of course. The real ace would be if he'd known about the plot to kill your friend, and confirmed it on camera.'

Perhaps I've been wrong about her, I thought: she sounds so committed. But I was still in my pessimistic mood anyway.

'Good luck with that. But I suppose I could try.'

'Attaboy.'

I knew what I had to do, but in my sudden mood of suspicion I decided not to tell her the details. Still, it was clear to me now that I'd have to put pressure on Boris Kulikov to persuade his FSB general to do the interview with me. That'd mean going back to Moscow, but I reckoned that with my magic Irish passport that shouldn't be impossible. I'd done the previous trip on my British one, in my proper name, and it seemed unlikely that the Russians would correlate the two personas.

She was frowning. 'But I won't be able to come with you. I've got my own problems with the management, and they certainly won't give me time off to do my own thing.'

I nodded. That meant I'd have to rely on Vara to help. Going alone might attract too much attention, and I could get her to make the arrangements on the ground and act as translator. Surely she'd be OK? To be honest, I'd got to the point where absolutely no one seemed entirely reliable to me. It's the response of the hunted, I suppose. I'm the wildebeest, with a long journey to make through lion country. And it's often hard to tell who's running with the lions.

I asked Alyssa if she'd get a message through to Vara that afternoon to ring me. She'd presumably be at the art gallery where she worked.

'And where can she get hold of you?'

Again, something in me suggested that I should keep shtum. I don't know why.

'I'll ring you at the Centre at let's say four this afternoon, to give you my number.'

'But where will you be?'

'I honestly don't know,' I said, but I honestly did know very well. I just didn't want to tell her.

There's a row of telephone boxes which are still more or less in working order near the Aldwych. I'd tried out one not long before, when I'd lost my mobile and had to report it. I would just find a way of passing the time until four o'clock. Lincoln's Inn Fields was a useful place, where I could settle down on a bench and wait. And think things over.

At five to four I rang Alyssa. This time I didn't put on my phoney accent. Why did I ring her five minutes earlier than I'd said I would? Surely you can guess. Mistrust.

'I wasn't expecting you to ring so early.'

Did I detect a soupçon of something in her voice? Maybe she was starting to wonder about me, just as I was wondering about her.

'Did you get through to her?'

'Yes, yes – all fixed.'

'That's really nice of you.'

I put as much warmth into my voice as I could. After all, the chances were that this girl with the superb profile was simply sticking her neck out for me, a good deal farther than a salaried employee of a nasty outfit really should.

'The number is . . .' I've forgotten it now, of course, but I had it written down in front of me as I spoke to her.

It wasn't the number I was speaking from. There was another bank of phone boxes a quick run away, outside the Law Courts, and I gave her one of those numbers. The phones there are usually in working order, because people need to let their nearest and dearest know when the case against them has collapsed. I'd timed the walk from one set of phone boxes to the other: thirty-three seconds.

I was there quicker than that, if anything. For a while the phone stayed silent: it seemed to me like several hours. At least in this mobile-using era, though, you don't get people forming queues outside and tapping on the window, impatient to make a call of their own.

It rang.

'Hi,' I said into the receiver. 'I hope you're well.'

'I'm just glad to hear your voice. Are you all right?'

Hearing Vara's pleasant contralto, I could imagine her warm half-smile.

As good as a wildebeest can be in lion territory, I thought, but I didn't want to tell her that. It would only complicate things.

'Yes, fine. Listen, do you remember the place we went to after the robbery?'

'Of course I do. When do you want to meet there?'

'Half an hour?'

The quicker the better, I thought: the chances were that nobody would be staking out her gallery, and if they were listening to this conversation – *if* – it would take them a bit of time to roust out some watchers to follow her.

'I'll see you there.'

I went round the corner to the Tube station at Holborn, and bought myself an Oyster Card, using cash. Nowadays the Oyster seems to be fading out, because people just touch the pad at the entrance gates with their bank cards. Not me, though: no bank. For crooks, transitories, people who want to stay under the radar, cash leaves no trace.

As I snatched glances at my reflection in the window opposite my seat in the Tube train, it seemed to me I looked pretty unrecognisable by now. I was a lot thinner than I used to be, and the beard seemed to have changed the outline of my face and given me a haunted, mean look. Also the grungy coat and old, dirty jeans.

The only item which had survived from my past was the shoes I wore: wrinkly old brogues, which had once been the colour of horse chestnuts and now looked a dusty brown. No, I reflected as

I got nearer the restaurant where I was to meet Vara: it'd be really hard to recognise the old Jon Swift in this get-up.

It was obviously a bit of a shock to Vara when she came in and saw me sitting there. As a result there was a new awkwardness to our interaction; apart from anything else, we didn't look as though we belonged at the same table. Several other customers seemed to feel the same thing, judging from the way they stared at us.

'We're attracting too much attention,' I murmured. 'When you've finished your coffee, let's get away from here.'

Outside in the street I suggested that we should separate and make our way to the café at the top of the big department store across the square. Much better. In Peter Jones there's always a mixture of Chelsea mums and characters off the street. True, they didn't seem to be sharing tables with each other, as we were. But here no one looked at us, which was a relief.

She got us another coffee each, and – a rather charming touch – she brought me a gingerbread man. As I bit off its limbs and head with cannibalistic relish, she looked me over.

'God, you've changed.'

'Yes, well, being an outlaw has its effects, you know.'

'For the better.'

'Thank you. I must go on the run more often, if you like it.'

I meant it to sound light and bantering: the old me. Instead it came out resentful, bitter, reproving. Her head jerked back, as though I'd threatened to slap her.

'I didn't mean—'

'No, please don't take any notice. All this living rough seems to have changed me. Once we get the whole thing sorted out, I'll be my old, jolly, overweight self again. You'll see.'

I grinned, but it didn't seem to make things better.

'What are you going to do?'

'I'm going to go back to Moscow and see this character from the FSB who seems to want to spill the beans. I wondered if you'd be prepared to come too.'

'Well, the gallery does seem to be getting rather tired of me. The owner came in the other day and said he hoped that everything which has been happening wouldn't affect our customers.'

'Does that mean you'll come, or you won't come?'

'It means I'll come. Of course.'

She lay her hand on mine. If anyone had been watching, it must have looked like Beauty and the Beast.

We headed downstairs on the escalator, standing a little apart, and in the electronics department she pretended to look at television sets while I examined the stills cameras. The one I liked the look of cost well over two hundred pounds, but these things can all shoot video nowadays and a stills camera is a lot less eye-catching than a video one. Assuming I could smarten up the way I looked, I'd make a much better approximation of a tourist with the camera round my neck.

I could see the sales assistant wanted to make some comment, probably something to do with my appearance and the fact that I had a fat roll of cash in my hand, but I gave him my nastiest glare and he quickly looked down at the till instead. I decided not to buy anything.

Vara and I took the escalator again, staying separate by mutual, unspoken consent, as though it was only chance that we were standing near each other. When we reached the men's department I stepped off and bought some unremarkable clothes to take to Moscow. She was waiting outside the main entrance, where we'd come in. I knew she'd be there, which was comforting; but was I in danger of becoming too dependent on her?

'There's one more thing,' I said as the wind swirled round us and a couple of leaves off a nearby plane tree flew past. 'Money. I've got enough for day-to-day stuff, but it's not much. I can't pay for our airline tickets because I don't have a bank account. It's going to cost a good two thousand for the whole trip. I'll pay you back at some point, but I'll have to ask if you'd be prepared to stump up.'

I couldn't even look her in the face as I spoke; asking women for money is something I don't do. Well, that's what I like to say.

'Please don't even think about it,' she said with a sweetness that belied her dark looks. 'I've got plenty stashed away. From the old days, you know.'

So that was a relief. We made arrangements about booking flights and getting visas which I won't bore you with, and agreed to meet up in a couple of days' time. With my new clothes and my new look, I felt better about the risk of being recognised. There was still the problem that I didn't have a credit card, which meant I had to think carefully about where I was going to spend the next two nights.

But around Paddington station there are plenty of small hotels that don't charge much and don't mind how you sort the bill out; in fact, they probably prefer cash. I showed my Irish passport when required, paid in advance, and shut myself up in my room for the evening.

I'd taken the precaution of going into a corner shop on the way and buying something to eat. Sitting on my narrow bed, I gnawed a sausage roll that tasted like cardboard drenched in DDT, and drank a couple of miniature single malts from the bottle. Chelsea were playing Arsenal on television, and that cheered me up too. Especially when Chelsea slipped in the winning goal in extra time. It felt like some sort of omen, though in reality it was just that Chelsea had managed to persuade Eden Hazard not to go somewhere else.

The following night I found another hotel not far away and repeated the dose. Instead of football, a rather pretty girl was prancing round my elderly television set pretending to be the Queen. But all the while, even as I watched, I was thinking about Vara. Had my wanderings made me somehow emotionally dependent on her? Was I, somehow, being disloyal to Patrick? And above all, was it safe? I turned over in the bed, in sheets that were surprisingly clean and pleasant, and fell into a troubled sleep.

Thirty-Three

We'd arranged to meet again the next day at a place which we both knew, and which was discreet and private. I'd been a member of the London Library, that vast private palace of books in St James's Square, ever since I left university. I suppose going there gave me the feeling of being still linked to academia, and I loved pottering around among ancient tomes coated with dust; the tomes, not me.

There it stands, anyway, tucked into the corner of the square. It was founded in 1841 by Thomas Carlyle, as nasty an old proto-fascist as you could find. Only the accident of time meant he couldn't earn a couple of hundred thou a year as a newspaper columnist, forever spluttering about some new outrage. But even so the library is a wonderful place, and in the streets leading up to it you can always seem to tell which are the members as they totter towards it for their latest injection of bibliophilia.

Once upon a time the London Library was like one of those gents' clubs in nearby Pall Mall, and the staff would greet you by name. When I lost a book and had to pay for it (a girlfriend of mine had thrown it at me when I was breaking up with her, and it landed in the fire; we carried on exchanging insults so long that the front cover, complete with London Library sticker, burned away, together with pages vii to 45), the rather attractive young woman on the returns desk looked at me disapprovingly for weeks afterwards, as though I'd kicked her Pomeranian.

Now, though, like the rest of the world, the library has become electronicised, and no one notices you. If you don't have a plastic membership card, you can't get in. But if you do, a low glass gate in the main hall opens sclerotically and allows you entry. Its action is so slow that you can shepherd several non-members in with you, and the nearby staff are usually too busy doing their jobs to notice. You could probably get the entire Crystal Palace football team through in full kit, before anyone stopped you.

One of the many things I like about the London Library is that it still classifies things as it used to back in around 1905, so you have to look in 'Austro-Hungarian Empire' if you want to find something about modern Vienna. As for the Soviet Union, it came and went while the London Library still filed it under 'Russia'. I suppose we should be grateful it wasn't called 'Muscovy'.

'I'll see you in the stacks in the old main part of the library, at the back,' I'd said to Vara. ' "History – Russia". Shall we say eleven?'

We said eleven.

I was passing the time looking at biographies of Nikolai Bukharin when I heard footsteps coming towards me. One of the weirder things about the old part of the London Library is that the bookcases are fixed in long parallel rows on skeletal steel floors. These floors have gaps in them, each the breadth of a butcher's knife; so if you look down, or up, you can see the tops of the heads or the feet of users on the other floors. Not for those of a nervous disposition, therefore.

Vara's feet made that hard, characteristic London Library sound of leather on metal, and her soft, gentle, low voice greeted me pleasantly.

'So how are you, Jonny?'

'Yeah, fine. Glad you found me.'

I liked 'Jonny'.

We chatted a bit about the library and its Russian books, and how amazingly up to date they were, and how they fitted them all in. And she handed me an envelope with a thousand quid in it.

There aren't many places to sit in this part of the library, but round the corner there's an area that's just big enough to hold a table and a couple of chairs; and for a wonder there wasn't anyone there, labouring away with half a dozen volumes piled up in front of him or her.

> *Remember*
> *First to possess his books; for without them*
> *He's but a sot, as I am.*

That's Caliban planning to whack Prospero. He got it spot on, and I'm the same.

We sat down at the empty table and whispered to each other. There was urgent business to be done. I had to contact Boris Kulikov, my dissident friend in Moscow, but I needed Vara to do it for me. The FSB would be watching Boris's messages, but he'd given me the number of a cut-out, a sympathiser who seemed to be unknown to the cops. I dug out the number and jotted it down on a bit of paper for Vara.

'Text "Has our mutual friend heard any birdsong yet?" to this number, would you?'

'Is that safe, Jon?'

I was obscurely touched.

'Nothing's safe. But this is better than any alternative I can think of. All we need is a yes from him, and a date for us to go to Moscow to do the interview.'

She nodded, and did the necessary texting while I sat there and watched. After she'd pressed *send* she looked up at me with a charming, rather girlish look as though she wanted my approval. Well, she had that anyway.

I was still looking at her when I heard another version of the leather-on-metal sound: heavier, longer, and perhaps I felt even then, more surreptitious. I don't know, though – maybe I've made that bit up. It came round the corner behind me, and something in the look on Vara's face made me lurch round in my chair.

A young man was taking the last step towards me. I took in the habitual grey hoodie, which covered most of his face. But most of all I took in the knife: almost a foot long, with those horrible serrations of the kind that remind you of ISIS snuff videos.

I'm not sure about the order of all the events which took place after that: Vara's low scream, the hoodie's lurch forward with the knife, the dual scraping of our chairs on the steel floor, my instinctive decision to put Trotsky's *My Life* to an immediate use. It was a quarto edition circa 1928, with lots of pictures of him making speeches during the Revolution, and it lay on the table in front of me.

The knife darted forward like a snake – I was scarcely aware of the wrist that wielded it – and seemed to be heading for that bit of my midriff where the ribs come to an end and there's no protection for the upper stomach: inadequate design by the Almighty, I would say. Without any real thought, I found Trotsky was in my right hand like a small but well-positioned shield. The knife went into it, and got as far (I found afterwards) as the events of 1905: the old boy's greatest achievement, really.

The hoodie hadn't been expecting this. His face, which I hadn't taken my eyes from, registered a kind of mild surprise and irritation. He tried pulling the knife out of the book, but the ISIS-style serrations made it impossible without a great deal more wristwork than the hoodie felt able to devote to it. He gave a kind of yelp, and turned to run.

I suppose I should have rugby-tackled him, but I'm getting on a bit for that kind of thing. So I sent Trotsky after him like a frisbee instead, with the knife still half buried in it. The edge of it took him in the small of the back, and he gave a gratifying low grunt, as though it had really hurt. I hope it did. But it didn't stop him. He lurched off down to the stairs leading to the basement, and disappeared from sight.

Vara was in tears.

'Oh God, Jonny! Tell me you're not hurt. I couldn't bear it. Why are these awful people trying to get you all the time? What do they want? How can we stop them?'

I didn't know what to say, so I went and picked up the life-saving *My Life*. It was pretty badly damaged from its experiences, but by holding it down between my knees and gripping the handle of the knife in my right hand I managed to separate the two. The blade gave a nasty sucking sound as it came out.

It was only when I held the thing in my hand and looked at how sharp it was, and how carefully designed to cause real trouble in your insides, that I started to realise my luck.

'They ought to ban these bloody things,' I said, sounding like a *Daily Mail* editorial. But it was pretty feeble.

Vara's head was down between her knees now.

'Look, dear girl, you can't be sick here. It'll go straight down to "Topography" if you do.'

Actually, if I'm honest, that's a bit of *esprit de l'escalier*. At such a time I couldn't possibly have remembered what the floor below us was dedicated to, or put it into words. But it's what I would like to have said, anyway.

Whatever it was I did say, she nodded and quickly got herself under control. It was only then that I started to wonder who the hell could have got into the library to skewer me, and why: why being even more important than who.

I must have said something of this out loud, because Vara said bitterly, 'These people will never leave us alone! Why don't they just kill me now, and put me out of my misery?'

Not the way I saw it at all, of course. I just wanted my old life back, where people didn't try to open my stomach up or kill my friends or send me dead cats and filthy pictures. Wasn't there something I could do to stop it all?

The answer, of course, was no. The only way to stop it was to bring the whole nasty business out into the open, so that everyone would understand what these people were doing.

And as if it were announcing some message from heaven, Vara's phone gave a little ping at that moment. She stopped emoting and looked at it. (Have you noticed how our phones take precedence over everything else – even near-evisceration?)

She read out the English words slowly and wonderingly.

'"Thinking of you at 3-month anniversary of our last meeting."'

I was still a bit bemused from my knife and frisbee experience, and the barbarism of calling three months an anniversary confused me. Fortunately, though, Vara was clearer-headed.

'He must mean he wants you to be in Moscow that day, don't you think?'

I sort of did, but it took me a look at my online diary and a couple of minutes' working out before I could settle on the correct date that I should be there. It was twelve days away.

Thirty-Four

Twelve days sounds pretty short, but think back over the last twelve days in your own life and you'll see it's actually quite a long time. And given that I was on the run and in danger of being spotted and handed over to the cops at any moment, it seemed like an eternity.

There was also the question of money. My hotel in Paddington might be cheap and crappy, but London prices dictated that it still cost £80 a night; and twelve nights would whittle my stash down by nearly a thousand quid. Not including meals or fares. After the little episode at the London Library, anyone I stayed with would be put at serious risk. No matter how careful I was, the bastards seemed to know everything about my movements.

It seemed unlikely that they would hand me over to the British police, but to be honest I'd rather be in the hands of the Old Bill than stabbed, shot, or otherwise dealt with by the Russians. Assuming they were the Russians.

The only good card in my hand was my Irish name and passport. I thought and thought about it, and in the end decided that the best thing to do would be to get out of Britain as quickly as possible, go to Moscow, and take as long over the journey as I possibly could. It would cost me, but at least I wouldn't be in such danger of being spotted.

When you're being hunted, as I was, all you do is think about yourself. You don't want to be burdened by anyone else, and you don't want to share any secrets. You go into social lockdown. When I met Vara, in a pub in Wandsworth where I'd never been before, there seemed no reason why I should put her in danger by telling her what I was planning to do. Instead I suggested a meeting place in Moscow, twelve days on.

'But how are you going to get there? Wouldn't it be easier and nicer to fly with me?'

'If they're checking your phone, and I bet they are, they'll be on the lookout for the two of us. If we travel separately, we'll stand a much better chance of actually getting there.'

'So when will you fly?'

It was on the tip of my tongue to ask why she thought I would be flying, but I decided not to.

'Maybe Monday week.'

The appointed date was Tuesday.

'If your plane gets in late on Monday evening, we can meet up around midnight,' I went on.

'But where?'

I'd thought this out already. The best places to meet, if you're likely to be followed, are fluid ones – by which I mean places where lots of people are coming and going, and there are plenty of exits. But I was also a romantic, and there's only one place in Moscow for romantics to meet: Red Square. Of course, well-trained spooks can easily follow you through the very thickest of crowds; indeed, the thicker the crowd the easier it can sometimes be.

But there are ways of lessening the odds if you choose your rendezvous with care, and if you keep a few tricks up your sleeve. I'd stayed awake until two in the morning thinking about it all in my Paddington hotel room. There wasn't a great deal else to do.

'Red Square, beside the Lobnoye Mesto.'

The Lobnoye Mesto is a round stone platform just in front of St Basil's Cathedral. Ivan the Terrible addressed the Moscow crowds from there in 1547 – it wouldn't have been a good career move to have missed that, I imagine – and the later tsars used to fetch up there on foot at the end of their Palm Sunday processions.

'But isn't that going to be really obvious?'

'Not at midnight, I shouldn't think. Red Square will be pretty empty then, and no one can get close to us without being spotted. After we've met up we can head off separately to our hotels.'

We'd already booked them: Vara was staying at the Four Seasons, which in Soviet days had been the horrible old Moskva, where Party officials hung out, while I was going to the ever delightful National, where I'd stayed so often in the distant past.

No arrangement was likely to be entirely FSB-proof, but this one seemed pretty reasonable to me. And I liked the thought of walking through Red Square at night.

'Whoever gets there first waits for the other, but only for four minutes. If we don't meet up, the whole thing is aborted.'

'Whew. That's a pretty tight deadline, Jonny.'

'Got to be. Set your watch by the BBC World Service news before you take off for our little get-together. So – Moscow, midnight.'

She grinned. 'Yes, captain.'

I grinned too, and kissed her. In a brotherly kind of way. I didn't want to foul everything up with any sudden urges.

'And now I'm going,' I said. 'I shan't see you again till then. Don't forget.'

Half mockingly she talked over me: 'Monday night.'

And saluted. I can't think when I've seen anything more attractive.

Thirty-Five

I know I went on a great deal some time back about what I looked like, but I feel it's important to tell you exactly how I'd changed. I'd shed enough weight to give me the kind of figure I last saw in my twenties. My beard was full and of hipster cut, and Vara had chosen to dye it the precise colour of the pipe tobacco my grandfather used to fume out his sitting room with. It didn't quite match my hair, but you often see men who go round like patchwork quilts in this way. Losing weight had given me extra wrinkles, including long downward valleys like railway cuttings in my cheeks. I used to look big, cherubic, and jolly; now I looked like a sadistic headmaster. That suited me: I was much more concerned to go on living than win a beauty competition.

To add to my sinister quality, the beating I'd had in Brussels had given me a slight limp, and I'd taken to using something that had been lying around in the flat ever since a trip to rural South Africa years before: an elderly knobkerrie made of mopani wood – a Zulu walking stick, with an intimidating bulge on top. I know, I know – you're thinking, here we go, Swiftie's setting everything up for a big fight scene later in the action, in which someone gets a whack from the knobkerrie. Well, don't be too sure. I know perfectly well that Anton Chekhov said, 'Never have a loaded rifle onstage if it isn't going to go off. You mustn't make promises you

225

don't mean to keep.' But this isn't a play, things don't necessarily end neatly in real life, and anyway my bloody ankle still hurt and I needed something to support it.

My real point is that I looked just different enough for people to look at me and think, 'He's a bit like that bloke off the telly – but you can see it's not him.' That, at any rate, was what I hoped. But what we hope and what we get are two different things.

I was back in the waiting room at the Russian visa section in London, sitting apart from everyone else, nursing my walking stick in one hand and my numbered ticket in the other and letting my mind go blank, when a hand fell on my shoulder. Not my favourite sensation.

'Sorry, it's Jon, isn't it? Jon Swift?'

What the hell was I to do? I'd run through one or two options in my mind over the previous few days, but I hadn't really prepared anything because I'd just taken refuge in the hope that it wouldn't happen. Now it had.

I knew perfectly well who this intrusive character was: a noisy, rather boastful ex-colleague of mine from way back, whose company I'd sometimes enjoyed and sometimes shunned. I'd done him a couple of good turns in the past, but for some reason – or perhaps that *was* the reason – he'd taken to bad-mouthing me behind my back.

'Don't trust him, is my advice,' someone who was genuinely a good friend had told me.

But here of all incriminating places, when I was just about to get a visa in a wholly different name, I had to do an emergency smarming number on him.

'Hello Robert – good to see you.' In fact, of course, I was as glad to see him as I would be if I'd just come across a plague bubo in my armpit. 'But would you mind keeping your voice down? I'm going off to do a bit of undercover filming in Russia, and I don't want anyone to know about it.' And then the killer: 'In fact, apart from my producer, you're the only person in the entire world who does know.' In other words, if it gets out I'll know exactly who to blame.

'Oh absolutely, old man, silent as the tomb. Not a word to anyone.'

At that precise moment an electronic beeper sounded and my number came up on the electronic screen above one of the counters. I pointed to it and to my bit of paper in dramatic fashion, shook hands with him, and hobbled over to the counter. But I was badly shaken. My appearance clearly wasn't as different as I'd hoped, and one of the people I'd least like to be spotted by had let me know.

Bugger. Still, I had no alternative now except to keep on going. If I stopped bailing, I'd sink.

Robert, fortunately, was tied up with his own negotiations at another counter when I finished, so there was no need to say goodbye to him.

I limped back to the Tube, and hopped on the first train that came through. Sitting there, with the roar of the train in my ears, the cables running past me in the dark tunnel outside the window, and only the closed-down faces of my fellow passengers to stare at, I thought my position through.

And bit by bit, as the Circle Line unfolded in a westerly direction, I worked it out. Not plane, but train to Moscow. It'd take me several days, but I had approximately ten at my disposal and I only needed to be there the night before I met up with Vara and went to see Boris Kulikov. Spending that much time on the journey would hopefully keep me off everyone's radar.

I didn't want to catch the Eurostar at St Pancras again, because I so often bumped into people I knew. But there's a weird station called Ebbsfleet, on the Kentish outskirts of London, where some of the Eurostar trains stop. It's a bit like you might imagine main line stations in North Korea to be – grey steel and entirely empty most of the time – but catching the train there meant I wouldn't have to start at St Pancras, and if I took the first available train in the morning and booked a seat, I could probably slip on board while everyone else was dozing.

The other advantage of an early start was that the staff at the station might well be a bit dozy too, and less likely to remember me. On the other hand, I might well be the station's only passenger at that time. It was a toss-up – but Ebbsfleet won.

I got out at Marylebone and bought a railway guide in the bookshop, then wandered out of the station without thinking where I was going. Opposite I saw an inviting-looking café and went in. The man who ran it had a welcoming manner, a loud Italian voice and a waxed handlebar moustache of the kind I hadn't seen since my childhood. The place was warm and steamy, and I ordered a sandwich with all the things the health sections of the newspapers go on about: white bread sandwich with fried egg, sausage, and bacon. Well, I was a wolf's-head, an outlaw, who could be turned in by anyone who spotted me; as far as I was concerned, all the usual rules were cancelled. Robin Hood must have felt like this on his day trips into Nottingham. It was no time to think of self-denial.

Sitting there over a cup of strong tea and my unwieldy, yolk-dripping sandwich, I looked at my railway guide. Rotterdam seemed like a useful intermediate destination, and the first train there which stopped at Ebbsfleet was at four minutes past seven in the morning: peak dozing time. And how was I to get to Ebbsfleet? From Stratford International in the east end of London, apparently. I'd gather my kit together, pass the time as best I could

– a film, maybe? – then go and settle at the Balans Café in Soho for the night. I'd done that once before, a few years back, and it had been perfect: goodish food, low lighting, couches to sit on, and staff who didn't keep prodding you to eat more or leave.

I still needed to buy a camera for the interview in Moscow, of the kind I'd checked out in Peter Jones. The quality of the video which a stills camera can shoot is nowadays almost as good as a proper full-sized television camera can get, only without attracting all that attention, with kids dancing round and making V-signs in the background. I dropped into a camera shop in Soho and bought one, plus several of those little flashcards the size of a postage stamp on which you record your stuff, and a classy leather case for the camera I'd chosen. Because I'm a snob, it was a Leica; in reality it's just a Panasonic with the little red Leica badge on it, but the lens is great and when I wave it around I feel I'm at one with the ghosts of Magnum: the photographers' collective, not the ice cream. You have to explain these things nowadays, I find.

When I'd got my clothes and equipment into the hold-all, and my books into the backpack, I headed off to the National Film Theatre on the South Bank, like my Dad and I used to do in the distant past, not bothering to check beforehand what was showing but just sitting down and letting the cinema surprise us (or, rather more often, bore us stiff). But tonight I hit the jackpot: W. C. Fields and Mae West in *My Little Chickadee*. Perfection. I sat there and laughed a bit too loudly, especially when some character on the train heading through the Wild West says 'Poker – is that a game of chance?' and Fields fans the cards with amazing professionalism and says 'Not the way I play it, no.' People started looking across at me, and a couple of youngish women sitting together moved to a different row.

After that I had six hours to kill. I wandered about for a while, still grinning, and headed for Old Compton Street at around midnight. Once upon a time there used to be lots of elderly tarts in torn stockings standing in the doorways, but now, like everything else, it's all less obvious and more demure. The bouncer outside the Balans Café gave me a superior look but stepped aside to let me in. Inside it was noisy and overly warm, but pleasantly womblike. I passed the time with whiskey, coffee, and orange juice, and around four ordered ham and eggs and strong tea, with my back to the rest of the room, reading and dozing. It felt good.

Thirty-Six

Ebbsfleet was everything I'd expected – more than a touch of Kim Jong-Un, and no problems with security. I bought a ticket to Rotterdam. When the train pulled in I clambered over legs and suitcases to my preassigned seat, past the early morning dozers, and was soon dozing myself. Changing at Brussels didn't feel fantastic, given my history there, but I got a train on to Rotterdam quite quickly, and then bought a ticket to Berlin.

So far it was all going disturbingly to plan. In Berlin I hopped out and went to one of those seedy little hotels that grow up round big railway stations like a skin rash. My plan was to move from one to another over a period of four days, though the third hotel I found was so pleasant I stayed a couple of nights.

From Berlin I took the train to Warsaw, where I repeated the dose: four nights, during which I read large amounts and wandered through the streets until my feet ached. To be honest, it's all a bit of a blur. In that entire time I don't suppose I spoke to more than ten people, seven of whom were standing behind a bar.

And then, finally, Friday afternoon came and I could load myself on to the Moscow sleeper at Warsaw Centralna, together with the hold-all, which contained my clothes and washing gear, and my backpack, which just contained books. I'd become deeply grateful for my stick, which propped me up as I walked and became a valuable tool for pushing open swing doors, getting attention and forcing my way through crowds. And of course it gave me the comforting feeling that I was armed and could defend myself if necessary.

I chucked the bags and the stick on the other berth and flopped down on mine. I'd rather splashed out when I booked this compartment, getting one that had only two berths in it and taking both of them to give myself some privacy. Twenty hours of travel lay ahead of me and I wanted to enjoy them without having to worry about some fellow traveller sitting there picking his nose or trying to get into conversation with me.

A Polish ticket collector came to fuss over my ticket and seat reservation, and a fat housekeeper-like woman made me stand up and follow her dumb-show instructions about pulling the folding bed down and making sure I didn't fall out of it. But they'd both buggered off some time before the train gave a little anticipatory shake and started to move off. I grinned: this was how I liked to travel.

> *I sprang to the stirrup, and Joris, and he;*
> *I galloped, Dirck galloped, we galloped all three;*
> *'Good speed!' cried the watch, as the gate-bolts undrew;*
> *'Speed!' echoed the wall to us galloping through;*
> *Behind shut the postern, the lights sank to rest,*
> *And into the midnight we galloped abreast.*

Yes, well, it wasn't like that at all. I just lounged around in my seat looking out at the grey Polish plain and reading Tolstoy, and occasionally thinking about going down the swaying corridor for a glass of something at the bar.

I'd never done this journey by train, but I'd heard all about how weird it was. Most of Europe, you see, follows the British railway standard gauge of four foot eight and a half inches, but the dear old Russians never have; ever since tsarist times, their gauge has been five feet. So after 130 miles, when we reached Brest on the Russian frontier, we jerked and shimmied to a stop, and after a while the sleeping cars were separated off one by one and shunted into a large shed. Mine came to a halt in the near darkness, with lots of noise and unnecessary blokes shining torches and shouting, and it was jacked up inch by inch while they stuck a new bogey underneath it.

It felt weirdly internalised and personal, like having an endoscopy. More shouting, more shunting, more clanking and shuddering, and then we were ready. And not long afterwards a Russian lady of a certain age with red hair and a grubby white uniform banged on my door and announced that if I wanted something to eat, the restaurant car would be open in twenty minutes.

I waited for an hour, since this was going to be a long journey. I'd been looking forward to Russian *zakuski*, though the Polish version had also been good: cold cuts, *pirozhki*, devilled eggs, mushrooms, salmon, sturgeon, the lot. Not Russian at all, originally, but copied by Peter the Great from Sweden. Still, the Russians have turned the whole idea into a grand national tradition.

Not, alas, on this train, though. When I got to her hangout, the red-haired lady smiled apologetically and explained that the food trolley hadn't made it to Brest in time to meet the train. Russia was still Russia, it seemed. All there was, she said, was borscht, ham, and bread.

'*Harasho*,' I said. 'I'll have borscht, lukewarm and watery, and some stale grey bread with ham curling up at the edges.'

I got exactly what I'd ordered.

Not my own joke, actually: adapted from one by Raymond Chandler. And of course I didn't really say it out loud.

Still, no one can spoil vodka. The bar-lady, embarrassed by her inability to feed me properly, revealed the riches she kept in a cupboard under the bar: *krupnik*, which is honey-flavoured; *pertsovka*, flavoured with peppercorns; *zubróvka* (bison grass); and *okhotnichya*, which means 'hunter's' and is flavoured with cloves, lemon, and ginger. It would have been rude not to try them all, I felt. And it's amazing how a good glass or four of vodka can perk up the kind of food you'd otherwise give to the cat.

Outside, the scenery had changed like a dissolve in a film. No more of the farms and carefully tended fields of eastern Poland; now the hills reached out, plain and untilled, towards the horizon, and birch trees in millions crowded up on either side of the railway line, with the occasional village visible between them: those low wooden houses you think surely can't survive much longer, and yet which always do.

I was back in my stuffy compartment when we rattled through a station with the date 1812 on it. This was Borodino, where the battle was fought: 'a continuous slaughter which could be of no avail either to the French or the Russians', said Tolstoy, in a passage in *War and Peace* which I'd ploughed through a couple of days earlier in Warsaw. Still, what happened in more or less the same area a hundred and thirty years later, when the Russians gave Hitler a bloody nose, was a great deal of avail to them and to the rest of us.

By the time we reached the farthest outskirts of Moscow it was past noon and I was sick of it all: sick of trying not to think about what was going to happen next, sick of being scared, sick of too much early vodka. All my stuff was packed and ready to go, long before it needed to be.

We clattered our noisy way between hundreds upon hundreds of ugly, featureless tower blocks of flats, each one with its own skimpy unlined curtains and cheap light fittings: the kind of flats that house the millions of people who obediently come out to vote for their president in election after election, because he's made them think their country's strong again.

The buildings were starting to look older, and concrete was giving way to red brick and the kind of parchment-coloured plaster you only seem to get in Russia. I felt suddenly at home. Soon we'd be getting in to Belorusskaya station.

I said my goodbyes to the lady of the vodka and the man who was in charge of my sleeping coach, climbed down the steep metal steps to the platform, and trudged off towards the ticket barrier.

An unexpected burst of self-confidence came over me. I was like some Bolshevik agitator slipping illegally into the tsarist heartland, a pathogen sent to infect the empire. 'Infect': where did I get that from? I knew: passing through the Gare Bruxelles Midi had brought it to mind, and it had stayed there, just below the surface of my memory, ever since. Auden, of course: 'Gare du Midi', which is why I thought of it. Something about snow falling, and a terrorist arriving, clutching a little case. You'll no doubt remember it, even if I can't quite seem to find the exact words. What it boils down to, anyway, is that this character has come to infect a city whose terrible future has just arrived. Sinister, eh? We've certainly had plenty of that in our own time.

No snow now, though, and the only terrible future seemed likely to be mine. Still, thinking yourself into someone else's poem is a rather pleasing form of self-dramatisation. Clutching a little case, plus backpack and knobkerrie, I made my way briskly through the barrier and headed straight for the newspaper stand.

I took my time, looking at the front pages and managing to glance around. No one seemed to be paying any attention to me. Well, they wouldn't, of course, but they'd have to be pretty brilliant to be this hard to spot, unless they were watching me through binoculars from some vantage point on the roof, which didn't seem particularly likely. For a while I messed around, taking the two papers I'd bought to a nearby tea stall and taking my time sipping from a cardboard cup. Still no one.

Quarter past five: six hours and forty-five minutes till our rendezvous.

Thirty-Seven

Maybe I was being much too cloak-and-daggerish about all this, I reflected. Russia isn't the country it was in the Soviet days, where everybody was watched and controlled and reported on all the time. It's a lot easier to say what you want. The problem is, of course, doing anything about it, against the official line. That's when nasty things start happening.

What I wanted to do here would certainly damage Russia's reputation, so the security service FSB (Federal'naya Sluzhba Bezopasnosti, in case you're interested) would most certainly try to stop me if it could. But one thing I've learned over the decades is that none of these much vaunted spy organisations are anything like as powerful and effective as the movies crack them up to be. They're basically just as slow-moving, understaffed, underpaid, dozy, resentful, bureaucratic, and disorganised as the outfit you or I work for. Even so, it's as well to treat the FSB, in particular, with respect.

I checked in at the National. No one behind the reception desk said Seánac Ó Fuada was a funny-sounding name, and a large wheezing porter insisted on carrying my camel bag and backpack for me. I lent heavily on my knobkerrie and slipped him five dollars. The room was charming. It was the one I'd stayed in, the night before Margaret Thatcher was elected prime minister, back in 1979, but nothing except the bare walls was the same now.

After that I decided to kill time by taking a Metro ride. As part of my FSB respect policy I got off the trains and on to others a couple of times, but I'm pretty certain no one followed me. I worked my way in and out of crowds, and slipped on to a train at the last moment. My stick got in everyone's way.

There was a time, in the Communist past, when everyone stared at a Westerner on the Metro; your clothes were so much better than theirs, and your shoes were made of leather instead of grey plastic. The other passengers would sit there, looking you up and down and pricing everything you were wearing. That's all long in the past, of course. Nowadays Russians have access to all the shops the West boasts, and sometimes more. I was definitely one of the worst-dressed people in each carriage I got into, I noticed with a certain self-congratulation.

The Moscow Metro is probably the loudest and most discordant underground system in the world, but I found the shattering roar comforting: it was a great aid to concentration. And I couldn't shake off the sense of being a secret agent.

I hung around in various places until past eleven o'clock: no need to help the FSB by going back to the National, I reasoned. I suppose my stick made me conspicuous, but if I'd limped along without it I'd have stood out just as much.

There was more activity in Red Square than I'd expected, but as I came through the archway from Manezh Square my footsteps echoed loudly off the walls. The arch looked as though it had been there for at least as long as Ivan the Terrible's speech from the Lobnoye Mesto, but I remember when it went up, not long after poor old Mikhail Gorbachev resigned, at the end of 1991.

I went up the incline, my stick working away on the cobbles, and came level with the square itself. As all those poor old sweating soldiers, male and female, know, the square isn't flat, but undulating. The floodlights were still on as I walked past GUM, with the Kremlin walls to my right, and I revelled in it all. It's as theatrical as St Mark's Square in Venice used to be, before the bloody tourists took it over.

My shadow stretched ahead of me, then faded and was replaced by another which moved round me on the cobbles. I limped on, my knee hurting. The Lobnoye Mesto was in view now, and the clock over the Spassky Gate showed eleven forty-eight. A car buzzed past, its tyres rippling over the bumpy surface, and a few small groups of people, mostly couples, were scattered over the vast area. What things had happened here over the years! Who can forget Aleksandr Solzhenitsyn's account of taking part in the grand Victory Parade in 1945 with all the other returned prisoners of war, cheered by weeping crowds, only to find they were marched down past St Basil's and put on to buses that took them off to labour camps for decades?

No one seemed to be hanging round the Lobnoye Mesto; there's nothing much to see there, so it's not a tourist draw, and certainly not at night-time.

'Looking for someone?' said a voice in my ear.

I raised my stick instinctively, but I'd already recognised her voice.

'Hello, little *shpion*,' Vara said. *Shpion* is Russian for 'spy'.

I kissed her with feeling.

'Aren't you taking this a bit far?'

'Not nearly as far as I'd like to take it,' I answered, and she laughed pleasantly and – I thought – rather provocatively.

Soon, though, she was serious.

'I've been there and checked him out.'

I approved of the way she deliberately avoided using Boris Kulikov's name, even here in the silence and immensity of Red Square.

'He'll see us tomorrow, at lunchtime.'

'Ah,' I said.

I was already starting to think of other uses for the evening.

Maybe there was a good secret agent reason for not taking her to the bar of the National for a drink, but I couldn't think of one. Anyway, it was the only place round here that was still open at midnight. And I wanted her to sample their vodka menu with me. Useful stuff, vodka.

'Tonight is downtime,' she said as we sat there, and looked away into the depths of her empty glass.

I come from a generation which did its lovemaking in the dark. Not true, actually, but it sounds like a good excuse for not writing about what happened after that. If I did, I would feel pretty crap about it, and so I'm sure would Vara. Anyway, we went back to the Four Seasons, her hotel, and spent the night there, on the grounds that everything in my room at the National creaked, from the floor to the furniture. It's why I love it so much, but in this case . . .

Guilt can produce a great erotic charge, and it did so for both of us. It seemed to me that there were times when Patrick was in Vara's thoughts, and sometimes he was in mine too. Not all the time, fortunately.

Breakfast in bed was a delight, though I had to hide in the bathroom when it arrived, shortly before eight o'clock. Surely the waiter must have wondered why a slightly built young woman would want barley porridge, rye bread, soft sausage, a three-egg omelette, and a jug of Buck's Fizz? But waiters at five-star hotels are trained not to show curiosity about such things; perhaps he just thought Vara had an appetite. If so, he was right.

There was no real reason to suppose that our conversations were being listened to in the Four Seasons, but in today's Russia you can never be entirely certain. So I occasionally wrote messages on her phone and handed it to her, and she answered them in the same way. It felt cute but clever at the same time. Vara insisted that she had to go round to see Boris that morning, rather than send him a message which would almost certainly be seen. We had something of a written argument.

I think much too dodgy!!!

Nonsense – you over-protective.

Then followed three heart symbols.

Must come too.

No that's really stupid.

I AM really stupid.

And so on. In the end she did what she wanted, anyway, while I went back to the National and dozed.

It was ten thirty when she rang my room from somewhere in the city.

'All OK?'

'No probs,' she said proudly.

'So we'll meet where we said?'

'Sure.'

I'd stressed to her the importance of short, inexpressive answers on the phone, probably because I'd seen lots of Second World War films about Nazi spooks sitting in detector vans trying to home in on signals from Resistance radio sets. To be honest, I have no idea whatsoever how modern spooks do it, seventy years later; but you don't have to be Alan Turing to guess that things might have got a touch more sophisticated since 1942.

The place where we'd agreed to meet was under the clock at Belorusskaya station, where I'd arrived the day before. It's a lovely bit of 1890s imperial architecture, painted the colour of pistachio ice cream. Crowds swept backwards and forwards across the station concourse at all times of the day.

Slight problem: there seemed to be two clocks, not one. Since I'd drilled into her that we had to maintain radio silence and not call each other, it was several minutes before we managed to find ourselves under the same clock at the same time. No matter: putting my arms round her and kissing her was a deeply enjoyable experience. And we wandered outside towards the charming bronze statue of a young woman kissing her wartime soldier goodbye, and repeated the process.

I meant to watch out for any sign that either of us had been followed, but to be honest I forgot. I suppose I was so excited to see her and find out what had happened that it slipped my mind. In fact I don't suppose anyone was watching us. Secret policemen are just civil servants, after all. They come on duty at regular times, five days a week, and pack up and go home eight hours later. And even in 1930s Moscow, with Stalin wanting to arrest everyone he'd ever known, the NKVD was complaining in memos that it was short-staffed. Nowadays the FSB are paid hugely better, yet there still aren't enough of them to go round. So I felt pretty justified in believing that no one had yet twigged that I was in town.

Vara's outer layers of sophistication had been stripped away by the experience she'd gone through; it was like watching a restorer cleaning the varnish off an pleasant enough portrait, and finding something even fresher and more lively underneath. We were still moving our stools into place in the station bar when she started telling me what had happened, her Russian vowels breaking into the almost unaccented English she usually spoke.

'I did it. I saw him. And he gave me the general's address.'

'Is he really a general?'

'That's what Boris calls him. He lives near Sadovo Samotechnaya, the ring road, not far from the puppet theatre. We always used to go there when we came to Moscow. Apparently his wife died recently – emphysema, he says – and the general has been left on his own because he didn't get on with the new boss, and he started finding fault with the line the organisation was taking.'

In the flood of words and ideas I noticed Vara shied away from mentioning which organisation she meant.

'And do you think he's willing to—'

But she was off again.

'At first he wrote a memo to . . .' – she dropped her voice – 'Bortnikov, the director. Bortnikov just ignored it, so the general sent a round robin to the heads of all the different departments, saying that they were wrong to be doing what they were doing – you know, the kind of thing we've been talking about – and Boris said he's seen a short version of it. He thinks the general will give us a copy.'

'Fine, great, but you know, we're here because of Patrick.'

'Yes, well, Boris says that must have been a planned termination.'

She'd never learned expressions like that in a London art gallery, I thought. Her eyes were flashing and her hands waved excitedly, and by now the waitress had noticed us and shambled over. I ordered a couple of glasses of tea in order to get rid of her.

'And will the general talk to us about it?'

'Boris says yes!'

'So when?'

'Boris is fixing it for tomorrow morning!'

Another night, I thought; and then I reflected that it would be a lot more sensible if we stayed apart until the next day.

While that was going through my mind, she leant over and kissed me full on the lips. I suppose some of her excitement and enthusiasm was transferred to me in that kiss. Maybe, just maybe, I might be able to clear myself of all the accusations made against me, and get my old life back. I kissed her back, with interest.

She accepted my suggestion that we should split up with a flattering hint of reluctance, and we said our goodbyes. She headed straight back to the Metro, while I ordered another glass of tea and thought things over. It was a full hour before I paid up and made for the Metro myself.

I stayed in my room at the National for the rest of the day, while boredom, desire, and excitement about the next day intermingled with one another. My night was boring too, Vara-deprived and lonely. But it was shot through with the thought that I might be about to sort out my problems tomorrow, with the general's help. At one point I dug out my camera and fiddled around with it, videoing myself quoting a bit of Macaulay in the wardrobe mirror. I put in a lot of actor-like expression, doing my Donald Sinden impression:

> *To every man upon this earth*
> *Death cometh soon or late.*
> *And how can man die better*
> *Than facing fearful odds,*
> *For the ashes of his fathers,*
> *And the temples of his gods?*

I had a lot of fun doing that. Then I took a couple of little recording cards from their holders and slipped them into my double shirt cuff. I always wear double cuffs with the same pair of cornelian cufflinks – my old man's, of course. When he died of a massive heart attack, lying in my arms, I slipped the cufflinks out of his cuffs in case the ambulance men or the hospital nurses nicked them.

'Sorry, old chap,' I said as I put the links in my pocket, and I've worn them ever since, in his honour.

Why am I telling you this? *The ashes of his fathers*, I suppose. I had the poor old bugger cremated, you see. He'd have been furious about that, but I couldn't afford a proper Church of Ireland funeral of the kind he'd have wanted. And of course I've managed to lose the biscuit tin with his ashes in it. But not the cornelian cufflinks. And no doubt about it – he'd definitely have agreed that they were more important.

Thirty-Eight

We'd arranged to meet up in the street which ran close to the puppet theatre. Oddly enough, I remembered this street from the distant past. It used to be called Oruzhye Pereulok, Gun Alley, and I knew it because Boris Pasternak had lived in a flat there: in the days when I was living in Moscow I spent an entire day working out where it had been. Naturally the building has long gone, bulldozed as part of a redevelopment of the area. Now a few words from a Pasternak poem floated into my mind:

> *In the churchyard, under the trees,*
> > *Death, a bit like some government official,*
> *Stared at my pale face, trying to working out*
> > *How big a grave I'd need.*

Not bad, eh? I wished I could quote it to Vara. Maybe she'd think it was creepy, though; she didn't like references to death, I'd noticed.

We had both made our rendezvous point on the corner of the street at precisely the right time, and were elaborately pretending not to notice each other. I found that quite a strain.

With elaborate carelessness we headed in the same direction, she on one side of the street and I on the other, twenty yards or so further back. She'd worked out exactly where we should go – she would, of course – and began making her way across a little patch of open ground to a red-brick block of flats a hundred yards away. I followed her, but stopped at the place where the cars went in while she carried on walking towards the main entrance to the flats.

While I waited, I fished out my phone and started checking it. Not that I actually expected to find that anyone had called me or messaged me; it's just that it's a useful way of disguising the fact that you're on some sort of stakeout. In the past I'd have looked like one of those menacing characters from a 1940s black-and-white thriller, wearing a trilby hat and a trench coat and standing opposite the hero's front door looking up at the window. Nowadays you're just another goop looking at his text messages, and it seems a lot more natural.

Vara, I should explain, had come here earlier in the day and trailed the general to a nearby convenience store where he did his lonely shopping. She'd bumped into him there, accidentally on purpose, and introduced herself. Then she'd made the arrangement to bring me round to the flat later.

I'd only been looking at my phone for a couple of minutes when it lit up: the message on the screen said '14'. I tried not to look as though I'd just had my instructions, and wandered casually towards the main door; except of course that my heart was beating so hard you could have generated electricity from it.

The familiar, throat-catching stink of cat piss, the general sense that no one was looking after the place, the out-of-order sign hanging on the lift door: it could have been any block of flats anywhere in Russia. Breathing heavily and muttering 'Horatius at the Bridge' to take my mind off the task, I toiled up the concrete stairs to the fourth floor. When I got there I had to wait a while until I decided I was going to live. The front door of number 14 was slightly open. Music came out at me through the gap, sounding like Tchaikovsky. I tapped with a fingernail and went in.

It could have been the flat of a writer or a musician, if it hadn't been for the stuffed head of something very large with horns over the bookcases. Photos of people I assumed must be friends and relatives were propped up in front of the books. It was a fussy place, with things piled up in out-of-the-way corners and a smell that caught you by the throat and refused to let go. Not bad or rank in any way, but the smell of a place that could do with having the windows open for a good long time and half the stuff in it sent round to the nearest charity shop.

'Genryk is being so lovely,' Vara gushed.

That jarred, I have to say.

Genryk was a tough old bastard with a hand that felt as though it had been crafted out of hard leather. A cop's hand, I should say, which had connected with a good many faces in the past. But something like a grin was occupying his mouth and eyes at the moment, and he was holding a large glass of vodka towards me.

'Hello,' he said jovially, in a kind of English.

'Zdravstvujtye.'

I gave the vowels my best shot, and we clinked glasses. I wasn't here to make value judgements about him; I'd come to do an interview which would hopefully set me free and clear the name of my friend.

What do we know about people's motives? I might have said that wickedness was written all over his face; and yet here he was, offering to spill the beans on everything and everyone, for the sake of conscience and decency. I hoped.

I know I shouldn't have put the entire operation at risk, but I suddenly felt I needed to know what the reason for all this was.

'Tell me why you want to talk to us.'

Vara looked as though she had felt a sudden sharp pain, but he merely cracked his reptilian smile, like a lizard spotting a butterfly.

'In my business we do a lot of bad things. In yours too, I think. But that doesn't mean we are pleased to do them. And sometimes we want to make . . . I forget the word.'

'Restitution?'

'Yes. That is what I am doing now.'

'But that's dangerous for you, surely?'

'Of course. I know what I am doing, though. And I think I have enough friends in my service to make sure that even if I am in trouble they will help me.'

He grinned again, and turned his wrinkled face from one to the other of us as he sat there, wrapped up in his fully buttoned grey cardigan and woollen scarf. That made him look more like a lizard than ever, because he seemed not to have a neck. I asked him to take the scarf off for the camera, but he refused. It seemed to be non-negotiable. I once interviewed Oleg Gordievsky a year or so after he defected to Britain, and failed utterly to persuade him to take off his ludicrous orange wig. It was much the same colour as President Donald Trump's hair, only a shade less pink.

It took us some time to agree on the ground rules. Genryk didn't want us to show his face, so I'd have to film him in silhouette. My heart sank. In any television interview, let alone one where a top spook spills the beans, you want to see the interviewee's face and make up your own mind about his or her character and motivation. Still, filming in silhouette can sometimes add to the drama of an interview.

We chatted for a while, and I tried to establish what exactly he was willing to say. But after a while I decided that too much preparation was likely to make the whole thing stilted and unconvincing – the very last thing we needed. And anyway all this chat was just delaying things.

'Let's go for it,' I said,

I got my camera out of its case and set it up on the little tripod I'd bought at Heathrow. I'm not the greatest technical expert around, but nowadays you don't need to be. Getting the general's face in silhouette was simply a matter of arranging the big old-fashioned standard lamp so he was completely in shadow. After that I pointed the camera at him, pressed the *on* button, and sat down with the camera running just behind and above my left shoulder.

Vara, for her part, had focussed her camera on me from much the same position behind Genryk. Now she switched it on to record my questions and get my reactions to what Genryk said, and, when I asked her, she came forward and clapped her hands so both cameras could see and hear it, just like they do in the movies. That way we'd be able to synchronise the two video streams when we came to edit our report.

I started off by asking him about himself and his career; in shadow he seemed less reptilian and a lot more impressive. His face took on a lively expression, and he even smiled once or twice when he talked about the past. It was a real shame that the viewers wouldn't be able to see all this, I thought.

It was hard to get him to say what he had been doing in the years before he retired from the FSB. But I persisted, and although he was reluctant to go into any detail it seemed pretty clear he'd become an internal critic of the approach and tactics of the FSB around 2016.

'But I still don't understand – why have you decided to take the risk of talking to me like this? Because it is a risk, isn't it?'

'Of course.'

There was a pause.

'It was my wife, you see. She died two years ago: fifteen October. In hospital she made me promise that I wouldn't do these things any more – that I'd be honest to them.'

If this was anyone but a Russian, I'd have thought it was play-acting. But I've been around them so much of my life, I found it quite credible. They're a funny lot.

Talking about his dead wife seemed to unblock the entire flow. And then something else happened.

'Look, if I am going to tell you everything, it'll be obvious who I am. So why don't you just film me like normal?'

I could have adjusted the lighting and started again from the top. But I wanted to keep this bit of theatre in, because it seemed to me to show the man as he really was: instinctive and gutsy. So I left the cameras running, and got up and moved the light so it shone full on his face. Then I sat down again. We'd use all of this material. Even before he'd said another word, it was starting to be dynamite.

Opening up to the camera meant opening up to me. He gave me his full FSB title, and an outline of what he used to do. And then we got down to the real business. It took quite a long time, because he insisted on going into detail about a number of dirty tricks he'd been involved in since the fall of Communism.

It was twenty minutes before I could ask the question I'd come here for.

'Did your department have anything to do with the death of the British MP Patrick Macready?'

It was a big risk. I should have spoken to him earlier about it, only I'd thought it would detract from the freshness of his answers.

'Well, by the time that happened, and I read all about it in the newspapers, of course, I had been moved to a different department of the service.'

There was a brief silence, while I kicked myself metaphorically. Then he started speaking again.

'But I planned a very similar operation against a Sweden journalist who had been revealing in his newspaper links between a Sweden government minister and the Federal government.' He meant the Kremlin.

I didn't need to nudge him along now. He described in detail how three of his men had gone round to the journalist's flat, undressed him at knife point, tied him up, put an orange doctored with amyl nitrate in his mouth and a plastic bag over his head.

'He died quick. This operation was successful and no one took interest in the case when it was discovered. And I should tell you that a few months ago, when I was invited to a dinner for the retirement of one of my colleagues, I asked him if they had used the same process against your politician. And he said me, yes, it had been successful against the Swedish journalist so they did it again in London.'

He sat back with a smile on his face: he knew how important this was to me. I grinned back. It was devastating stuff, and my heart sang as I listened to it.

There was plenty more, but nothing quite to match that moment. Still, once he'd started singing, the general clearly decided he was going to finish the opera.

'Now I have told all,' he said at the end, standing up abruptly without asking me and ripping the microphone from his lapel. 'You and your intelligence service will be very happy.'

'And you?'

'I too am a little happy. I have done what I promised to my wife.'

We were packing up the cameras now, and I turned away to make sure he wouldn't see me taking the little recording card out of my camera. I replaced it with the mostly blank one on which I had recorded the stuff about Horatius, and slipped the one with the interview on it into my shirt cuff. Then I turned to get Vara's camera in order to take the card from that too.

Only before I could flip open the little port on the underside of the camera, there was a heart-stopping noise from the hallway.

Someone was beating loudly on the front door. It didn't sound like a neighbour asking for a cup of sugar.

The general's face took on its reptilian mask again. Vara gave a little gasp, then sat down resignedly, as if this was what she'd expected all along.

I just said 'Fuck' under my breath.

The general went and opened the door. There were several of them, and the first one I knew very well. Why wasn't I altogether surprised?

'Hello Jon,' said Yuri, my fixer and friend for twenty years.

He moved aside, and three other men came in: indistinguishable, undifferentiated heavies. They even seemed to be dressed the same.

Two of them grabbed the general and took him into the next room. He didn't say anything, and the door slammed behind them.

Yuri gave an impersonation of himself in our good old days together. He even smiled as he held out his hand for my camera bag. I gave it to him. There didn't seem any point in resisting: the thug standing beside him would have got it off me in a matter of seconds anyway, and the only difference in the two transactions was that this way my wrist and fingers would stay unbroken.

Something, I felt, needed to be said. There was always, of course, 'Yuri, you utter piece of shit, you'd sell your sister for two roubles and charge your mother to watch.' But although it would have made me feel better, it was unlikely to improve our situation.

If I'd obeyed the instructions of Anton Chekhov, this would have been the moment when my faithful knobkerrie came into service. I confess I was tempted to whack Yuri on the head with it, and could even see it propped up against the wall where I'd left it. But there wouldn't have been any point. And anyway I was sick of being thumped up by Russian and Russian-paid thugs. I left the stick where it was.

Yuri, knowing nothing of my little internal debate, picked up Vara's camera, switched it on, and spooled back to get a quick look at the pictures she'd recorded: me asking questions and giving the occasional wise nod. He nodded himself, and turned to my camera.

I forgot to tell you that, in case of some such catastrophe as this, I'd added a minute or so of pictures of the general sitting in his chair on to the card that contained me intoning Horatius at the bridge. I don't know why I did it: instinct, I suppose. Anyway, after recording a bit of him I'd switched the cards. The interview proper was sitting unobtrusively in my left shirt cuff.

Of course Yuri should have run through the card to check it was the right one. If he had, my impression of Donald Sinden would have shown up almost immediately. But he didn't. He assumed that because the other card had been OK, this one was as well.

Bad call.

It just goes to show how important chance and timing are. If Yuri had looked at the card in my camera first, and played it for a bit, he'd have spotted the switch.

'Don't worry, little Varvara,' he said in Russian. 'No one's going to hurt you or your boyfriend here. We're just going to take you to the airport.'

And to me he said, 'We've even booked you business class. You see, we care about you.'

He grinned. I gave him the dirtiest look I could summon up. Privately, though, I was thinking, 'You poor sucker – someone's going to get extremely angry with you, quite soon.'

It made me feel a great deal better.

But there was one last ordeal we had to endure before they took us away. Yuri pulled a document out of his jacket pocket and showed it to us.

'You have to sign this,' he said.

All my career I've refused to sign things. Especially when they're held out towards me by people who've pretended to be colleagues of mine and were in fact secret policemen all along.

'Sod off,' I said, without actually looking at it.

'Now, now, Jon. Just take a look. There's nothing to worry about in it.'

I gave him another of my you-lump-of-ordure looks, but even so I took it and read it. Then, to gain myself a bit of time, I handed it to Vara. It said we acknowledged that we had broken Russian Federation law by interviewing someone who had not expressly given permission for their views to be broadcast outside the country.

'Of course he gave me permission.'

'So where is this permission?'

'Ask him.'

Whether the other plug-uglies were waiting for this moment, or whether it was just chance, I couldn't tell. Either way, in the brief silence that followed Yuri's last couple of words there was a loud and rather dreadful groan from the next room. The general was having a bad time in there, and signing documents about broadcasting permission was not uppermost in his mind.

I still didn't say anything.

'*Harasho*, Jon. You force me to tell you that if you do not sign, both of you, Varvara will have to stay. She is a citizen of the Russian Federation as well as a British citizen, and when she is here on Russian territory she is fully subject to Russian authorities.'

Did I have an alternative? There was no question of leaving without Vara.

'All right, all right, I'll sign.'

You could feel the tension in the room lift a little, and Vara thanked me. I grabbed the pen from his hand.

'Seánac Ó Fuada', I wrote.

'What is this shit?'

He hit the paper with his open hand.

'My name. The one that's on my passport.'

Yuri checked. 'You must put "Swift".'

We argued about that for some time, but I could see he was getting nervous. Maybe he was calculating the time it would take to drive to the airport, or maybe he was worried about his bosses. In the end, though, I agreed to put 'Jon Swift' in brackets after my Irish signature. Your friends won't like this, all the same, I thought. You'd have done better to stay on our side: at least our organisation doesn't order executions, though it probably would if it had the power.

We weren't allowed to say goodbye to the general, and the car ride to the airport passed almost in silence. Yuri sat in the front, beside the driver; Vara and I sat side by side in the back. I put my hand over hers, but there was no answering pressure. She seemed paralysed with fear.

As we got closer to Domodedovo airport, Yuri turned round to us.

'I thought you'd like to know your cases are in the back of the car. I packed them myself, very carefully.' He laughed and turned round to face the road.

It was the last time he spoke. At passport control he shook hands with both of us silently, and grinned as we joined the passport queue. He was still smiling as I turned round, unwillingly, to see if he'd gone away.

Thirty-Nine

A shadow fell across me, and I looked up sharply.

'Have you decided, Mr Swift?' said the waiter.

Vara and I were sitting in the coffee room of the Kildare Street Club in Dublin. I've been a member since my father's day. It's expensive, and I don't get there very often, but it seems like a tribal duty.

'My guest will have the potted shrimps and the lamb, Charlie, and I'll have the soup and the steak. Undercooked.'

We hadn't stayed in London: too many dangers there. I'd thought it out on the plane, and told Vara. Directly we landed at Heathrow we'd changed terminals and clambered on the next Aer Lingus flight.

Here at the club they knew exactly who I was and what I'd been accused of, but they'd have smuggled me away over the rooftops rather than tip off the Gardaí. There'd been Swifts at the Kildare Street Club since it was founded in the 1780s, and my father and I had stayed on as members when it merged with the Dublin University Club and the old clubhouse in Kildare Street was sold. Nowadays it's established, very comfortably, in one of the grandest houses in Stephen's Green.

The dining room was dominated by grand paintings of old bucks and beautiful women: Anglo-Ireland as it once saw itself.

Below them sat today's members, convivial, noisy, and fun. Not so many of them Anglo-Irish now, of course.

How many of them had spotted me? Most, I would guess, and the story would be all round Dublin by the evening. But if I knew the Ministry of Justice, it'd be a bit of time before they got the paperwork together and sent it to London. The Irish are a civil and peaceable lot nowadays, but they still see the law as something to get round, rather than as a fixed totem that everyone has to worship, like the bloody Brits do.

I waved at a festive chap in a technicoloured waistcoat with his napkin tucked into the neck of his shirt.

'How are you, Fin?'

'You' came out as 'ye'; being back in my native atmosphere had produced a vowel shift. Finian waved back jovially and raised his glass, but he didn't come over. He must have guessed it might cause me embarrassment.

'I love this place,' Vara murmured.

I knew why: it was the kind of thing she thought she'd be getting when she grew up in London, only to find that by the time men asked her out for a meal the old grand stodgy London had mostly disappeared. Nowadays it's all bright lighting and tiny portions there.

'I've got something to tell you,' I said.

She looked up sharply, worried. But her face changed as I explained how I'd switched camera cards and smuggled the real one out; I thought she was going to jump up and kiss me then and there. Fin and the others would have loved that, of course.

I opened my wallet and pulled the little beauty out to show her.

'I've got a friend . . .' I started.

In Ireland you've always got a friend. This one was a jovial lady with an edit suite of her own at home. She made documentaries, but somehow they never earned enough money to give her the income her talents deserved, and she had to make ends meet by doing the editing for other people. I'd known her for years: she was another one who'd never dream of calling the cops on me.

After lunch we went up the grand club staircase to our room. It was the kind of place that made you think you were staying in some great house in the West of Ireland. After the superb claret, at some unfeasibly cheap price per bottle, I needed a lie-down. I had an awkward feeling that Vara might want something a bit more, but she had to understand that there were limits.

An hour later I rang Roisin.

'Hello little rose,' I said.

'Jon, you old swine.'

Don't worry, it's the way she always greets me.

I explained the situation, knowing there wasn't a possibility on earth that either the Kildare Street Club's phone was being listened to, or hers. She asked an occasional question, but mostly I did the talking. Roisin is a good listener, which may be why she's one of the best picture editors I've ever worked with.

'You'd better come round,' she said when I'd finished.

Roisin O'Donoghue's editing studio was in Dalkey, a pleasant little seaside town on the southern edge of Dublin. I'd rented a flat here myself in the distant past, which is when I'd first come across her. She lived and worked down a side alley off the main street – the one with the two mediaeval castles in it. Don't ask why there should have been mediaeval castles in a seaside town outside Dublin. As with everything else in Ireland, you can blame the bloody English for them.

She's a big girl, fortyish, blonde and rangy, and a good and generous friend.

'So let's have a look at what you've brought back with you. If you filmed it I expect it'll be rubbish.'

You have to put up with a certain amount of that kind of thing from Roisin. Maybe she wants you to talk back in the same way. I don't know, because I've never tried it. I'd be too nervous.

We watched the first five minutes or so of the interview on the big screen above her editing machines. Actually I didn't think it was too bad, though it clearly wasn't professional. Roisin seemed to think the same.

'Well, the exposure's not very good – I suppose you just put it on auto, like beginners always do. But the sound's OK, and I can see that it's the words that count here.'

I'd played the interview a couple of times on the camera, back at the Kildare Street Club, so I knew that everything we wanted was there. To have an FSB general on camera describing in detail the murder of a Swedish journalist was brilliant, however he was framed or lit.

'Your questions are all completely off mike,' said Roisin severely.

'Yes, well, the sound was recorded on my camera and Vara did the cutaways. My questions were on hers, but they grabbed it with the card still in it.'

'That sounds like the kind of thing I don't want to know about, thank you very much. But the content's there all right even if the quality's bad.'

What I needed was for her to edit it down and make some copies: so many copies that even the FSB couldn't get them all. I'd worked it out that ten would do it. Roisin grunted, and promised to have it all done by the next day.

'I can't give you any money, Roisin.'

'I can,' Vara said.

Roisin shook her head.

'Look, I'm a paid up member of Amnesty International, for fuck's sake.'

There was a particularly good Italian restaurant about fifty yards down the road. The three of us had an enjoyable meal there, and if anyone spotted me they didn't say anything about it. No doubt the beard helped. Also the beanie pulled down over my eyes, which stayed in place all through the linguine and the torta di San Gennaro con crema, though it finally came off for the grappa. God knows how I managed to eat and drink so much, after a club lunch. Vara was a lot more restrained. Perhaps as a result, her night with me back at the club was particularly lacking in restfulness.

We swung by in a taxi the next morning and picked up the copies Roisin had made. Then we walked to one of the banks in the main street. I'd had an account here in the distant past, and for some reason I'd never entirely drained it dry: I suppose I just forgot about it.

The manager was a jovial type in his late fifties, the kind who liked to tilt his chair back and put his feet on the desk.

'Well, Mr Swift,' he said. 'I might as well start by saying I've been reading all about you in the press.'

However this looks on paper, it didn't sound nearly as censorious as you might think.

'I'm living proof that you can't believe everything you read.'

He laughed uproariously. Ten years before, this is the point at which he'd have pulled a bottle of whiskey out of the bottom drawer. But Ireland's changed now, more's the pity, and he merely asked me if I wanted a cup of coffee.

'I've had an account here for a long time. Could I ask you a favour?'

For an instant the joviality faded. Bank managers are bank managers, after all; even Irish ones.

'Would you look after this for me? Just in case I might need it?'

He looked at the spare DVD Roisin had made for me. 'I'm hoping there's nothing bad on this,' he said.

I'd prepared myself for this, and hauled my laptop out of my bag.

'Very bad indeed. Take a look. It's an interview I've just done with a Russian spy.'

We both laughed. I spooled through it so he could see there was nothing there except the interview.

'And you're thinking the Russians might want this back.'

'Yes.'

'Well, as long as they don't blow up the bank.' He paused for effect. 'Though plenty of people would say that'd be no great pity.'

He promised to keep it in the drawer where, in the distant past, the whiskey would have lived.

Vara and I took the ferry from the Port of Dublin to North Wales: there was less surveillance than there was with flying. I suppose the chances of someone hijacking the ferry and sailing it into the Houses of Parliament aren't too great. My passport was scarcely glanced at, and the journey gave us a lot of time to decide what we'd do next.

Forty

Os brought us in a pot of tea. His sitting room was as full of memorabilia as a game lodge in the Timbavati: good photos of lions and cheetahs, a couple of big paintings of elephants, a zebra skin on the floor, some tribal stuff. It seemed a bit out of place in suburban Wimbledon. My knobkerrie might have fitted in here rather well, but by this stage I'd decided I didn't need it any more.

Os's world-view was made up of primary colours, with few complicated shades. He loved the idea of what we'd done in Moscow, and – typical of him – was prepared to break all the house rules in order to help me now.

'The general told us that the FSB has an outstation in a block of flats on the Marylebone Road. Mostly Brits there, with a couple of Russians in charge. We need some shots of it for our film. Not just wide shots, I'm afraid – up-close stuff.'

'No probs, boss.'

I thought he hadn't really grasped it.

'These are very nasty people, Os. You'd have to get really stuck in.'

For once he dropped the bantering 'boss' stuff.

'And when did I ever say no to doing that?'

I thought of him on Mount Zuč, outside Sarajevo, laughing as he filmed the phosphorus shells falling around us, or in the streets of Robert Mugabe's Harare, recording a piece to camera with me when the penalty would have been seven years in a Zimbabwean prison. Os Malan wasn't the type to say no.

'The trouble is, I can't go with you.'

That annoyed him just a touch.

'You know, Jon, I *can* work on my own.'

I soothed him down. What I actually meant was that I hated sending him to do something dodgy, without being able to share the danger too. I think he realised I meant it.

I gave him the address: Bickenhall Mansions, off the Marylebone Road. 'There are some hard people there,' the general had said. 'English, mostly. They do the bad things.'

We spent the rest of the day planning it all. We'd get him a parcel and a delivery man's jacket, and fit him up with a miniscule camera set in the front of the jacket. Vara and I would stay at his house and watch the pictures coming in on a recording machine.

He looked rather impressive in his yellow hi-vis vest, I thought, and there was no sign whatever of the beady little lens set in the logo on his breast pocket. We spent a couple of days practising it all, and finally we tried it out on an unsuspecting householder in a street not far from Os's house. What the householder thought of the shoebox with a broken plastic toy in it, wrapped in a copy of the *Surrey Comet*, I've no idea.

My plan was to have Os deliver the parcel to the flat in Bickenhall Mansions, and hang on as long as he could in the hope of getting thirty seconds' worth of usable pictures, over which I could talk about the FSB and its habit of hiring local bad guys: 'gurriers', we called them in Dublin in my day, though I'm told the word is dying out now.

On the morning of the operation, there was a hitch. Os, so brave in the face of danger, had a living to earn, and he was worried about his bosses. He thought he ought to tell them what he was doing, otherwise they could get back at him afterwards, when they saw the film. I couldn't blame him for that, but I couldn't talk him out of it either.

'All right,' I said eventually. 'But don't ring them up about it, write them an email. That way they can't instruct you immediately not to do it.'

He agreed, and we concocted an email to his spineless boss, Sam. Both of us knew that Sam would run to the head of news the moment he saw what Os had said, and I was unpleasantly aware that the jig would then be up. The only thing that might just possibly delay the moment when they got on to the cops was the hacks' instinct that there might be a good story in all this.

There was no alternative. Os wouldn't do the filming without this lifebelt, and he was the only cameraman I could get to do the job for me. And without being able to show pictures of this FSB-operated hornets' nest bang in the centre of London, our film would have a large hole in it.

'Well, all right,' I said finally, and Os sent the email. It explained a good deal, though not quite all, about what had happened: that I had interviewed the general (no mention of Vara, naturally), a little of what he had said, and an explanation of what I'd asked Os to do at Bickenhall Mansions, and why. Then I hurried Os out of the house, in the expectation that the apparatchiks at the Centre would need to have at least two meetings to decide what instructions to give to him. I couldn't persuade him to leave his mobile phone at home, but he did promise to keep it switched off for the duration of the shoot.

As he was getting his stuff ready, he came across another little GoPro camera.

'I might as well mount this inside the car, so you can see what's happening the whole time,' he said.

'Sure.'

To me, it didn't seem to matter very much: I couldn't see how we'd use any driving pictures, but you never know.

The important thing was that I was sending him off to risk his life. I thought it over once again: couldn't I go with him? But I knew the answer. The people he was going to see were familiar with the way I looked, and if they spotted me the entire game would be well and truly up.

Os's wife and kids were back in South Africa with her parents for the school holidays, so the house was empty. He offered to let us stay in it while he went off and did the filming. He'd use a personal hotspot to feed us the material from his car and from the block of flats, and he showed me how to record the output from them on the couple of laptops he set up for us, one for the camera in the car and other for the one in his jacket.

'Well, that's everything, boss. Help yourself to anything you want in the kitchen, and I'll be back when it's all finished.'

'You're a great man, Os,' I said, and gripped his hand hard.

'Always a pleasure, boss,' he replied, his blue eyes on mine.

He shook hands with Vara without saying anything; he always seemed a bit nervous of her.

She and I went into the kitchen and made ourselves some coffee. It'd take at least forty minutes for him to reach Marylebone. But when we went back into the room where he'd set up the editing equipment, there he was, already chatting away from the car.

'Just thinking about how we did that live from Jameson Street,' he was saying, and he gave his great leonine laugh, throwing his head back. Typical of him to call a street in Harare by its old colonial name.

That had indeed been one of his, and my, better moments, but since there was no way for me to talk back to him, it seemed a little strained.

'Good times,' he said, and looked straight into the camera at me.

Outside the car it was getting dark by now, and the camera was struggling to cope. Os stopped talking. Did he feel nervous? Did he ever feel nervous? You couldn't tell with him – it wasn't the kind of thing he talked about.

He found a place to park close by, and got out of the car without looking at the camera or saying anything further. Vara and I switched our attention to the other screen, which was picking up the camera in his jacket. I could see he was carrying the parcel which the three of us had put together for him to take to the flat. It seemed distinctly odd to be seeing everything from the viewpoint of Os's chest.

He had parked not far from the main entrance of the flats: a red-brick block built around 1890. A large character was hanging around outside, but he took no notice of Os. We watched as Os pushed his way through the outer door, went up some stairs, and pressed the button for the old-fashioned brass and steel lift. Inside it, he pressed another button, and the lift went juddering up to the fifth floor. I could hear Os whistling quietly through his teeth, and remembered that was what he usually did when he was going into action. At Mount Zuč, for instance.

The lift jolted and stopped, and Os pushed the folding door open. A big man stood there in front of him, the size of Os himself.

'Yeah?' Native English speaker, I would say.

'Delivery for flat 21.'

'I'll take it.'

Big hands reached out towards the camera.

'Sorry, mate, my instructions are to get a signature from the person that lives there.'

'And how do you know that's not me?'

Os had a remarkable way of being friendly with the most unpleasant people: I remember how the Bosnian Serbs loved him in the hills round Sarajevo, when we went to film their artillery positions. It had something to do with his size, as well as his joviality.

'It probably is, but I'd need to see you standing in the doorway.'

I could sense him grinning, and the amazing thing was that the thug grinned back.

'Let's press the buzzer,' said the thug.

The door opened quickly, as though someone had been standing just inside. Os was holding the parcel right in front him by now, and it obscured the camera a bit. But there was no mistaking the accent that spoke next:

'Yes – what do you want?' Pure Russian.

'Signature, please.'

'We haven't ordered anything here.'

'Well, someone's sent you something. Maybe it's a present.'

And at that point the whole scheme went wrong. No one said anything else, but the Russian must have made some sort of sign to the two thugs outside. They grabbed Os and shoved him through the door. We saw a passageway with pictures and open doorways and the occasional head, and then an empty room. Os was pushed down onto the floor and the picture went black. But the camera was still working. You could hear Os breathing heavily, and then there was the sound of cardboard being ripped.

'The fuck is this?' said a British voice. 'We didn't order any plates.'

Vara and I had put six cheap side plates into the box and wrapped them up.

'Wait,' said the Russian voice, and went into another room.

Half a minute later the voice was back.

'Check him.'

A lot more confused pictures, then a shout.

'You fucker. Look at this.'

It was the camera. After that the screen went blank.

Vara looked deeply shocked, her eyes stark and open, her mouth trying to form words. I must have looked pretty much the same.

I pulled out my phone and called 999. A crisp and very together voice asked me which service I wanted. After that, I was talking to a policewoman.

'There's a friend of mine been kidnapped in Marylebone. Bickenhall Mansions. London W1.'

'And how do you know they've been kidnapped, sir?'

'I've just watched it. He had a camera attached to him, and it was feeding pictures the whole time till they found it.'

'And who were they?'

'Russians. I don't know. You've got to hurry.'

'And why were you recording them?'

'We thought they were planning something. It was for a television news report.'

That really went down badly.

'If this is some kind of stunt, sir . . .'

'No, no – please send someone round to the flat. God knows what they could be doing to him.'

'All right, I'll pass the details on and a car will go round there.'

It didn't sound as though she thought it was very important. I heard later that by the time a patrol team got there, the thugs were gone and the flat was quiet.

Vara and I were still looking at each other and not saying anything when the first screen caught our attention. All this time it had just silently shown us the interior of Os's parked car, but now the lights suddenly went on. I imagine the thugs had been pressing the button on Os's car key, and found it that way. The back door opened, and Os was pushed inside. He had gaffer tape over his mouth, and his wrists were taped up behind his back. The two British thugs jammed him in the middle between them, more or less sitting up, and the car jerked away.

I hadn't heard the driver's voice before.

'Check him over again,' he said. Also British, London, black. 'See what ID he's got, that sort of thing.'

They spent most of their time going through his pockets.

'Nothing.'

'Well, he must be working for someone. Never mind – we've got a job to do.'

Vara was white in the face.

'They'll just drop him off somewhere,' she said. 'Won't they?'

'Yes, of course.'

But I didn't really think that was how it was going to end.

They carried on driving, until they must have reached the outskirts of London. The traffic was light and they didn't seem to be passing anything much in the way of houses or shops now.

'We've got to call the police again,' Vara said, her voice trembling.

'And say what?'

But I did call. The same procedure, with different voices. I said I wanted to report a kidnapping. Some people had caught a friend of mine and were driving him off.

'Can you give me the registration and make of the car, sir?'

'Well, I'm afraid I don't know.'

'Or the colour?'

'Sorry.'

'All right, which direction is it going in?'

'I don't know that either. But they started off about ten minutes ago from Bickenhall Street, Marylebone.'

'And how do you know all this, sir?'

'I've been watching the live video feed from a camera that my friend mounted inside the car.'

'And why would he do a thing like that?'

'Well, it's for a television documentary.'

I'd actually lost the man on the other end at around the moment when I said I didn't know where the car was going, but this sealed it. Nothing was going to be done.

Vara and I watched the pictures. It was like one of those dreams where you can't make anyone hear you, and you're trapped somewhere. And all I could think of was how the whole thing was entirely my fault.

'It's down here somewhere,' said one of the thugs in the back.

'I know where it is, don't I?' That was the driver.

The crazy thing was that the pictures were so clear. Each one of the three thugs was easily identifiable. As for Os, he moved around a bit without making any noise. Maybe he thought he'd save his energy.

The car stopped.

'OK, you get out,' said the driver.

When the door was open I could hear the engine noise of another car: they'd got backup.

'Cut him loose.'

They reached in and started cutting the gaffer tape round his wrists. Os started to flail round with his arms, but as we watched, one of the thugs hit him round the face and head really hard with a cosh of some kind. Vara called out in horror. Os sank back, his head lolling. One of the thugs pulled the gaffer tape from around his mouth.

They weren't going to leave any signs.

'Don't look any more,' I told Vara, and she went and sat on the other side of the room, crying quietly.

But I went on watching. I saw one of the thugs – the one Os has first spoken to, back at the block of flats – carry over a small jerry can and start pouring it round the inside of the car. Then he poured the rest over Os.

A match flared up and disturbed the balance of the picture for a moment. But the camera quickly coped with it.

I guessed that the car was moving slowly forward now – I suppose the three thugs were pushing it. The doors swung open, Os still lolled in the back, and the flames caught him. He flared up, and then the car jolted and started falling. I still couldn't stop watching.

Then the picture blacked out, and I didn't have to watch any more.

Vara was lying on a sofa, weeping silently. I just sat there, my face frozen. This was my doing. I'd killed one of the people I loved and admired most in the world, for my own stupid, selfish, unforgivable purposes. I retched, but nothing came up.

I can't go on living with this on my conscience, was my first thought after that. My second was, those bastards have got to be made to pay.

There was nothing I could do about Vara. Her crying was unstoppable, and came from somewhere deep inside her. I led her into Os's bedroom and put her on the bed. She paid as much attention to my words of comfort as if I'd coughed.

I sat in front of the two blank screens and thought. No good asking my wet, useless organisation to sort this out. And suddenly it became clear who I had to ring: Malone Road, the MI5 man. I ought to have kept in contact with him the whole time, I now realised.

'Hello,' said the mellow vowels. It sounded as though he knew who I was before I told him.

I ran through what had happened, trying to keep the horror and guilt out of my voice and words.

'I'll get on to the boys in blue,' he said calmly. It was the jaunty kind of slang you used to find in sixties spy novels. 'They'll pay more attention to me than they would to you.'

No doubt about that.

He asked me to check the video and time the journey from Marylebone to its unthinkably dreadful end. That way, he said, they'd have some idea which police forces to check with. While he held on, I ran the pictures back at high speed. I couldn't bear to focus on them.

'Forty-three minutes,' I told him. My voice was really cracking up now.

Forty-One

Malone Road sat across the plain deal table from me and sympathised. Well, he said he did, though I expect he thought I was the most pathetic fuckwit he'd ever come across. If so, I'd have to agree. We were in an interview room at Paddington Green police station, the place where they take terrorists after they've been nicked. Maybe we were there because it was fairly close to Bickenhall Mansions. But it could have been something to do with Malone Road and what he'd told them.

To be honest, I wasn't paying as much attention as I should to the proceedings, so they led me round like a performing bear. The reason my mind wasn't on it was that I'd had to ring Os's wife an hour before, and tell her.

'I've got some bad news,' I said over the line to Jo'burg.

'It's Os.'

She wasn't asking. This was the call she must have been dreading throughout their entire life together.

'Yes.'

I won't try to repeat the exact words I used, because they were stupid and clumsy. At first there was silence. Then she started yelling at me. I don't want to recall her words too exactly either, but she said I'd always let him take the danger while I'd lurked behind in safety, and that I didn't care about him because all I was

275

interested in was my stupid pointless career, and that he was a far better man than I could ever be, and what was going to happen to her and the children now?

Some of it was unfair and some of it wasn't. I couldn't answer her question.

'We're staying here,' she said. 'When you find Os you must send him out to us. This is his home. He belongs here.'

I promised I would make sure it happened, though I had no idea how. I'd have promised her anything, just to get her to stop blaming me.

'Wife cut up rough?' Malone Road interrupted the voices in my head.

'What do you think?'

'I've had to do a bit of that over the years. You should have let me speak to her.'

'Yes, well, he was a real friend.'

'I know.'

Suddenly I felt intensely grateful to him. It meant I could start thinking again.

We must have sat there for an hour and a half – long enough for two tea cycles, with uniformed officers bringing us cups of strong, sugary builders' brew. At one point, as I sipped the stuff, the present horror parted for a moment like a mist, and I remembered that I was wanted for possession of child porn and had skipped the country to avoid arrest. It may seem completely unlikely, but I promise you I'd forgotten all about this in the awfulness of Os's death.

I said something about it to Malone Road.

'Standard Russian procedure, planting that kind of porn. Don't worry about it – it's gone away. Directly I heard about it I got the office to ring the Met. No charges or anything like that. Anyway, we've got something much worse to pin on them now.'

I suppose I should have felt relieved, but I didn't feel anything much – just that sharp, grieving voice in my ear telling me I always let Os do the dangerous stuff I wasn't prepared to do myself.

There was a knock at the door, and a chap in a dark suit came in. He whispered something in Malone Road's ear.

'You've got to be kidding me.'

'Well, that's what the crew on the spot are telling us,' said the suit.

He went out, looking curiously at me and Vara.

'They've found the car at the bottom of the gravel pit.'

Vara gave a little sound and covered her mouth with her hand.

'The extraordinary thing is that your friend's alive. He's got some nasty burns but the coppers on the spot say he's conscious and no great structural damage seems to have been done, apart from a broken collarbone and maybe a couple of broken ribs.'

I couldn't believe it for a second or two. A great rush of relief and emotion washed through me, and I had to cover my face to hide the tears. Then I looked up at Malone Road.

'The coppers say he's swearing pretty loudly. In fact that's how they found him – he was shouting "Fuck" quite a lot, apparently. He'll be on his way to A&E in Maidstone by now.'

Malone Road fixed up a fast limo to take me there; it must be great to be a secret policeman. Before I went I rang Os's wife again and told her.

She didn't answer for a bit. I heard sniffing and some nose-blowing. Then she said, 'I've been so ashamed, ever since I put the phone down. Thank God he's alive. Thank God. And I'm so sorry. He thinks the world of you, you know.'

There wasn't time for much else, except that she said she and the kids would be on the next plane they could catch. 'And tell the big man I love him.'

I arrived at the hospital too soon to be able to see Os, because his burns, in particular, were taking a bit of time to sort out. But after I'd hung around a bit, a young doctor came and found me.

'Oh, I didn't realise it was you. A Mr Clark rang to say we should let you see Barend Malan. If you come this way . . .'

Mr Clark was the man I've been calling Malone Road; he could even organise hospitals, it seemed.

Various people were still fussing round Os when I arrived in the doorway, but no one stopped me talking to him. Or him to me.

'Bugger me, boss,' Os's voice boomed out. 'Those bastards.'

I did a lot of 'How are you feeling?' stuff while the nurses kept on putting ointment on him and winding bandages round his arm, but to be honest all that mattered was that he was talking at all. I was so relieved I could scarcely speak. I'd helped to get him murdered, but he'd refused to stay that way. Os was a force of nature: no burns, no broken bones could conceivably shut him up.

If it'd been someone else I might have told them the truth – that I loved him. But you don't use words like that to a massive Afrikaner with arms like the hams in a butcher's window, so I limited myself to letting him know how fantastic the pictures had been. For him, that was far more important.

Forty-Two

The following morning, Vara and I were at a little café round the corner from the Centre, with Alyssa and someone she'd brought with her sitting opposite us. Mark was a thin, ascetic-looking character – not the kind you would want to make jokes to.

> *if my name were liable to fear,*
> *I do not know the man I should avoid*
> *So soon as that spare Cassius.*

A few hundred years back Mark would have been haranguing armies of Crusaders or organising a mass burning at the stake; now he was the best forensic programme-maker our outfit possessed.

I set out the whole position to him, though without mentioning Malone Road; I thought he might not approve of that bit. Alyssa's sharp, intelligent gaze kept searching my face, as though there was more I wasn't telling them. Well, there was a bit, but not all that much. The basic story was clear, and stronger than anything I'd ever reported on before.

'All sounds good to me,' said Mark decisively. 'We'll obviously have to put it out as quickly as possible. I'll need the powers that be to agree, though.'

'Aren't you the powers that be?'

'There's always someone further up the ladder.'

We agreed that we'd start editing that afternoon. Mark offered us his best picture editor.

'Whew,' said Chris, as he watched the pictures of Os inside the car, burning and falling down into the gravel pit. 'That's a bit strong.'

Alyssa was sitting bolt upright in the edit suite, her face set in a shocked mask. She hadn't seen the pictures before either. Vara had refused to come in, and she was walking up and down in the corridor outside; I could see her through the glass.

Chris was pleasant and friendly, but he was one of those types who wouldn't usually let himself be impressed by the pictures people like me brought in. These were different.

'We won't be able to use any of the stuff after they set him alight.'

Alyssa winced.

'But we could blur them,' Chris added.

I agreed. It was important that our audiences should see for themselves what those swine were capable of.

We worked out a schedule. Mark and his boss had agreed to drop their next programme, which was scheduled for Monday, and broadcast our stuff in its place – if we could get it ready in time. It was Thursday now, and the edit would have to be finished and locked up by Sunday evening: three days and nights. Chris was up for that. He was as stirred up about the project as the rest of us.

We worked out a division of labour. To start with, Alyssa and I would make a rough outline of the film, while Chris would start cutting the pictures down and edit them into sequences. We could tidy it all up later, but at least we'd have blocks of material to work with. I'd tackle the business of writing the script. Alyssa would move backwards and forwards between us, keeping an eye on us both. We'd need Vara to go through the interview with the general and select the best bits.

I decided to do the writing in this café. My brief and only incursion into the Centre since I'd been back hadn't been a big success, and I couldn't go round telling everyone that MI5 had killed off the charges against me. A leper ringing a bell and exhibiting his more spectacular sores would have got a warmer reception than I did. People I'd known and liked for ages had avoided eye contact.

The lift was the hardest place. I wanted to explain to everyone standing in it that it had all been the Russians' doing, that I was completely normal, that the most blameworthy thing on my computer was an old series of *Curb Your Enthusiasm*, but I thought if I did they'd probably section me. So I fixed a stupid half-smile on my face and wandered around not looking at anyone.

Writing a television documentary isn't like writing an article for a newspaper. Nor is it about you showing how clever you are and how many long words you know. It's about showcasing the pictures. You have to put them first. The best way to write for television is the George Orwell way: clear ideas and simple words. It's an exercise in modesty, therefore, and not everyone finds that altogether easy. Certainly not me, the vainest show-off around.

In this case, though, the pictures were so extraordinarily strong that I wouldn't have much writing to do. They told their own story. We had a general of secret police admitting freely that they killed people, often in bizarre ways; we had the death of a British MP in precisely one of the bizarre ways the general described; and we had the attempted murder in graphic detail of someone who was sent to investigate a Russian secret police operation in London.

Even if I held back on the words, though, it'd still take a good fifteen or twenty hours to write the script for a thirty-minute documentary. The staff at the café where I was working didn't seem to mind having me there. The Lebanese boss had spotted me right from the start and told the waitress to look after me, and she came past every twenty minutes or so to top up my glass of tea or offer me some delicacy. And at two-hourly intervals Alyssa would arrive with newly edited video for me to look at on my laptop and write to.

But it's hard to sustain this kind of work rate too long, and Chris, the picture editor, had to obey the regulations about working hours. Not that they applied to hacks like me, of course: they expect us to work round the clock. By the end of the first day Alyssa was pretty whacked, while Vara seemed drawn into herself and depressed. When the café closed, shortly before ten, I decided to go home. I was tired too, but a new mood had come over me: exultation, almost. This documentary was the method by which Patrick Macready's murder and the attack on Os Malan were going to be avenged, and I would be the instrument by which it would happen.

I took the Tube back to Sloane Square, and walked home from there. I'd slept in my flat for a couple of nights after we got back from Dublin, but I'd suffered from nightmares and ended up sitting at the kitchen table listening to Radio 3 on autopilot – me as well as Radio 3. It had been a miserable time.

Now, though, I felt different. This was fightback time. I was proud of what we'd done so far; Mark, the documentary maker, had come in to see what we'd done and had been almost human.

'This is going to knock their socks off,' he said.

Whose socks, he didn't specify.

I don't know whether anyone was trailing me; it certainly didn't feel as though they were. But directly I let myself into the cold, dark flat I had a bad feeling about it. Should I have stayed the night at a hotel? No money for that, of course, but maybe I might have asked Vara if I could go home with her. I could have slept on the couch and at least had a bit of company.

Being here took me back to the worst parts of what we'd been through: the silence, the loneliness, the gloom. I lay down and did a bit of reading, but maybe the life of Wilfred Owen wasn't the most uplifting thing I could have selected. I slung him into the corner and pulled some P. G. Wodehouse out of the bookcase beside the bed. *Joy in the Morning* – delightfully light and funny, yet written at a time when poor old Plum felt particularly down, and was regarded as a traitor by the Brits. I knew the feeling. The familiar jokes made me grin, and I was starting to feel a tad better.

Then I heard it. Just a single sound, no louder than if someone had clicked their fingers. But it was wrong. It could only have been made by a human being. Inside the flat with me.

I remember reading something that Joseph Conrad wrote, in one of his more lugubrious novels, which struck a chord with me. Something to the effect that courage is mostly just an aspect of your self-confidence and your sense of being in charge of your life. Lose that, and you're like a dog who's strayed on to someone else's territory.

I was in my own property, I'm a moderately tough character, and I'm not easily scared. But maybe, after weeks of being a fugitive, wanted for a crime I hadn't committed, I'd lost something of myself.

Anyway, I felt my insides melt with fear. I was so scared I couldn't even reach for the phone. And anyway I hadn't had much luck with dialling 999 recently. I just lay there in bed, frozen with funk.

If I hadn't heard the original sound, I probably wouldn't have heard the footsteps. There were at least two sets of them, possibly three. My senses hadn't switched off, you see, just the guts and drive that would normally have had me roaring out and charging at the bastards. That's worked for me before in various nasty situations, but it wasn't working now. I stayed in bed.

There was silence: I suppose they were gathering in the little hallway outside my bedroom door. The light must have been shining under it, to tell them which room I was in. I hadn't even had the balls to switch it off.

The door opened a few inches, noiselessly, then a few more. A head in a black balaclava poked round it. The eyes in it, dark and wide with tension, connected with mine. It was only then that I did something reminiscent of the old me.

'Fuck off,' I said. 'I've called the police. They'll be here any moment.'

'Says he's called the cops,' said the owner of the eyes, turning back to the others outside.

'Bollocks,' said another London voice. 'He's just a fuckin conman.'

The two of them came into the room. Strangely, now that I could see them I didn't feel quite so scared. I've had to cope with men in balaclavas and black outfits all my professional life.

A third man came in. He hadn't bothered to cover his face, though he was also wearing black. I looked at him: he had the fleshy face and light-coloured eyes of a northern European.

'Go on,' he said, and the other two came over to me.

It didn't help that I was sleeping in the buff. Somehow, being naked in front of your enemies is a particularly discouraging business. Your dangling parts feel horribly vulnerable.

They grabbed me as I was standing up, and threw me face down on the bed. One of them jammed my face into the bedclothes.

Fuck, I thought, they're going to smother me, like the Princes in the Tower.

The sons of Edward sleep in Abraham's bosom, And Anne my wife hath bid the world good night.

Actually, I've just thought of it. No one, not even Laurence Olivier, would have remembered *Richard III* at a time like that.

But they didn't smother me. They held my hands behind my back and yanked me to my feet again.

'This is just professional,' said the northern European, and I realised he was Russian. He would be.

Odd thing to say.

'That's an odd thing to say,' I spluttered out loud.

'I mean, there's nothing personal. We won't hurt you unnecessarily.'

'You won't hurt me at fucking all,' I shouted, my courage coming back at long last, and I wrestled my way out of the grip of one of the balaclavas. But not out of the other; and now the first one grabbed me again.

'OK, give it to him,' said the Russian, and balaclava number one reached out his free hand and took a syringe from him gingerly.

I shifted around to make it hard for him to get a clear shot, but he managed to stick it into my arm, even so. Maybe, though, he wasn't able to get a quality jab. Anyway, if this was supposed to knock me out it didn't really succeed. I was woozy, but for the next few minutes I think I was always at least partly conscious.

They weren't nice minutes. The bastards grabbed my legs and pulled them wide apart – I was on my stomach on the bed – and tied my ankles to rails at the end of the bed; not the first time that had happened here, but with different motivation. Then they wound something round my left wrist and tied that to the bedhead. I expected them, in my semi-conscious way, to grab my right arm as well, but they didn't.

It wasn't just because I was thrashing around, making it hard for them: I think it was so that what followed would look more natural. After all, an auto-eroticist couldn't tie himself up hand and foot and then do everything they were going to do to me now. Even the cops might wonder about that.

The Russian grabbed my hair and pulled my head back. Then he gripped my chin and forced my mouth open. I managed to give his gloved hand a bite, which felt good, but by this time it was five–nil to the visiting team and I might as well have just let them do what they wanted.

My teeth closed on an orange – of course – and I felt the juice running down on to the sheet below my head. The bastards were giving me the Patrick Macready treatment. My drug-addled brain tried to cope with the question of whether this might be a tad obvious, but I wasn't up to the intellectual effort and blacked out.

The pit I'd swum into should have been the blackness of death. Instead, almost immediately, as it seemed to me, there was a light shining in my eyes. I was lying on my back and someone's voice, unnaturally loud as he bent over me, was saying, 'I think he's coming round.'

'Well, that's one good thing.'

This second voice was familiar, and the vowels were those of Malone Road.

'What kept you?' I croaked.

Not bad for someone who'd just been almost murdered, I thought.

'Nothing. We were here all along. You didn't hear us coming in.'

I was really groggy, and had a horrendous headache. It was hard to focus my eyes on anything, so I shut them.

'Where are they?'

'On their way to Paddington Green, I should imagine.'

I realised there must have been a bit of a gap in my awareness of things.

'We were watching outside in the street when these charming characters arrived. Something told us they might want to pay you a visit tonight. We gave them a bit of a head start, just enough to see what they were planning to do, and then we moved in.'

'What, you gave them time to jab me? I could have died.'

'True. But you didn't.'

Bastards. Even if they *had* saved my life.

'Another thing.' My head was hurting badly, but despite the steam hammers operating inside it I was starting to string some thoughts together. 'I can't believe they were going to do the same thing to me that they did to Patrick. I mean, surely that would have been a bit obvious.'

'You'd think so, wouldn't you? Maybe they don't have much imagination. I hope it was that. The alternative is that they thought we – the entire British state and people – were so stupid they could play the same trick and no one would question it. Well, you're lucky no one thinks you're an auto-eroticist as well as a paederast.'

That was the cue for me to laugh. For some reason I didn't.

'And if it hadn't been for the doctor here, you'd be dead.'

The doctor was a young, fresh-faced chap.

'I've always been a great admirer of your work,' he said.

'Yes, well, thanks to you I can carry on doing it.'

I had no bone to pick with him; it was Malone Road I was angry with.

'You could have stopped them as they were getting in,' I hissed at him.

'We shouldn't have had a case against them. Breaking and entering, that's nothing. This is attempted murder, and now we'll be able to get them on the Macready case as well.'

It annoyed me that he was so pleased with himself, but I could see why.

I looked down: I was still stark naked.

'Couldn't you at least have covered me up while you did all this?'

'Really, Mr Swift, you do seem to be doing an awful lot of complaining. Now, though, we've got some things to sort out with you. Do you feel well enough to talk?'

The young doctor was shaping up to help me, and passed me my clothes. Given that I had the upper hand again, I didn't want anyone dressing me, so I struggled into them by myself. Then he helped me downstairs to the kitchen. The kettle was making encouraging noises over in the corner.

'You shouldn't have anything to eat, but you can have a cup of black tea if you want. Unsweetened.'

Life seemed to be improving, until Malone Road came in to talk to me.

'Seriously, how did you know these bastards were going to come for me?'

'We had a tip-off. An anonymous call. It went to the police, and instead of screwing it up as you'd expect, they got on to us. Quite quickly, actually.'

'Any way of knowing who the caller might have been?'

'No, the voice was disguised – one of those little gadgets you get at joke shops. I listened to the tape. Kind of Donald Duck effect.'

'Very droll. But I suppose I should be grateful to whoever it was.'

'More than you've been with me. We've tried to work out who might have made the call, but it's really impossible to say. Someone connected with the operation in some way, though. You'd be amazed how many people have a conscience in this strange world of ours.'

'Yeah, great. Fascinating.'

I sipped my tea, and listened to him talk. He was mostly concerned about the documentary.

'Well, with this on top of everything else we've got them bang to rights,' I said.

'Yes.' It didn't sound hugely enthusiastic.

'Well, we have.'

'Far be it from me to interfere with the freedom of the press, but in general terms we always prefer to keep these things quiet. If you blurt out everything they've done, they tend to get resentful and want revenge. Keep it quiet and they do too.'

'Look, I don't want any part of your little Cold War games. A friend of mine was murdered in a way that's made his name a laughing stock ever since. Everyone knew that I had child porn on my computer, and if we don't run this documentary I'll have that hanging over me for the rest of my life. Just because you want a nice quiet life with your Russian buddies.'

He smiled sweetly and put his fingertips together. The doctor was messing around with his gear in the corner, and Malone Road turned round to him.

'I wonder if you'd mind giving us a couple of minutes on our own, Dr Parsons.'

Then he turned back to me.

'Perhaps I didn't explain myself very well. This doesn't really matter too much to us. We've often caught the Russians at their tricks, and they've often caught us at ours. I agree that this is a bigger case than most, and it involves the murder of a government MP so it's pretty important. Even so, that was in the past and the world has got on pretty well without poor Mr Macready. We don't have to rake it up again. Simply catching them at it is a punishment in its own right, and it'll make them go quiet for a time.'

He sipped his tea, his bushy eyebrows coming together as he thought. There was a moment's quiet.

'No, surprisingly enough I'm thinking about you. You and that rather attractive Russian girl.'

'Vara.'

'Exactly. Vara. She's in a very exposed position, you know. They really don't like their own people turning against them.'

'She's one of us, for Christ's sake.'

'They don't see it like that. They won't forgive her, and they won't forgive you.'

'Forgive me? But I'm the one who's been attacked.'

'Again, I have to say, you're getting it all wrong. As far back as Ivan the Terrible' – I was afraid for a moment that he was just getting started – 'you can see that they've been a vengeful lot. If you do something against them, they'll make sure you pay for it. At some point. And I don't just mean refusing to give you a visa.'

'You're not just going to turn the other cheek?'

'No, of course not. We've collared a middle-ranking FSB character here as well as a couple of local hard men, and the hard men will give us the names of the others. They always do. So the Marylebone lot will be rolled up. But there are plenty of others we won't be able to touch.'

'Gronov, for instance?' He was the Russian I'd met at the embassy do.

'Oh, you know about him, do you? Yes, we might chuck him out. But to be honest it's better to keep him where he is. All of this has holed him below the waterline, and we know just about everything he does and who he deals with. They could easily send someone in his place that it'd take forever to get on top of.'

'It all sounds very cosy.'

'Yes, well, that's how it is with us. The question is, are you going to go ahead with this documentary of yours?'

'Of course I am.'

'Well, don't say I didn't warn you. But it's your decision.'

Forty-Three

Actually, as it turned out, it wasn't.

Despite my headache, which was starting to wear off anyway, I went in to the Centre and turned up in the edit suite at the time arranged. I'd agreed with Malone Road that I wouldn't tell Alyssa or Vara about what had happened to me during the night. What his reasons for asking me were, I don't know. I just thought it would be bad for business.

Vara seemed really pleased to see me, which was nice. Alyssa was friendly in a slightly bossy way, which I also enjoyed. Chris, the picture editor, was clearly fired up with enthusiasm. Altogether it felt good to be there. And we were even on track in terms of time. I was just arranging with them to bring me the latest chunk of material which they'd edited, when a nervous young chap whom I rather liked, Ahmed, put his head round the door.

'Daniel wants to see you, if you've got a minute.'

We both knew that my having a minute or not having one played no part in this transaction whatever. It was the equivalent of the three-line whip.

I went round to Portchester's office: another glass box.

He was looming inside, looking rugged. I imagine he'd decided it was better to stand if he was going to force me to do something.

What that something was, I'd been trying to decide all the way up in the lift and along the corridors.

It turned out he, like Ahmed, was only the messenger.

'The Owner would like you to go up and see him.'

This was disturbing: The Owner only manifested himself on rare occasions. Most of the time he lived in clouds of glory in Monte Carlo. For him to come down to earth and be made flesh here in London meant that something big had happened. I assumed it must be a lot more important than me and my concerns, but it gave me real pleasure to see how nervous Porchester was.

And because I'm a bully, I couldn't resist giving him a little extra fright.

'Well, look, I'm really sorry, but we're at a key point of the edit and I'll have to get back downstairs right now. I only came to see what you wanted. Tell The Owner I won't be free for another hour.'

Christ, that felt good. I just wish I'd said two hours.

Porchester wagged his head from side to side in anguish.

'No, come on, Jon, you know what he's like.'

I almost felt sorry for him. If his shirt collar hadn't been turned up, I would have said something that sounded like a compromise. But I didn't.

'You've got my mobile number. Get him to ring me around two.'

Actually, I knew perfectly well I'd have to go upstairs right now; all this was just role play. I was trying to show Daniel I thought he was a nervous-nelly helot, fearful of his boss, while I was a free agent, in bondage to no one.

> It matters not how strait the gate,
>   How charged with punishments the scroll,
> I am the master of my fate:
>   I am the captain of my soul.

293

Stirring, I grant you, but sheer bollocks of course, and that old bullshitter W. E. Henley (another hack, you know, who had a wooden leg and was the model for Long John Silver) probably realised it. I thought of quoting him out loud – W. E., not Long John – but decided this would be going too far. The scroll would be even more charged with punishments if I did. By now, anyway, the recognition that I was just having him on was starting to creep across Portchester's irritatingly good-looking face.

'Yes, well, I think we'd better go up there right away.'

We did. The Owner brought his own team of creeps with him whenever he travelled, and they were there in the outer office, being obsequious to him and domineering to everyone else.

'He's been waiting, you know.'

That pissed me off.

'*J'ai failli attendre*, eh?' I sneered, in the secure knowledge that no one would spot the reference or speak good enough French. And then, because the look on his PA's vacuous face annoyed me – though she had a really good figure – I translated.

' "I nearly had to wait." It's what Louis XIV said when someone was only just on time.'

It was clear that neither she nor any of the other creeps knew what in God's name I was talking about.

Two people were required to take us across the carpet to the door of the holy of holies, knock, and open it. There was almost nothing inside: no pictures on the walls, no furniture except a mid-eighteenth-century oak table, possibly genuine, and three armchairs grouped together. Plus a hard-looking mahogany dining chair, uncushioned and straight up and down.

Two of the armchairs were empty. The central one contained an ancient bag of bones in an expensive suit and a collar two sizes too large for him. My guess was that he'd had his shirts made by someone very good at least ten years before, and couldn't bear to give them up. I liked his violet silk tie, though.

'Take a seat.'

His voice sounded like a very old cellar door that hadn't been opened for some time.

There was no alternative to sitting on the mahogany dining chair. I thought of forcing The Owner to shake hands by stretching my arm across the desk towards him, but at that moment a completely different feeling came over me. I'm embarrassed to say that it was one of awe. You might not approve of him – not many people did – but it was undeniable that he was amazingly grand. And not just ultra-rich, but very clever and successful.

He looked at me for a few seconds, the sharp old eyes like agates in the dull grey ostrich skin surrounding them. Then he said, 'Go on, wait in the other room.'

I stood up.

'No, you stupid idiot – him.'

He waved his veiny old claw and Daniel Porchester slithered humbly out.

'Wanna drink?'

'Wouldn't say no.'

'Ha!'

There was a bottle by his feet which I hadn't noticed. His hand shook as he passed it over, together with a glass. It was a type of single malt which I happened to know was seriously expensive.

'Can I pour you one?'

'Can't,' he said, and pointed to his heart.

'Surely life's not worth living without it, is it?'

A dreadful noise emerged from him. It took me an instant to realise he was laughing.

'Now, you moron,' he grated, 'you're doing some programme that's causing trouble with Russia.'

'No, I'm doing a programme about how Russian agents have killed a politician, a friend of mine, and almost killed a cameraman who worked for you.'

'Nonsense. It's all nonsense. I know these Russians. They're tough to negotiate with, but they don't kill anyone.'

'We've got the proof.'

'Got the what? Speak up – everyone mumbles nowadays.'

'We've got the proof.'

'No you haven't. You've just got a lot of accusations. We're not broadcasting rubbish like that.'

I stood up.

'If you don't broadcast it, I'm walking out of this organisation.'

'And good riddance if you do.'

There was a pause of about a second.

'But before you go, have another glass. It's not every day someone turns me down to my face.'

He creaked again, and one hand shook in time to the noise. His Adam's apple seemed to have taken on a life of its own, inside the encircling shirt collar; it moved as though it was operated by an entirely different control system.

'I'll drink your single malt, because it's memorably good. But if you don't broadcast my piece, I couldn't possibly stay in your outfit.'

I found it surprisingly easy to give it straight to this creaking old gnome. At the same time, he must have been pretty formidable in his day. Around the time of the Boer War, possibly.

'Well, I'm not going to broadcast it. It'll cause too much trouble. I've got interests in Russia, you know. Maybe I could find a different job for you, though.'

'I don't think I'd take that either, thanks very much. This place is too full of arse-lickers. I can't be doing with them any longer.'

It felt really liberating.

'Arse-lickers!'

He liked that, so we had the creaky laugh again.

This time it went on so long I thought it might do him real damage. I didn't want to be responsible for killing him. How would I break the news to the toadies next door?

'You're too much of a nuisance. But I'll give you good severance terms, because you've made me laugh.'

Of course I should have told him where to put his severance terms, but at his age I didn't think he'd be able to find it.

'You're an idiot, you know,' he creaked. 'You could have done well here. I'd have promoted you.'

He looked down, and the agate eyes seemed to fade, like lights that had been switched off.

I tiptoed out.

'Everything all right?'

Porchester seemed solicitous, until I realised he was asking about himself.

'I think he's going to sack you as well as me.'

The reaction was highly satisfactory, though after a moment he guessed I was joking. So I told him I'd resigned, but that The Owner had said he'd give me generous terms.

That was awkward for poor old Porchy. He only had my word for it, and I didn't think he'd dare to go back and ask The Owner if it was true.

'We'll sort something out,' he said.

I had to break it to the three downstairs – Vara, Alyssa, and Chris – that all their efforts, all their enthusiasm, had gone for nothing. This was what Os had nearly given his life for, and it was going to be chucked in the bin because it might interfere with The Owner's business interests.

Except that it wasn't. Even as I sat there telling them this, the solution came to me.

I asked Chris if he'd be kind enough to make three copies of everything we'd done.

'I'll take it to the BBC. They're mad enough to run anything.'

'But the copyright?'

'Screw the copyright.' Then, 'No, actually, I can think of a way to get it.'

I ran out of the edit suite and jumped into the lift. At the very top, I opened the door to The Owner's suite.

'Yes?' asked a rather glamorous woman in a tight emerald-green suit. I hadn't noticed her before, though I should have.

'The Owner needs to know something.'

'Yes, well, you can't possibly tell him now.'

'Oh, I think I can.'

I strode over to the inner office door and opened it. Various lackeys were crowding round him as he signed something.

'That's him – there he is,' said The Owner, emitting his wheezing, crackling laugh. 'I'm just writing something about you.'

'Well, thanks. But what I really want is your permission to take the material we've gathered for our documentary and give it to someone else. I need the copyright.'

The lackeys looked startled.

'And why should I give it to you? So you can cause me more trouble?'

'Well, if I take it to someone else – the BBC, say – they'll get all the blame from the Russians and you won't get any. And you know what? You were a really good journalist, once upon a time, and this is a great story.'

Funny: all these creeps around him, but not one of them ever seemed to have the balls to praise him for something he actually deserved praise for.

His face went mottled, and he grinned, though it looked at first as if his ulcers were playing him up. But he said yes then and there, and told one of the creeps to put it in writing for me. While that was happening he started laughing again. Even when I closed the door of the inner sanctum, I could still hear him through the wood. Well, the wood substitute.

Forty-Four

A few hours later I dialled Vara's number. She must have seen that it was me, but she just said bleakly, 'Yes?'

'Can I come round?'

'I don't know. I suppose so.'

'Feeling low?'

'A bit, maybe.'

'Then let me try and help.'

'OK.'

Her voice was dull, uninterested.

Why I thought a bunch of flowers and a box of supermarket chocolates might help, I don't know. That was my default response when I got into trouble with women, I suppose. Usually it worked. Not, though, when she'd just seen a man she'd worked with and liked being almost burned to death. She gave the stuff a look, said a mechanical thank you, and put them on a side table.

She looked pretty rough: grey, lined, unresponsive.

I put my arms round her, but felt no answering pressure.

'I'm responsible for what happened to Os,' she said eventually. 'Watching those pictures . . .'

'Bollocks. I was the one that sent him off. It was my idea, and I almost killed him.'

Being a bloke, I think sex with Vara would have helped us at that point; I suppose that's part of the reason I went round to see her. There was no question about it, though – she didn't. She lay on her bed, looking at the ceiling, and I closed the door, got a large drink, and went and lay on the couch in the next room. Tiredness and booze did the rest, and I blacked out completely. But a few hours later, when it was starting to get light, she was still lying there on the bed, her eyes wide open.

'Did you get any sleep?'

'Not much,' she said.

I had a lot to do that morning. I had to go round to our great competitor, which I'd left under a cloud a few years earlier, and persuade them to drop everything and put out a documentary which an altogether different organisation ought to be broadcasting. I had my letter from The Owner in my inside pocket, and a DVD with all our precious material on it. I said goodbye to her and went out.

Gronov was sitting outside Vara's front door in the back of a large black Beamer with the windows open.

'Mr Swift,' he called in a loud, friendly voice.

I got in beside him: there seemed nothing else I could do, if I wasn't simply going to ignore him. But I couldn't help thinking this was what Os had done, and it had nearly killed him.

'Look,' he said in his pleasant Russian-accented English, 'I know all about it. We don't have to exchange insults or threats. I just want to ask you if you really have to broadcast your report.'

'I'm going to the BBC with it right now,' I said, waving the DVD in his face. And because I'm a mischievous bastard, I added, 'You can give me a lift there.'

'Why not?' said Gronov, and laughed.

He gave the chauffeur the necessary instructions in Russian.

We headed across the Albert Bridge.

'So what's your answer?'

'First, I've got a question for you. How did you know where I was?'

'We know things.'

'All right, so how do you know where I'm going now?'

'That's a second question. I am still waiting for your first answer.'

'My first answer is "Fuck you."'

'Very charming, and just what I would have expected. You are Irish, I understand.'

'You understand right. But even if I was a fucking Hairy Ainu from the Kuril Islands I'd still say the same thing.'

He laughed. He had style, this bastard.

We were driving up Whitehall now.

'I know you are short of money. I know also that you have no job. We can address all that. You wouldn't have any more worries.'

'Look, I'm sorry. I quite like you, and I don't want to piss you off too much. But your thugs have killed one friend of mine, nearly killed another, and bloody wrecked my life, and I want to settle the score. And that's what I'm heading off to do right now.'

'You oblige me to put things another way,' Gronov said, sounding once again as though he was in a Bond film. 'We do possess certain capabilities, and we could make things very unpleasant for you.'

'Oh yeah – right. What'll you do? Load my laptop with child porn and kill my best friend?'

'Please accept my condolences for all of that,' he said quietly, and, sap that I am, I actually think he meant it. 'But anyone who has your interests at heart' – God, his English was good – 'would have to say at this point that you would be unwise to continue with our present journey.'

I decided to keep the conversation low and insulting. Anything else might give a wrong impression.

'Fuck off, Gronov. I may be an old lowlife, I may be hard up, I may be increasingly useless at my job. But what your lot never seem to understand, and I don't just mean the Russian ones, I mean all the sodding spooks everywhere, is that some of us believe in what we're doing and can't be bought off or scared off either. So you're wasting your breath.'

As a journalist, I'm good at spouting high-principled guff, you see. He looked out of the window, and didn't answer.

Piccadilly Circus now, heading into Regent Street. Writing this, I've been wrestling with myself a bit before putting this conversation down on paper, because it sounds altogether too cheesy, too holier-than-thou; the kind of thing Woodward and Bernstein might have said at the end of a Watergate film, with the audience clapping and agreeing with each other that journalists are today's real heroes. They're not, and I'm not. But I was buggered if the FSB was going to make a takeover bid for my conscience.

Gronov was a gentleman, no question about it. He patted my shoulder in a way that seemed almost approving. But as we fetched up in Portland Place he turned and looked me full in the face.

'I must warn you, Jon – you are making an enemy of the most powerful intelligence agency in the world. But I am your friend. If you change your mind, you can contact me at any time on this number and I will try to help you. But seriously I urge you to think again.'

I was out of the car by now, and he handed me a card through the open window. As they drove off, I looked at it. No name, just an expensively embossed phone number: a Moscow mobile. That was real class, I thought, as I went through the revolving doors.

Forty-Five

Everything was sorted out eventually, like the end of a Shakespeare play. A comedy, that is, not one of the ones where the actors are left lying around all over the stage with Kensington Gore coming out of them.

> *Jack shall have Jill,*
> *Naught shall go ill,*
> *The man shall have his mare again*
> *And all shall be well.*

Scotland Yard tried to stop us putting out the pictures of Os's kidnapping and death, but just at the moment when they got most self-righteous they suddenly caved in – which, I imagine, showed the hand of MI5.

The three thugs in the video had disappeared, so there was no question of anything being *sub judice*. Presumably the FSB whisked them out of the country. There was an amazing amount of red tape from the Corporation, but I wouldn't have expected anything else.

Two weeks after I'd taken the video to them, *Death of an MP* went out on the main channel at peak time, with a maximum of public attention. I asked Vara if I could watch it with her in her flat. She nodded, in a dispirited kind of way. It didn't seem as though anything mattered to her now.

She did a lot of weeping while it was on. Me too. As I've grown older I've suffered more and more from a sudden welling up at anything emotional. Seeing pictures of one good friend talking and smiling and altogether being alive, and watching another being nearly burned to death counts as emotional, I promise you.

At the end we just sat there in separate armchairs. There was nothing to say.

'I'll make some coffee,' I said, though I'd rather have had alcohol.

She shrugged, and didn't drink any of hers when I brought it in.

Finally I decided I couldn't take so much concentrated gloom any more, so I gathered my stuff together and headed back across the river to my flat. There was a light drizzle, but I didn't mind that. Walking fast in the rain helped to clear my head a little. The street lamps shone on the pavement and flickered on the dark waters of the river. My footsteps made the only sound. One or two people hadn't bothered to close their curtains, and I peered in, trying to imagine what their lives were like, and whether they'd been watching *Death of an MP*.

When I turned the corner into my side street, my stomach lurched. There was something hanging from the front doorknob. When I got closer I could see it was just a bit of cardboard, roughly torn off a box, I should imagine.

DON'T THINK WE FORGOTTEN WHERE YOU LIVE, someone had written on it in ill-formed letters. I've declared war on a hostile army, I thought, and this is just the start of it.

Still, nothing else happened during the night, and it was obvious that things had suddenly picked up for me in terms of my reputation. Recalled to life, I thought, like the coachmen said when they were going to pick up Dr Manette from prison in *A Tale of Two Cities*. Our documentary was rebroadcast all over the world – I heard they even ran it in Cambodia – and for a couple of weeks I was in demand everywhere.

Except of course on Russian television. They just pretended the whole thing hadn't happened, like a marchioness does when someone breaks wind at the dinner table. One channel ran a feature on the way the Western media were starting a new propaganda campaign against Russia, but they didn't get round to mentioning what was actually being said.

People who had crossed the road or walked into their offices to avoid me now shook my hand in both of theirs and assured me they'd never believed the allegations against me in the first place. There were a couple of small paragraphs in the papers about my chances of winning a BAFTA. If only this had all been about some other subject, I'd have been happy.

But something was gnawing away at me. It'd first come to me as I was walking over the bridge after leaving Vara's flat. How had the FSB known that Os was coming round to the flat in Marylebone? They'd clearly been expecting him. I'd watched the video – the bits that I could bear to watch, anyway – again and again: it was the way the man outside the flats waved him to the lift, and the way the two roughs outside the flat door greeted him. I couldn't get it out of my mind. And I had the impression they knew exactly where his secret camera was when they started searching him, too.

The prime minister made a tough statement in the Commons that afternoon, about how the murder of a democratically elected MP was an outrage which no country could accept. She didn't actually mention Russia at any point, but I didn't mind that. A bit later the State Department said much the same thing – also without naming Russia. I was just watching their spokeswoman on BBC World when I got a call from some department at my new employers' called Compliance and Co-ordination. They have that sort of thing at the Corporation.

'We don't seem to have had a release form from a General Shep—Ship—'

'Shepanikov. No, I didn't ask him for one. I reckoned he'd think I was asking him to sign a confession.'

'Well, I'm afraid I don't think we can authorise payment of a fee to you. The regulations are quite clear on this.'

Wonderful. On the day the world finally blows up they'll still be disallowing people's expenses claims. Maybe that's what Kipling meant.

As surely as Water will wet us, as surely as Fire will burn, The Gods of the Copybook Headings with terror and slaughter return.

Though actually I don't understand what that means, any more than you probably do.

After that, other things started happening: stupid things, often, that people would have thought were crazy if I'd talked about them. Didn't Moriarty give Sherlock Holmes a spot of bother like this? Or was it Colonel Moran? Both bloody Irishmen, anyway. Once something dropped close beside me from the scaffolding on the building next door as I was walking past. Then, a day or so later, I was on a zebra crossing near the flat when a motorbike drove straight at me. I had to throw myself on to the pavement. Oh yes, and something vile smelling was stuffed into the little round plastic vent set in my kitchen window. I retched a few times, and tears streamed down my face, but it fell into the sink and I quickly drowned it in soapy water.

In the end I couldn't take it any more, and called Malone Road. He met me in a bar in Westminster, dark and quiet, and listened to my story.

'These people know exactly what they're doing,' he said at last, draining his whiskey sour. 'If they wanted to do you in, they would. This is all about reminding you about how badly you've upset them.'

'So I'm in the clear?'

'Not in the slightest. It's just that they'd be stupid to do anything too rash to you now, just after it's all come out. No – they'll bide their time, and come for you later, when everyone else has forgotten about it. But they want to make sure you'll remember all about it.'

'Very reassuring. I'm so glad I consulted you.'

'We can help, of course, but it'd be a big commitment for us. Our chaps could be with you day and night. We did it with that writer chap – what's his name? Salmon something.'

'Salman Rushdie.'

'Yes, but we had to put him up in the Cavalry Barracks on Hyde Park.'

'I think I'd rather die.'

'Attaboy. Do it for England. It's a lot cheaper for us that way.'

It took me a moment to realise he was joking.

'No, if the worst comes to the worst, we'll look after you, of course. You've done us a real favour, after all. But I'll tell you what would be a good idea in the meantime: write a book about it. They don't like that kind of thing, because it'd all be out in the open. Name names and places. The full monty.'

'I'll name you.'

'If you do, we'll have to charge you under the Defence of the Realm Act.'

'I'm pretty sure that was repealed in 1919.'

'Ah. Well, we'll find something, anyway.'

'I hope you're getting on with that book,' he said, when he rang me a couple of weeks later.

'You're sounding like my agent.'

'Yes, well, we both have your interests at heart.'

The fact is, I've been writing faster and faster. If only I can get this out into the open, I'll feel a hell of a lot safer. I mean, how much of a headbanger would you have to be, to bump someone off after everyone had been tipped off about you? Answer, the characters who are after me, I suppose.

Forty-Six

A week or so ago I sent off the manuscript to my agent, in the hope that he'd find a publisher who would do it justice. I'm rather proud to have written a book. For those of us who deal in two- and three-minute reports, ninety thousand words seems close to infinity. I'll miss doing it, though, which is why I'm carrying on writing this journal. I find it's rather good for clearing the channels of thought.

After a few days Julian – my agent – wrote back to me. The publisher he had in mind had had a look at what I'd written, and seemed to like it enough to want to buy it. To be honest, I didn't really care how much they'd pay, though Julian tells me that kind of thinking is a betrayal of authors and their agents the world over and must be suppressed. Fine: but I think my life will be hanging on the line until the book is out.

Whatever relationship I had once had with Vara seemed to be completely finished. I'd only seen her a couple of times since all these big events, and her eyes were red with crying both times. She scarcely took any notice of me.

And that was the point at which I understood that I really, genuinely loved her. The way she'd been in Russia haunted me. I heard her voice again and again saying 'Hello little *shpion*' in Red Square, and 'Come here again, my ugly old Irish brute' in bed in the Four Seasons. I know as I write it that this is corny stuff, a bit teenaged and probably more than a little embarrassing, but that combination of sharpness of mind and an occasional playful gentleness had utterly captivated me. Surely Patrick must have felt exactly this. The way she settled her dark blue eyes on mine as she sat across the table from me, then looked down again, had also captivated me. And I loved her hands, long and slender, with the veins on them as blue as her eyes. And now she took no more notice of me than she would of the postman.

Of course I should have cut her out of my life, just as she was busy cutting me out of hers. Somehow, though, I was obsessed with this sorrow of hers: I felt I had to try to understand it. Things had turned out extraordinarily well, after the violence and murders.

I didn't really expect her to feel about me the way she had clearly felt about Patrick, but I couldn't deal with this blankness, this sudden eradication of whatever little there had been between us. I'd been wiped as though I were a memory stick. How could she feel there was so little left after all that had happened?

There must, I felt, be something behind it. But I couldn't work out what, and there was no point in asking her.

Out of the blue, I got an email from an old friend of mine, Peter Grenville. He was coming back to London from Syria, and wanted to have dinner. Peter is famous, an American television reporter who hit the big time and has written a number of books on the Middle East. He likes good-looking women, so I thought I might as well ask Vara. Peter was so annoyingly good-looking it might, I thought, cheer her up. And to be honest I just wanted to see her. So I wrote back to him and suggested the restaurant at the Frontline Club in Paddington, where a lot of our friends hang out. Let's meet in the bar first, I said.

Vara didn't seem to care one way or the other when I rang her, but after a bit of toing and froing she agreed listlessly to come. I picked her up in a taxi and we went on to Paddington. Peter had said eight o'clock; we got there a bit earlier. Hugh Jenkinson, who founded the place, was standing in the bar when we arrived, talking to a guest. Hugh was a superb character, a combat cameraman of the front rank, who'd won a large number of awards and was famous for having been hit by a sniper's bullet in Kosovo. The bullet lodged in his mobile phone, so he wasn't seriously injured. The joke went round that it had hit his wallet.

I talked to him for a while, then showed Vara the display cases along the wall: Hugh's mobile, naturally, with the bullet in it, but also the prosthetic arm which the great cameraman Mo Amin used to wear after he lost his own. Mo worked with me under the scariest of circumstances in Baghdad, but was most famous for his superb pictures of the Ethiopian famine of 1984, with Michael Buerk. He died, finally, when a plane he was in was hijacked and crashed into the Indian Ocean.

Alongside that was memorabilia from another friend of mine, Rory Peck, a fellow Anglo-Irishman, who was shot and killed outside the television station in Moscow during the fighting there in 1993: the camera he was using when he died, his Russian press pass.

I couldn't help quoting Tom Moore at a time like this, naturally:

> When I remember all
>   The friends so linked together
> I've seen around me fall,
>   Like leaves in wintry weather;
>   I feel like one,
>   Who treads alone
> Some banquet-hall deserted,
>   Whose lights are fled,
>   Whose garlands dead,
> And all but he departed!

Vara, being Russian, perked up at all this gloom and she and Hugh talked at length about Kosovo. Then Peter Grenville walked in.

'So how are things?' Peter asked, shaking hands. His eyes were already on Vara, I noticed.

And she liked him. For the first time in ages her eyes took on a sparkle, and she even laughed. It showed me, as though I needed to be shown, that I no longer played any serious part in her life.

Peter was full of good stories and insights, and the wine and whiskey flowed. It must have been around ten fifteen when the restaurant went suddenly quiet. Four men, their faces covered with scarves, were standing in the doorway. One had a hatchet, and the others had those big kitchen choppers that always look so frightening.

'Christ!' Peter whispered. 'It's ISIS.'

That was a joke, and I laughed: not a good move. Two of the masked men came leaping across the restaurant towards me, yelling and holding their kitchen knives in the air.

'Put your fuckin' hands on the tables! Anyone with rings on, take 'em off or we'll chop 'em off!'

Hard not to visualise that. I wasn't wearing any rings, but I still put my hands on the table; I like them the way they are – eight fingers and two thumbs. Vara had gone white, and her mouth was wide open. Peter was Peter. He still had an amused half-smile around the mouth.

The two thugs seemed to pick on us, charging over and grabbing Peter by the shoulders and hair.

'Take your fuckin' rings off.'

'No rings,' I said, as evenly as I could.

'Then take your fuckin' watch off.'

I did, as slowly as I dared. The man with the meat cleaver went over and put the edge of it against Vara's neck.

'This gets sliced if you do anything stupid.'

The other two were going the rounds of the tables now, collecting up the rings people were only too glad to hand them.

'We're takin' the girl,' said the one who was doing most of the shouting.

'We'll go together,' said Peter calmly.

'Me too,' I said, rather feebly.

They grabbed the three of us and pushed us out in front of them. One of the thugs stayed by the door as we were being pushed through it.

'I'm staying here to see nobody makes any stupid phone calls.'

But clearly someone already had. In the distance I could hear a police siren.

All four men now pushed out into the cold, shoving us in front of them.

'Let the fuckin' girl go.'

They pushed her, but she fell over in a heap. We were dragged towards a black van standing nearby.

I seemed to have had an awful lot of this recently. And for some reason I said it out loud.

'Shut your fuckin' face.'

A heavy fist hit my cheekbone, but at least it wasn't a meat cleaver.

'All right, Mr fuckin' clever-dick Swift, get in.'

It was only then that I realised what this was all about.

'I'm sorry, Peter—' I started to say, but a shower of blows shut me off.

He lay on the ground, and I saw a couple of nasty kicks going in.

'Get out of here!' shouted someone, and they started pushing me into the back of the van.

But I'm a big bloke, even though I wasn't quite as big as I had been, and (as I've boasted before) I used to play rugby. Good game, rugby: it teaches you that your own personal pain matters less than the pain you can inflict on others. I smashed my left elbow back into the stomach of one of them, and grabbed at the meat cleaver in the boss's hand with my right.

I was never going to get it: he had room to swing, and his wrist evaded my outstretched hand by a couple of inches. He brought the cleaver down on my head. I twisted away, but it hit me on the left-hand side, just above the ear and sliced some scalp off. There was blood everywhere, also a good deal of instantaneous pain. Then I did the most intelligent thing I'd done for quite some time: I fell down.

I like to present it as a conscious action, but it was probably just the inevitable result of having my head cloven.

And at that moment the cops were everywhere. Hoisting me into the van didn't seem to be an option. The thugs threw themselves in it and roared off, with the door still open.

'You all right, sir?'

The writer Martha Gellhorn, American by birth but British by adoption, once said to me that the calm sound of the British policeman's voice was the most magnificent thing in the world. Well, she was more of an Anglophile than I am, but I understood at this moment what she meant. It's also inclined to make you talk in stiff-upper-lip terms yourself.

'Yes, fine – just a bit of blood, that's all.'

You could imagine Charles the First saying that on the scaffold.

'Can you tell me, officer, does my ear still seem to be attached?'

We television people know the importance of how we look, you see.

'Yes, it seems to be fine, sir. But you're going to need a bit of attention.'

They led me back into the club. Peter was already in the bar, telling a large group of hacks what had happened.

'Jesus, Jon, what happened to you?'

' "Never shake thy gory locks at me," ' I quoted, but since I was the one with the gory locks it didn't quite work.

Hugh was already getting cloths and cold water and also a bottle of Irish whiskey over to me, and I was just applying myself to them in reverse order when the ambulance turned up.

They decided my injuries were slight enough to be sorted out on the spot. I emerged from the ambulance dramatically bandaged, and put down three Jamesons in quick succession. Well, you don't hold back at a time like that, do you? Vara was in the restaurant giving a statement to the youngest of the policemen, but I scarcely had a moment to speak to her before the police were asking me for a statement as well. After that she drifted away. The other cops were speaking to the remaining guests in the dining room. It turned out that two of them had managed to get photographs of the thugs on their mobile phones. Don't attack a room full of journalists, is my advice.

Eventually the cops left, and there was a general feeling that the evening was over. Vara was sitting on her own in a corner of the room.

'Can I take you home?' I asked.

'No – yes, actually. Thank you.'

She didn't look at me.

When the cab reached her block of flats, she said something completely unexpected.

'Would you mind coming in, Jon? I'm worried there'll be someone there.'

'Well, there won't be, but I'll go in with you anyway.'

By this stage in our relationship – if, that is, we'd ever really had one – there seemed nothing more for me to do than simply check the place for her and leave. I could just walk across the Albert Bridge when I'd made certain everything was all right.

She didn't wait while I paid the taxi, but headed straight for the front door. We walked in together.

There wasn't anyone in her flat, naturally, but even I felt a bit nervous as I went from one room to another, checking.

'All OK,' I said, expecting her to show me the way out.

But she didn't.

'Come and sit in the kitchen.'

She messed about, making us some hot chocolate. Neither of us said anything.

'You look really weird with that bandage,' she said as we sipped our chocolate. 'A bit like an Egyptian mummy.'

And she laughed. It was a sound I hadn't expected to hear from her, ever again.

'What's going on with you, Vara?'

'Oh God, so much. I couldn't even begin to explain.'

'Is it about you and me, and Patrick, and all that?'

'Well, that's part of it. But I think the main thing is how much of a shock everything has been. It'd be hard for any relationship to survive that, let alone everything that happened after Patrick – you know . . .'

She laid her fine hand on mine, and looked into my eyes.

'You do understand, don't you?'

I knew this was a kind of valedictory, but at least it wasn't that withdrawn coldness of hers.

'I'd better be heading home.'

Then words I never thought to hear from her again.

'You don't have to. I'm a bit spooked tonight. It'd be good to have you here.'

I told myself there was nothing more to this than her fear that the thugs might come for her in the night, but it didn't matter. I could live with that.

I made some remark about sleeping on the couch, but she insisted that I slept in the bed with her. The whole time I tried to keep my distance, knowing that anything else would just bring a load of pain. But at some stage, although I must have looked even more than usually ludicrous with my bandaged head, I moved across and held her.

After that, one thing led to another.

Somehow, though, it was clear to me that we'd reached some sort of invisible end point. There was an elegiac feeling in everything we did; and afterwards the same feeling hung over us as we lay there in the darkness, and when we got up and went back into the kitchen for something to drink.

'I really loved you,' I said, using the past tense deliberately.

'I know you did. But you do understand?'

'Yes, I understand.'

After that I slept another hour or so on her sitting room couch. At seven o'clock, when I couldn't sleep any more, I got up and dressed. Her bedroom door was closed, and I didn't open it. Instead, I slipped out of the flat, pulling the front door shut behind me, and walked back to Chelsea.

It seemed like a long, long way.

Forty-Seven

The most important thing now was to get my bloody book – this book – out and into the shops. Over the next couple of days, while I recovered from my injuries, I wrote away.

Always scribble, scribble, scribble! Eh, Mr Gibbon?

Well, that was me.

Peter had had a nasty time but was up on his feet again; it took more than the boot of a thug in Russian pay to keep him down. I didn't hear from Vara, and I was so fixated on getting my writing finished that I kept putting off ringing her. And when I finally did, I just got her classy, off-putting message about how she was too busy to speak to anyone at the moment.

I couldn't ignore Alyssa, though. She was clearly stirred up still about what had happened with *Death of an MP*, and furious with our company for refusing to broadcast it. She rang me in that bossy way of hers and insisted that she'd come straight round to see how I was getting on. I managed to persuade her to put it off till the next day; and by that time I'd sent off the last knockings of the book.

My flat had become a prison, and I was determined to get out of it for a while. But I was looking distinctly rough and didn't want to be stared at, so I suggested we should meet in Battersea Park. There's a row of seats alongside the statue of Buddha where you can look out at the river and not be too much in the public eye. Alyssa agreed to meet me there.

It was mid-morning. The sun shone down through the young, yellow-green leaves. Ducks and swans messed around on the river. A barge, painted red, moved slowly past me with a small white terrier standing on the bows, looking excited. Was it sentimental of me to think that these things were indicators that my luck had turned? Probably. Anyway, in my more rational moments, which are few enough, I don't believe in indicators, or in luck either. But I still felt good. And, for the first time since Daniel bloody Porchester had started trying to force me out of my job all those months earlier, I was optimistic about the future. The hair was even starting to grow back on the side of my head.

It was at that point that I spotted Alyssa. She wore black, of course. Not from mourning, but because everyone does nowadays. Her coat came down to her ankles, and she'd topped everything off with a quirky little hat. Women speak with their clothes, so this presumably meant something; but it was as if she had a heavy accent, and I couldn't understand what it was. Nothing bad, though.

'Hello, Swift.'

'Hello to you, Ms Roberts.'

'Nice day.'

Et cetera, et cetera. I won't reproduce the stuff we started off with. It was code for something else, anyway, but what? Surely . . . No. Not that.

But there was the hat, all the same.

She didn't smile.

'I'm pissed off with you, Swift.'

Ah.

'You could have taken me to the BBC with you. After all, it was my story too. And instead you just walked out on me.'

'I didn't—'

'Oh yes you fucking did. Don't give me that.'

'I—'

'Don't try and justify yourself. You're a selfish, thoughtless bastard.'

Guilty as charged, of course, but I didn't feel it was good for business to admit it.

'And what's much worse, you're a successful one too. That was a great bit of work, and—'

'But—'

'Don't interrupt me. Just listen, for once in your stupid, thoughtless life.'

To be honest, I tuned out after that. The ducks and swans didn't seem quite so meaningful, now that I was getting this dumper-truckload of abuse.

Finally, it came to an end.

'And you know what?' she yelled. 'You look bloody ridiculous in that woolly hat.'

She had a point there. I'd needed something to cover the shaven side of my head, and the only thing I could find that was stretchy enough was a blue-and-white knitted effort with CHELSEA FC on it and a pom-pom on the top. I'd bought it ages before at Stamford Bridge when the temperature was well below freezing and we were playing Watford. It's a dangerous thing to wear outside Chelsea, naturally, but Battersea is just on the border and doesn't have a football team of its own.

'It's to cover my injury.'

'I don't care. It's really stupid and if you're going to be seen with me I'd be grateful if you'd take it off.'

Meekly, I did. She got a look at the shaven area and the plaster.

'OK, put it back on. You look even worse without it.'

'If you'd come with me, you'd have got the sack.'

'No I wouldn't. All right, I would've. But I'd have got a job with the BBC.'

'They haven't given me one.'

'Yet.'

'Well, you may be right, but I've got no money and my only hope is this book I've been writing.'

She wasn't interested in my book. A pity, because I thought it might take the heat off me, my shortcomings, and my ludicrous appearance.

'And I suppose you've been shagging that Vara in the meantime.'

'I haven't seen Vara in the past few days – no one has. And with my injury I couldn't shag anything.'

'Don't give me that. Word is, you'd be shagging even if you were on your deathbed.'

'Word is wrong. I live the life of a recluse, a monk. I am sad and lonely and don't have anyone to care for me. I'm the King Lear of Chelsea.

> *I am a very foolish fond old man,*
> *Fourscore and upward, not an hour less,*
> *And to deal plainly*
> *I fear I am not in my perfect mind.*

She gave me a wintry grin.

'Well, at least you've reached a measure of self-awareness.'

I grinned back. She was interesting, this girl. Also, as I've probably told you, she looked like Nefertiti.

At my suggestion we got up and wandered along the riverside. I still had a bit of a headache, but talking made it better. Talking to her, anyway.

'I could always offer your services and mine to the Corporation as a team. Os's too. If you wanted. They've kind of hinted at it already.'

'Would that mean I'd just have to work with you?'

'Many people would have their eye teeth removed without anaesthetic to work with me.'

'Yes, well, I like my teeth the way they are.'

And she bared her gnashers at me. They were particularly fine.

''Nother thing. If I did work with you, no funny business – got it? There's nothing worse than couples on the road.'

'My dear girl, I assure you you'd be entirely safe with me. Assuming I actually wanted to work with a loud, aggressive termagant as my producer, of course.'

'No, you don't understand. I've got a new boyfriend, so if we're going to be working together it can only be purely professional. And anyway, you're definitely not my type. Got it?'

For a moment or two I couldn't think of any reply. And then her phone began to play some stupid tune. She pulled it out of her pocket, and said nothing for a bit while we walked on, side by side. She was reading a message, then replying to it.

Eventually: 'That was Vara.'

Her face was impassive, impossible to read.

'Really? What did she want?'

'She was saying goodbye, and she wanted me to pass on a message.'

'What message?'

Alyssa didn't say anything. She handed the phone to me so I could read it for myself.

Ps tell Jon I'm so sorry for everything I've done. I can't speak to him & cdn't live with myself any longer in UK. Am on Moscow flight, just going to take off.

I dropped down on to a bench. Alyssa looked at me.

'You know what I think, don't you?'

I shook my head, but I had a pretty good guess.

'I think she was on their side all along. I think she was telling them everything that you were doing.'

'No, that's complete bollocks. Not a shot on the board.'

But even while I was saying it I was thinking, that would explain how they knew to expect us in Moscow. And how they knew what Os was doing when he went round to film the thugs in their block of flats. The knife attack in the London Library. And us going to the club the other evening. And Gronov waiting for me outside her flat. Little betrayals and big betrayals.

And there was one last thought.

'She must have told them all about Patrick,' I muttered.

Alyssa just sat and watched me. She knew exactly what I was thinking.

I dialled Vara's number in a fury. There was just that cold, haughty message:

I can't take your call at the moment – I'm probably busy. Leave a message at the beep . . .

But I didn't leave a message. I walked on in the sunshine with Alyssa beside me. And, thank God, she was sensitive enough not to say anything.

Forty-Eight

I never got another visa to Russia, of course; I didn't even apply for one. My book still isn't out yet, but everyone seems to know everything about it anyway: I assume the publishers have been sending out extracts to the press. The other day the Russian propaganda channel got a bunch of people into the studio to say what a useless swine I was, and how nothing I said or more particularly wrote could be trusted. So the channel gets some things right, you see.

The BBC did give me a job, which was good, and they agreed to take Alyssa and Os on as well to work with me, which was even better.

Os came out for a drink with me to celebrate.

'Is Jackie all right with this?' Jackie being Os's wife, and this being the fact that he and I were going to be working together permanently.

'Well, sort of.'

'You mean she isn't.'

'No, not really. But she's happy about the money.'

The money was quite a bit better.

'Look, I'm really sorry . . .'

He laid a massive hand on my arm. Usually he didn't try to control me, but clearly this was different.

'Listen, Jon, let me say one thing. You don't take me anywhere; I go with you of my own free will. Right?'

I felt really abashed.

'Right,' I said meekly. And I meant it.

'Now, how about a real drink? Waiter, a triple brandy, please. And a Coke on the side. I'll do the mixing.'

As for Vara, I've seen her once since she got back to Moscow, but not in the flesh.

It was about a month after my drink with Os. The president was giving his annual televised press conference, a master-class in how to charm people, make policy on the hoof, and generally persuade the voters to give him yet another term.

Vara was standing next to the stage on which he was speaking. That meant she must have some official position now. The cameraman only showed her a few times, and then just in passing, as he panned round from the president to the crowds of journalists in the theatre stalls. But it was her all right.

She'd landed on her feet.

The annual press conference is intended for the Russian media, and the journalists come from all over the former Soviet Union. Every newspaper, every magazine, every radio and television station still standing (an awful lot have been closed down) has its representatives there. They wave cards, and even banners, with the names of their outfits on them, and a hugely efficient press secretary picks out the ones who are allowed to ask questions. And don't think that only the pro-government ones get selected; this isn't Stalin's Russia, not quite anyway, and the opposition often gets a look in.

A smooth, well-dressed character a bit like a Russian Peter Grenville, tall and dark-haired, got the nod from the press secretary and stood up. I'd seen him before: he worked for an opposition

326

television station which had just managed to stay in business as a result of some clever and determined footwork.

'Mr President, good afternoon. I have a question about the allegations that have been made in the West about the deaths of several people there. In Britain and other countries they're saying that these attacks are the work of our Russian security organs. Can you enlighten us about this?'

Clever stuff, and quite brave too. There had been no official response in Russia to my documentary, or to the condemnation that the British and other governments had heaped on the Kremlin. Now, thanks to the Peter Grenville lookalike, there would be.

The president tapped his pencil on the desk lightly.

'It goes without saying that the government of the Russian Federation, or any of its organs, has not carried out any attacks on individuals in the West. We are a democracy, and a disciplined one, and we respect international norms. These accusations are made as part of a provocation by Western intelligence agencies to damage the prestige of our country. We do not accept them, and we will never accept them. The principles that govern our policy at home and abroad are respect for the law and for human rights.'

So far so good. But then the president looked straight at the main camera, and his voice took on a new strength.

'But I can assure you of this. Russia will always defend its interests in the ways it sees fit, and this right cannot be questioned. Nor can the way in which we carry it out.'

No one had mentioned the name of Patrick Macready, or of anyone else for that matter. Yet I felt that his murder had now been acknowledged.

The bulk of the audience stamped and shouted their support. Then one of the journalists stood up, his back straight and his arms by his side, and started singing. It wasn't the insipid anthem of the Russian Federation, all about the wings of the Russian eagle; it was the stirring chorus of the old Soviet national anthem:

Long live our Soviet motherland,
Built by the people's mighty hand.
Long live our people, united and free.
Strong in our friendship tried by fire.
Long may our crimson flag inspire,
Shining in glory for all to see.

More and more people around the auditorium stood up and joined in, and the cameras swung round, capturing it all. For a brief while, one of the cameras zoomed in on Vara Kuznetsova. I could see her well-cut dark hair, her fine features, even the tattoo of the little bird on her neck.

She was standing to attention, singing proudly with the rest, her handsome head thrown back like a bloke's. And as I watched she turned those fine eyes, which had once shone with what I thought was love for me, to the camera. For an instant I looked straight into them. They were brimful now of some other love. For what? For whom?

Was she thinking, even at that moment, that I might be watching her and remembering everything she'd said and done?

Hello, little shpion.

But she'd been the spy, not me.

God, that made me feel bad.

From Byron, Austen and Darwin

to some of the most acclaimed and original
contemporary writing, John Murray takes pride in
bringing you powerful, prizewinning, absorbing
and provocative books that will entertain you
today and become the classics of tomorrow.

We put a lot of time and passion into what we
publish and how we publish it, and we'd like to
hear what you think.

Be part of John Murray – share your views with us at:

www.johnmurray.co.uk

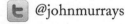 johnmurraybooks

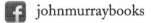 @johnmurrays

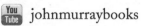 johnmurraybooks